M000285749

SALVAGE MERC ONE

JAKE BIBLE

SEVERED PRESS
HOBART TASMANIA

SALVAGE MERC ONE

Copyright © 2016 Jake Bible
Copyright © 2016 by Severed Press

WWW.SEVEREDPRESS.COM

All rights reserved. No part of this book may be
reproduced or transmitted in any form or by any
electronic or mechanical means, including
photocopying, recording or by any information and
retrieval system, without the written permission of
the publisher and author, except where permitted by law.
This novel is a work of fiction. Names,
characters, places and incidents are the product of
the author's imagination, or are used fictitiously.
Any resemblance to actual events, locales or persons,
living or dead, is purely coincidental.

ISBN: 978-1-925342-89-5

All rights reserved.

ONE

When you're a Marine, you're taught that you only have two friends in battle: your H16 Plasma Carbine Multi-Weapon and the Marine standing next to you.

Everything else can go to Hell. Mainly because it's your job to send everything else there.

Great philosophy if you're still fighting dirty Skrangs and their B'clo'no allies.

But, damn if the second the War ended I didn't end up having both friends taken from me. I really miss that H16. She was the best multi-weapon a hard-edged Marine could ask for in a tight spot. Killed more than my share of Skrangs with that baby. But I get it, you have to turn in your weapon at the end of your service. The Galactic Fleet is funny that way.

How'd I lose my second friend? The Marine standing next to me during all those firefights with the muscle-bound lizards and snot monsters? Okay, I didn't lose him. Crawford stayed in the Fleet. They didn't ask him to leave. He had all limbs and organs accounted for. Never had to cash in a single replacement chit. He was 100% human.

In other words, he was financially viable.

Me? I spent my two allotted repchits my second year in the Fleet. Lost both my legs below the knees when I stepped into a B'clo'no mating trap. I don't know if it was a male or female or both in that pit, hard to tell with those mucus things, but after I was through with it, it was dead. Don't care if it was holding a billion eggs like the lady ones do or if it was holding only a million like the guy ones. I wasted that pile of sludge as it ate away at my legs. Hooah to my H16!

With my two repchits spent, and some seriously heavy duty battle legs to maintain, the Fleet decided I wasn't cost effective. The Galactic Fleet really clamped down on spending once the War funds began to dry up. All that money being spent on peace instead of trying to wipe out the Skrangs and those damn, sticky B'clo'nos.

Crawford got to stay, I got the boot.

Ain't no thing, really. Not anymore. Sure, at first it hurt like a mofo, but that's life. I drank myself silly for quite a few months until I happened into a wubloov tavern on that one planet... Xippeee. That was it.

I know, I know, who names these planets? Xippeee with three E's? That crud drives me ten kinds of crazy. But, they have to be named something, I guess.

Where was I?

Xippeee, right.

So, I'm getting stunk drunk in this tavern and in walks this woman. She's a halfer, one of the rare mixed breeds that happen in the galaxy. Part human, part Gwreq. She totally had the Gwreqian stone skin going on, but had two arms like a human, not four. And she was fine. I mean, stop conversations, make heads turn, *fine*. Men, women, herms, asexers of all races dropped what they were doing to watch her walk into the tavern.

Now, I was drinking wubloov, which after six pitchers takes you on one seriously messed up hallucinogenic ride, so I thought I was looking at something my brain invented. I honestly had no idea she was real. I'm not kidding. This halfer crossed the tavern, ignored everyone staring at her, and took a seat at my table. The second she sat down, I ordered another pitcher of wubloov because I wanted that trip to keep on going.

It wasn't until she pulled out her KL09 hand cannon and set it on the table that I started to suspect that maybe she wasn't a figment of my imagination. Which was really a bummer since I knew I had a shot with her in my imagination. In reality? No way a gorgeous woman like her was going to get with a scarred-up, washed-out, mostly drunk ex-Marine like me. Even with my sexy battle legs.

"You Sergeant Joe Laribeau?" she asked me after the barmaid had set down my pitcher of wubloov. She waited until the barmaid was gone then poured herself a pint, downed it, and pointed at me with the empty glass. "I'm speaking common, so I know you can understand me. Are you Sergeant Joe Laribeau or not?"

She said the last sentence really, really slowly, like I was an imbecile that couldn't track words faster than three a minute. And considering I was about to pour a pint from my seventh pitcher of wubloov, she was probably right.

Except I have a gift. No idea how I got it. Fleet doctors think it's an alien virus that I contracted during one of my campaigns, but none of them would say for sure because then the Fleet would be contractually obligated to pay for any long-term health care issues that may come from it.

My gift? I clarify. Fast.

Simply put, no matter how drunk, sick, injured, or whatever I am, I can get laser focus in an instant. The noise of life disappears and I see the world in crystal clear detail. It came in handy during battles. Turned me into a man that couldn't miss. It was like everything around me slowed down and I could track my targets down to their molecules.

You'd think the Fleet would want to hang onto a man with that kind of gift, but, like I said, they had budget cuts and didn't want to worry about me putting in a health claim if I suddenly lost my gift and grew eight toes out of my forehead. I've seen that happen. Not pretty.

Plus, it isn't a reliable gift. It doesn't always kick in. But it did with the halfer woman, so I paid attention. A halfer knows my name, and pours a pint from my pitcher without asking, I don't care how hot she is, I get suspicious and perk up right quick.

"Who?" I asked.

"You're him," the halfer said.

She started to pour another pint, but I clamped my hand on hers and shook my head. She raised an eyebrow, which considering her rocky skin, looked like a row of pebbles was turning into a small arch above her eye, and looked down at my hand on hers.

"Who the hell are you?" I asked, hand still on hand, her eyes still on hands, my eyes still on her, the whole tavern quiet as a dead nuft.

"Remove your hand, please," she said.

I glanced at her KL09 and she switched her focus from our hands to the heavy pistol.

"I wanted it on the table so you knew I didn't have it under the table pointed at your junk," the woman said. She sighed and pushed the weapon across the table with her free hand. "You can have it. I've got a dozen more on my ship. All I need is for you to confirm that you are Sergeant Joe Laribeau and hear me out for five minutes."

"Five galactic minutes or Sterli minutes? Because I was on Sterli once and those minutes can last forever," I responded.

"Real minutes," the woman replied. She sighed again. "Please let go of my hand."

I did. Only fair since she'd pushed her pistol across the table to me. She took her hand off the pitcher and leaned back in her chair. The bare skin of her upper arms rubbed against the seat back and half the tavern cringed at the sound. Not quite fingernails on slate, but damn close.

"Do I have to ask again?" she said, almost pleading.

That tone changed things. Why would a halfer be pleading with me to confirm my name? Didn't make sense. Especially since she could probably reach across the table and crush my skull with her bare hands if she wanted. If she got the Gwreq strength to go with the skin, that is. If she wanted me dead then she could have just done it. Hell, half the people in the tavern would be too afraid to report her and the other half were so hot for her that they probably would have forgotten the whole thing if she gave them a sexy smile. I could have been a puddle of blood and bone with two battle legs in the middle and she would have walked away free.

"Yeah, I'm Joe Laribeau," I finally answered.

The look of relief on her face was priceless. There was a bleeping from her belt and she pulled out a small scanner. She put it to her eye and held it there for two seconds. Once it stopped bleeping she relaxed, put the scanner back in the pouch on her belt, and sighed a third time. The third sigh came with a smile that could melt a ship's hull.

"I'm Hopsheer Balai," she said and offered me her hand.

I shook it and pushed her pistol back to her.

"I've got one," I said as I reached down and patted the heavy pistol strapped to my thigh. "Don't really need a spare."

"You always need a spare," Hopsheer said and pushed the pistol back to me. "We go through firearms like candy in our line of work."

"We? Line of work?" I asked. "You want to tell me what this is all about before my wubloov kicks back in."

"Kicks back in?" Hopsheer laughed. "Your pupils are bigger than a Venti moon. I'm actually surprised you're able to use your speech centers. How many pints have you had?"

"Pints? No clue," I said as I filled my empty one with more drink. "But this is pitcher number seven. Pour yourself another, if you want. But only if you tell me what the foing hell is going on."

"Thanks," Hopsheer said and did pour herself another pint. She tipped the glass to me and then downed that one. "Oh, man, that is good. Only stuff in the galaxy that can get through my metabolism. Being half Gwreq pretty much nullifies my enjoyment of substances."

"That is the saddest thing I've ever heard," I replied. "I had no idea that was even a possibility."

"Only for halfers like me," she said as she reached for the pitcher again then stopped. I nodded and she poured a third pint. "Genetic anomaly when Gwreqs and humans mix."

"I'm no bigot, but that there is an argument for keeping bloodlines pure," I said and smiled, making sure she knew I was joking.

"You're telling me," she said and sipped at her pint instead of pounding it. "I was shot six times in the belly and went through seventeen hours of surgery without the anesthetic doing more than making my skin tingle."

"Fo," I said.

I waited for a few seconds, watching her closely because who the hell wouldn't want to, but she didn't say anything else.

"Yeah, so this is getting kinda creepy," I said. "You're hot, but I am not into crazy chicks. Sorry. I've been there, foed that. Took me three weeks to ditch this Nemorian woman. She actually loaded up her water tank onto a GF freighter to track me down. Left her water planet just so she could tell me how much in love with me she was."

"Nemorians are a nymph race," Hopsheer said. "They bond emotionally when they have sex. You should have known it would get messy."

"Yeah, well, my gift didn't make that part very clear," I said. "All the fun stuff we did with each other was super clear, but future stalker stuff wasn't."

"Your gift!" Hopsheer basically shouted.

Some of the staring patrons turned away. Halfer or not, no one wants to be caught looking at a Gwreq when she raises her voice. That's how a person loses an arm or two.

"That's why I'm here," Hopsheer said. "Your file was given to the SMC and my bosses saw the notation about your gift. Perfect clarity under stress." She pointed at the pitcher. "Explains the drinking and still talking thing."

"And...?" I asked. "Wait, did you say SMC? As in the Salvage Merc Corp?"

"The very one," she said and gave me that smile again as she took another sip from her pint. She set it down and leaned forward. "The SMC is looking for new recruits. We've had some unfortunate losses lately, mainly due to the Edger separatists racing around the galaxy and gumming things up. They see a salvage merc coming and they get nervous, think the number is gonna take them for a ticket punch."

"Aren't they?" I asked. "Hold on, what's a number?"

"Huh?" she asked, looking over her shoulder as two men walked into the tavern.

"What's a number?" I asked again. "I know that getting a ticket punched means you have claimed a salvage, but I have no idea what a number is."

"Me," Hopsheer said, her eyes still on the men that moved from the doors to the bar. "Us. Mercs. We all have numbers. I'm Salvage Merc Eight. We call each other numbers. It's an inside thing." She turned her attention back to me and her hand casually went to her pistol that was still on the table. "You'll learn all of that back at headquarters."

"I never said I was going with you to your headquarters," I replied.

The two men at the bar ordered then turned around and stared right at our table. They were strapped with sawed-off scatter blasters. Rusty things that looked like they'd explode in their hands if they pulled the triggers. I automatically assumed they wanted the blasters to look old and useless. That probably meant they were in perfect shape and would take my head off with one shot.

"I think you really should," Hopsheer said and nodded backwards. "Those guys? They aren't here to drink."

"I guessed that," I said.

"When I said my bosses got a hold of your file, well, that's because someone leaked every file of every decorated ex-Marine onto the Grid," she said. "Not a problem for the average spacehead, but for someone like you, with your gift, and those battle legs of yours, that is a problem."

"How so?" I asked. "I've been out of the Fleet for nearly two years."

"Doesn't matter," Hopsheer said, her hand tightening around her pistol's grip. "Those guys are bounty hunters. They've been sent by someone to collect you so you can be used by whatever organization is paying them. All it takes is an AI chip in the back of your head and you are one controllable killing machine."

"AI chips are illegal galactic wide," I said. "Life in prison for anyone that uses them."

"Which tells you that the organization that hired those two isn't exactly the law abiding kind," Hopsheer said. "Looks like I found you in the nick of time."

"Galactic time or Sterli time?" I asked, smiling. I loosened my KL09 and eased it from its holster. "That's a joke."

"Funny," Hopsheer said. Then the look in her eyes hardened. Literally, as her eyes turned to rock hard stone. "I need to know if you are interested in becoming a salvage merc."

"Why?" I replied.

"Because my ticket was only to find you, not to claim you," Hopsheer said. "You have to return with me of your own free will. That means, I legally cannot defend you with lethal force unless you specifically say you are interested in becoming a salvage merc. The second you do that then you are under the protection of the SMC and those two men are fair game."

"I'd be a moron to refuse you," I said. "I mean that in a sexy way, too."

"Don't be a terpig," she said and frowned. "We've been having a good time until you said that."

"Sorry," I said and finished my pint. I slammed the empty glass down on the table and stood up. "I am officially interested in becoming a salvage merc. When do we leave?"

"Right now," Hopsheer said as she stood and turned to face the two men that had pushed away from the bar and were slowly walking towards us. "Stay behind me."

"I can take care of myself," I said.

"Not with these foing Jirks," she said.

"Jirks?" I gulped. "Skintakers? Okay, yeah, you take the lead."

I could see her skin hardening under her clothes. The material tightened and her movements became more deliberate. Not stilted or clunky, just more deliberate. She was ready to get her fight on.

"No claim on him," one of the Jirks said.

The skin he wore was a light purple which meant he'd recently killed someone from the Tersch system with that bright red sun. His eyes were sparkly gold and when he smiled, he showed finely sharpened teeth. He was of a low caste for a Jirk.

It's the teeth that give away the lower skintakers. Jirks take on every aspect of their victims except the teeth. The high born ones can handle the teeth as well. Most Jirk assassins are high born which makes it hard to catch and convict the bastards. They get all the protection.

But not those guys. They were Jirk labor. Drones sent out to do the dirty work.

"He's a free man," Hopsheer said. "Hasn't broken any laws, local or galactic, so no claim can be put on him."

"I'm allergic to claims, anyway," I said. That was the wubloov talking. I shouldn't have said anything, but I get a smart mouth when I drink. I have a smart mouth when I don't drink, but it usually stays closed in potentially violent situations. My gift doesn't extend to my lips, unfortunately. "Sorry. Ignore me."

"We're leaving," Hopsheer said and the second man, also purple skinned, stepped next to his buddy so our way was blocked.

"Come on, guys," Hopsheer said. "I don't want to kill you and I doubt either of you want to kill me. Jirks hate being halfers, right?

You kill me and you'll take my form unless you spend a lot of energy fighting the change."

"I'd rather just take your form without killing you," second Jirk said. "That means I want to fo you like a—"

"Yeah, I know what you mean," Hopsheer replied.

I couldn't see her stone eyes, since her back was to me, but I assumed she rolled them.

"You've punched your ticket, merc," first Jirk said. "Your job is done. You found your guy, now walk away. Let us take it from here."

"So much taking, so little giving," I said. "I think there's plenty of me to go around. Listen gentlemen, or whatever you really are, how about I go with this unbelievably beautiful woman to SMC headquarters, hear their pitch, then I come find you, go to your employer, hear that organization's pitch, weigh my options, then make an informed decision. If the people that hired you have a better offer then I'll gladly sign up with them. No one has to fight, no one has to die, no one loses their skin or anything nasty like that."

"Why'd you have to call me beautiful?" Hopsheer asked without looking back at me. Her focus was locked onto the Jirks. "You could have just called me a woman, but you called me an unbelievably beautiful woman. There's no need to bring up my looks. My attractiveness doesn't define me."

"Okay, sorry?" I said, really confused. Calling a woman beautiful had never backfired on me before. "You're right? I should have just called you a woman?"

"Why are you talking in questions?" she snapped.

The two Jirks looked from her to me and both laughed. Their laughing ended when Hopsheer put a blast dead center in their chests. I didn't even see her raise her pistol. The guys crumpled to the floor, nothing but piles of clothes and empty, dead skin. After that, the tavern turned into a screaming mess as the patrons bolted for less deadly environs outside.

Hopsheer flashed her SMC credentials to the bartender and he nodded at her as he pointed up at the vid camera in the corner.

"SMC badge or not," the bartender said, "the authorities will decide what happened."

"I know," Hopsheer said. "But I wouldn't mind if your story was leaning in my favor. We all know what direction that interaction was headed."

"I'd like to go on record and say I felt my life was being threatened and Salvage Merc Eight here did the right thing by removing the threats," I said as I looked directly into the camera. "If she hadn't killed those Jirks, they probably would have kidnapped me and delivered me to Eight Million Gods knows what kind of evil criminal organization."

"Don't say things like that," Hopsheer said. "It doesn't help."

Hopsheer didn't move from her spot until the bartender gave her a slight nod.

"Thank you," she said. "I'll be sure and let my bosses know of your cooperation with this. That'll be good for you and your business."

"Better be," the bartender said.

Hopsheer reached back and grabbed my shoulder, yanking me with her to the doors.

"Hold on," I said and tried to pull free. Tried. "Uh, let go, okay? I need to pay my tab."

"On the house," the bartender said. "Just leave."

"Nope, not gonna," I said as Hopsheer let me go.

I walked to the terminal on the bar and placed my wrist against it. It brought up my bar tab and debited my account what I owed.

"I always pay for my tab," I said. "Bad luck to stiff a place."

"If you say so," the bartender said, his eyes locked onto the bounty hunter mess on his floor. "Can you leave now? I have to clean up and close for the day once I call the authorities."

"We're leaving," Hopsheer said. "Thank you again."

"Yeah, thanks," I said as I followed Hopsheer out into the pale yellow light of what was left of the day.

I glanced up at the two overlapping suns that shone down from the Xippeee sky and shook my head. I'd gone in that tavern for some pitchers of hard beer and came out a guest of a salvage merc, headed to SMC headquarters for what was maybe a job interview.

The galaxy is weird.

TWO

Six months later and I was standing outside a cave on the smaller of planet Hepnug's continents. I had the SMC version of a Fleet H16 Plasma Carbine Multi-Weapon in one hand and my ticket instructions in the other. Sitting to my left, unceremoniously cleaning himself, was my Leforian assistant, Mgurn. Basically a mix between an armored beetle and a Great Dane, Leforians are crazy loyal, dig faster than a gump on steroids, and see for miles with perfect focus. They do other things too, of course.

Great sidekicks if you can ignore the licking.

"Will you stop that?" I hissed at him. "Why do you always clean yourself right before we're about to make a claim?"

"I get nervous," Mgurn replied as he smacked his segmented jaws together, his prehensile tongue sliding back into the darkness of his mouth. "You know that."

"This is why Leforians can't ever get their number," I said. "You get weird in the field."

"Then why keep me around?" Mgurn pouted. "Why not ask for an Ichterran or Klav assistant?"

"Ichterrans freak me out with that water leaking from their gills thing," I said. "And Klavs are nothing but balls of eyes. Yeah, they are super smart, but I don't know where to look when I talk to one."

Mgurn did that huffing thing he does when he's annoyed with me, but I ignored him and focused on my ticket.

Salvage Ticket #4867345231:

Recovery salvage. Science team last seen on Hepnug in the Brgeete System. Data collected by team is primary salvage. Rescue of team members is secondary. Two thousand chit bonus for full recovery of data and team members. Added two hundred chits for every team member alive. Time sensitive. Recovery and return within one week.

That last thing was the tricky part. It takes a full day's travel to get to the Brgeete System from SMC headquarters. Three days of searching the planet since the damn thing has seventeen continents on it. Then, if I find anything, two days return trip to SMC headquarters due to the energy flux given off by Brgeete's suns. It messes with the engines of pretty much any ship not Behemoth Class or above. That timeframe cuts things tight.

I was on day four of my planet-wide search because apparently it was the lava season. No volcanoes, just vast quantities of lava that rains down from the sky at random intervals during the days and nights. Yes, I had a personal protective environmental shield, so did Mgurn, but that wasn't the point. The point was lava falling from the skies. Made things tricky.

"Sensors indicate that the team and their equipment are inside this cave," Mgurn stated. He glanced up at the sky and blinked. "I would estimate we have three to five hours before the next downpour. We will need to hurry to make that window of safety or we could end up losing another day."

He said "another day" like it was my fault. Which it kind of was since I'd ignored his suggestion and landed on the opposite side of the planet instead of right where we were standing. Leforians have an uncanny ability to sniff out the right landing spots, the right places to set up camp, the right equipment to bring on a salvage mission, and the correct way to cook almost any food in the known universe. Mercs joke about calling their Leforian assistants "Mom" sometimes. Never to a Leforian's face, though. They hate that and it makes them unbearably pissy.

"Any signs of life?" I asked as I swiped the salvage ticket from the screen on my wrist holo and brought up the list of items that needed to be retrieved to punch my ticket and make my claim. "I'm good either way."

"Are you?" Mgurn asked. "Because I would prefer to find the science team alive so we can collect the bonus chits. Need I remind you, that by not being a full-fledged merc, I only receive a fraction of the chits that you do."

"You don't need to remind me," I said as I started walking towards the cave mouth. "You have been very clear about the chits since we started working together."

"My sister is on her second litter of pups, Joe," Mgurn said. "Second litter. Where's the dad? Hell if I know. Lazy son of a gump skipped out on her the second he heard. One litter he's fine with, but two? Oh, no, that's just way too much for him to handle!"

"I know, Mgurn, I know," I said. "I can kick you some extra chits, if that's what you need."

"Charity? Bah!" Mgurn scoffed. "I work for a living, Joe. I work my carapace off, thank you very much! I don't need your handouts!"

"Man, I was only offering to help, okay? Don't snap my head off," I said, pausing at the mouth of the cave, my H16 aimed into the darkness, its scan function running at full power. "Are you seeing this? I'm not picking up any life signs at all. Not even native species. This is a dead cave."

"Dead cave?" Mgurn asked, his rant over with. I could tell by the way his quad segmented jaws clicked together that his normal nervousness had turned to wary fear. "We don't like dead caves."

"No, we don't," I replied.

I turned the H16 on the rock around the cave mouth, getting close for as fine of readings as possible. I wasn't even picking up mold spores. And every planet has mold spores. I'd be willing to bet that the center of the largest sun has mold spores. You can't get rid of the stuff.

"There are a few explanations of why there are no signs of life," Mgurn said. "None of them good."

"No mold," I said.

"Yes, I can smell that," Mgurn replied.

"You can? Why didn't you say anything?" I snapped.

"Because I wanted to confirm with actual scans," he said and tapped his scanner against his armored forearm.

Leforians don't have tech implants due to their insect-like circulatory systems. It interferes with the holos functioning properly or something. Yeah, they have hair like mammals and look like large beetle dogs, but their blood and fluids are just not compatible with internal tech.

Mgurn tapped his scanner against his forearm again and I watched his brow lower and eyes narrow.

"Problem?" I asked.

"Unreliable reading," he said. "Even with my external scanner."

He squatted, picked up a cargo bag, and pulled out a second scanner. He set the first one down and turned on the second then went through an entire scan protocol of the cave.

"This isn't how we save time," I said.

"It is how we save our butts from getting eaten," he replied.

"Eaten?" I asked.

"Eaten," he nodded and showed me the scanner.

Nothing. Absolute zero.

"Oh, man," I muttered.

"Yeah," Mgurn agreed.

"B'flo'do," we said together.

B'flo'dos are a feral race that sap all energy from their environment. They come from the same system as B'clo'no's, but are a different species. Still made of mucus, but all black and nearly impossible to see if you look at one head on because they suck in light energy as well. Not what a merc wants to come across on a mission. I had to deal with them as a Marine since the B'clo'nos use them as grunt soldiers, mostly for kamikaze attacks.

"It touches us and we're over," Mgurn said.

"I know," I replied.

"We won't be able to see it in there," Mgurn said.

"I know," I replied.

"You ever seen a B'flo'do drain a person dry?" he asked.

"You know I have," I said.

"Plan?" he asked.

"I don't have one," I said. "Draw it out? One of us is bait while the other recovers the salvage?"

"I'm stronger than you and can carry more equipment," Mgurn said, "and you have your Fleet battle legs which makes you a faster runner. Normally, I wouldn't say that about a human since we Leforians are quite spry, but you are an obvious exception."

"Yeah, that occurred to me as soon as I suggested the plan," I said. "Great."

"Lure the thing away from the cave and towards the east," Mgurn said as he stretched his limbs and rotated his torso back and forth. "Give me, let's see…fifteen minutes? I should have the equipment salvaged and loaded on the ship by then."

"Then what?" I asked. "It'll suck the engines empty if I try to get back to the ship with it on my tail."

"Then lose it out there," Mgurn said and pointed at the desert to our east. "There is almost no life out there. B'flo'dos tire quickly. Lead it into the middle of the sands and it won't have anything to feed off. It'll slow down enough for you to return to the ship before it can catch up. We'll be off planet in seconds once you are aboard."

"There are a few dangerous flaws in this plan," I responded.

Mgurn shrugged which always looks weird on a Leforian as their backplate lifts into the air. "It's your plan," he said. "Fix the flaws on the go."

"Great," I said. I pointed to a small natural alcove a few feet from the cave mouth. "Hide there. Do not show yourself until we are far enough away that it won't sense you. Then book your bug butt inside and get the salvage done."

"I believe we should talk chit split on this ticket," Mgurn said. "I am doing all of the salvage work. I'm not asking for the majority of chits, but half would be acceptable."

"I could scrap this ticket, take the penalty, and then get nothing," I suggested. "How is that for a chit split? Pretty sure half of nothing is nothing."

"Your mathematical skills are dizzying," Mgurn grumbled. "Fine. Extra ten percent?"

"That works," I said. I took aim at the dirt directly in front of the cave. "Hide. We need to get this over with."

Mgurn didn't argue and hurried to the alcove. He kept his back facing out which would give him some extra protection due to his armored flesh. I, on the other hand, had only my SMC uniform to protect me. Like an idiot, I didn't wear any battle armor, just my enviro shield, because it wasn't one of those planets. There's nothing on Hepnug. Not anymore. Not that it would matter since the B'flo'do would have just sucked my armor of all of its power, turning it into a lot of heavy garbage.

I pressed the trigger of my H16 and a wide beam began to scorch the dirt in front of the cave. It was a sweeper beam, not as powerful as a projectile plasma blast, but very effective when you need to burn your way through things. At that moment, I didn't need to burn as much as I needed to entice. No way the B'flo'do could ignore a tasty sweep beam right outside its door.

Or maybe it could.

I stood there for a full five minutes and began to worry that I'd drain my H16 myself before the damn B'flo'do showed up.

"Is there a problem?" Mgurn's muffled voice echoed out of the alcove.

"It's not coming," I said.

"It could have fed enough that it's in a sleep state," Mgurn replied. "That has been known to happen."

"Yeah, after eating a whole ship's worth of energy, maybe," I said. "Not sucking some scientists and their gear dry. It may be on to us."

"B'flo'dos are dumb as rocks," Mgurn said. "I highly doubt it is on to us."

"Then where the hell is it?" I asked.

I got my answer half a second later.

A thick tendril of blackness shot out at my H16. I jumped back and barely managed to avoid the strike.

"It's here," I whispered.

I walked backwards, sending a beam into the ground every couple of steps as I tried to draw the thing out of its hidey hole. The tendril followed, but the rest of the B'flo'do wasn't taking the bait. It was a cautious bastard which isn't like B'flo'dos at all. Mgurn was right, they are dumber than rocks, and usually chase down any hint of energy. This guy was playing it safe. That had me more worried than if it had come rushing at me head on.

Not that B'flo'dos have heads. They are just mucus creatures like their B'clo'no cousins.

A few more meters and the tendril stopped. It stretched all the way from the cave to me, nearly twenty meters long. That's a big B'flo'do. At that size, it should have been on me in seconds. None of its behavior made sense. The only reason it would be cautious like that was if a larger predator was close by.

But Hepnug was a dead planet. No predators at all because there was no life on the damn planet. Except mold because, as I have stated, mold is everywhere.

The tendril stopped, shook itself a couple times, then shot back into the cave. It made a rubber band snapping sound as it withdrew and I watched Mgurn jump in his alcove.

"What was that?" he called out.

"The B'flo'do," I replied, raising the barrel of my H16 and resting it against my shoulder. "It bailed. Went back in the cave."

"No, not that, the rumbling sound," Mgurn said and turned around. "You can't hear that rumbling sound?"

"No, I can't," I replied. "I'm not a bug dog."

"Really?" Mgurn snapped. "You are such a bigot sometimes."

"I was just kidding," I said. "Calm down."

His four eyes went wide and he straightened to his full height of seven feet. I could see the muscles under his hairy armor flex and pulse and I knew something very, very bad was about to go down.

"Is it behind me?" I asked.

Mgurn nodded.

"Is it really, really big?" I asked.

Mgurn nodded again.

"B'flo'do?" I asked.

"Oh, yeah," Mgurn said. "B'flo'do."

I took a deep breath and slowly turned around. Yep. It was a really, really big B'flo'do. I could see why the one in the cave was not coming out no matter how much energy I tried to bribe it with. B'flo'dos aren't generally cannibalistic, but the mass of black sludge in front of me was almost as big as my ship, so I could understand the smaller one's hesitation. Ones that big were known to syphon smaller B'flo'dos' energies if they were especially hungry.

I was willing to wager that the big pile of black snot was especially hungry since it seemed to have found itself on a dead planet.

"Okay," I said. "This is a problem."

First thing I did was activate my emergency beacon on my wrist. My implant would send a trans-space signal directly to SMC headquarters. No number wanted to have to send that signal since it made them look weak, but too many numbers learned the hard way that not sending it meant you kept your pride but lost your life. I was more than willing to take the ribbing I would get back at

SMC headquarters than risk dying before SMC decided to send out a search party and turn me into a salvage ticket.

There was a high-pitched screech from behind me and I whipped my head about to see Mgurn being dragged into the cave by the smaller B'flo'do. Big Problem Number Two.

It was right then that I wished I had control of my gift. Some uber-focus and clarity would have been nice. Slow things down, give me that extra split-second I needed to weigh all my options. Put things in perspective and make the smart choice first before making the not so smart choice that I usually have a fifty-fifty shot at stumbling towards.

Okay. Okay, okay, okay. Mgurn needed my help. He'd be a drained pile of exo-armor and endo-bones in minutes if I didn't go take care of B'flo'do Junior.

I took one step and Big B'flo'do shuddered, its mass lurching at me.

I stopped stepping. I even had my left foot raised off the ground and held it there, afraid the monster slime would grab me if I set it down. Battle legs or not, standing on one foot is not the position a number wants to be in when facing immanent death.

Mgurn screeched again. Then flat out screamed.

"JOE!"

"Hold on!" I yelled.

"JOE!"

"I know! I know!" I shouted back. "I'm working it out now!"

I was. My brain was in overdrive and I was taking a mental inventory of all of my options. The first ten options on that inventory list were dying, so I skipped to option eleven and looked down at my H16.

Now, while the galaxy may seem like a lawless place, especially in the chaos after the War, weapons weren't exactly a chit a dozen. I had to pay for my SMC H16 out of my own earnings. Same with the upgrades to my ship, the armor I wasn't currently wearing, and any and all supplies needed to punch a salvage ticket. So, my decision in that moment wasn't rash and wasn't without trepidation.

I very slowly opened the power coupling under the barrel of the carbine. Even that movement got the Big B'flo'do all hot and bothered. It slid its slimy bulk closer to me, and it took all of my will not to turn and run screaming.

My fingers found the regulator inside the power coupling and I twisted it carefully until it popped loose. Making sure I didn't lose the regulator, since those babies cost almost as much as the entire weapon itself, I tucked it in my pocket, took one last look at my handy multi-weapon, said a quick prayer to all Eight Million Gods, and pulled the trigger.

That got Big Smushy excited.

Without the regulator in place, the power coupling would overheat in only a few seconds. An overheated power coupling would normally trip the regulator and the energy levels would instantly drop and normalize, making for an even shooting experience. But my poor H16 wasn't going to normalize. It was going to do the exact opposite and die one painful death.

I'd die a painful death too if I didn't get my butt out of there fast.

That's where having battle legs comes in handy.

With my superheating H16 still in hand, I turned and ran as fast as my trusty legs would carry me. Mgurn stopped screeching as B'flo'do Junior came rushing from the cave, its energy hunger driving it out of its safety place. I ran straight at the alien, knowing I had maybe a full second to pull off what I needed to pull off.

Now, it is that kind of pressure that gets my gift to kick in. Running headlong at an alien, while also fleeing a much, much, much larger alien, both of which wanted what I held in my hands, meant the world started to slow, my vision became crystal clear, and any extraneous thoughts in my head were pushed away.

I threw the H16 high into the air and dove to the ground. Junior sprang from its globby position in front of the cave and went right for the carbine. I know Mr. Big was doing the same thing because I could feel the whoosh of air from its massive body press against my back as I rolled my shoulder and tumbled underneath the springing Junior.

I came up in front of the cave and scrambled into the safety of the darkness beyond. I was back on my feet and stumbling around in the dark as I counted off the seconds in my head.

"Joe!" Mgurn yelled as I came around a bend in the cave. He didn't look so hot. Half his armor was grey and his bottom jaw, both of them, slumped down against his chest. "Where is it? What's going on?"

I rushed over to him, picked him up by the hairy scruff of his exoskeleton, and started hurrying his bug dog butt deeper into the cave. We came around another curve and I could just barely make out the outlines of science equipment and possibly a few desiccated corpses when the world outside went thermonuclear.

Okay, okay, not precisely thermonuclear, but pretty darn close. Anyone standing within a half-mile radius outside the cave would have been seriously foed.

Mgurn screeched some more, because that's what he does, and I forced us both to the ground as rock and dust exploded all around us. I had pebbles up my nose and a lungful of Hepnug dirt before I even had a chance to cover my head. Luckily, the cave didn't collapse down on us, so head covering wasn't the thing that separated my exciting life from a brutal death.

"Joe?" Mgurn coughed as he rolled over and blinked his eyes a few times. "What did you do?"

"I blew my H16," I said. "It got Junior and Big Boy all hot and bothered. No B'flo'do in the galaxy could resist going after an overheating multi-weapon."

"You are right," Mgurn said. "That was quick thinking. Expensive, but quick. Your gift does come in handy."

"I thought that one up without any gift help," I said as I stood and unsuccessfully tried to wipe the dust from my uniform. "My gift didn't kick in until I was already running away."

"Oh," Mgurn said.

Despite the fact I'd just saved both of our butts, I had a distinct feeling he did not approve.

"What?" I asked. "What did I do wrong?"

"It isn't a matter of what you did wrong," Mgurn said. "Because you may have done nothing wrong at all. It's just that your gift allows you to see all angles and consequences at once."

"Yeah, I know how it works," I said, tapping at my temple. "It's my gift in my head. I don't see the problem. We had two B'flo'dos trying to kill us and I took them out. Where's the angle in that?"

"No, no, that is wonderful," Mgurn said, getting to his feet. He bent over and took several deep breaths then pointed towards the cave mouth. "But, and I'm only guessing here, but what if those two weren't the only B'flo'dos in the area? That kind of energy discharge and detonation would bring any others to us from halfway across the planet."

"Huh," I said as my brain caught up with his logic. "Crap."

"Have you activated your emergency beacon?" he asked.

"Yeah, I did that first thing," I replied.

"Good, good," Mgurn said and smiled in that multi-jawed way of his. "Then we should have backup in only a few minutes since I am certain there are other salvage mercs in this system working other claims. It is unfortunate we'll have to split our claim with them, but better than dying."

"That's how I saw it when I activated the beacon," I said. "I'm not too proud to split a claim."

There was a loud noise from outside the cave and Mgurn grabbed me by the arm.

"Not a battle arm, man," I said as I pried my bruised bicep out of his grip. "Ease off. Even if there are more B'flo'dos out there, the energy residue leftover from that explosion will keep them occupied long enough for help to arrive."

"I hope so," Mgurn said.

"Come on," I said and patted him on his shoulder. "Let's take a look. Just a quick look to see what we are up against."

"Oh, no, I don't think that's a good idea at all," Mgurn said, shaking his head back and forth fast enough that he got dizzy and plopped down on his shelled butt. "I'll sit right here. You go look, if you want. Try not to die."

"That attitude is making me think I should have picked a Klav for an assistant," I said as I walked away.

"They're too smart," Mgurn called after me. "They'd never sign on with you."

Yeah, he was probably right.

I had to squeeze through some cave-ins to get to the mouth, but I made it fairly easily. Just a couple more scrapes to add to the pile of bruises I would be sporting by the next morning.

When I reached the mouth of the cave, I sort of wished I'd stayed back with Mgurn in his safety net of ignorance.

The entire landscape outside the cave was filled with B'flo'dos. Hundreds of them. All sizes. A couple were bigger than Mr. Big had been.

Two things raced through my mind:

One- why were there so many B'flo'dos on a dead planet? Two was weird enough, but hundreds? Not a random thing.

Two- OH, MY CRUD! I WAS SO FOED!

I will say that I kept my composure and did not embarrass myself with any unwanted bodily functions. As quietly and slowly as I could, I crept back into the darkness of the cave. The B'flo'dos were rapt by the explosion's energy residue, so they didn't register my life force freaking out in the cave. Even still, I tried to keep my breathing steady and slow my heart rate in case a couple of them got curious about what could be hiding in the cave that had basically become my trap.

"What did you see?" Mgurn asked as I returned to the back of the cave.

"Not much," I said and sat down next to him.

"Oh, dear me," he whispered and his jaws started clicking in his native language.

Pretty sure he was praying to the Eight Million Gods too.

"We should stay put and wait for help," I said. "Outside is boring."

Mgurn started praying harder. I decided I should be quiet and not upset him any further. I was a considerate boss that way.

THREE

The beer spilled over the rim of my mug, but I didn't care. I was in the middle of my story and every eye from every merc at the table was locked onto me as I told it.

"Hundreds! I am talking hundreds!" I exclaimed.

"We know," Hopsheer laughed as she elbowed Salvage Merc Thirty-Five, an ugly cuss named Tarr Holenbeak. The guy was more scar tissue than healthy skin.

"Yeah, Laribeau, get on with it," Tarr said. "We saw all the B'flo'dos when we landed to save your ass. A heads up would have been nice."

"I was busy," I replied, taking a drink of beer. "So was Mgurn. That guy was doing that fear gas thing Leforians do, and I have never smelled anything so rank in my life. No wonder none of the B'flo'dos came into the cave. They got one whiff of his stink and they slithered their nasty slime butts as far away as possible."

"It was one puff of gas and they did not slither away," Mgurn called from his seat across the SMC headquarter's mess hall where he sat with a group of other assistants. "They were attracted to the new ships that had landed."

"Keep telling yourself that!" I laughed and finished my beer. I slammed the mug down and snapped my fingers for a refill.

"You're in the mess, Joe," Hopsheer said. "You have to get your own beer."

"Dammit," I said, picking my mug back up. "Stay where you are. There's more to the story."

"We were there," Tarr said.

"We weren't," Ig Vrtnig said. She was Salvage Merc One Fifteen and a full Groshnel. They're a race that has no bones, eight arms, and gulps air every few minutes to keep their bodies solid. They are known for their amazing singing voices and complete inability to use salt properly when cooking. "Come back and finish the story. It's been boring as Hell around here lately."

"Be right back," I said, giving Ig a quick nod and tip of my empty mug as I turned and headed to the taps in the far wall.

Almost any type of drink known to the galaxy could be found in one of those taps. The SMC headquarters was a rambling, sprawling complex that had been added on continually for decades since the Corp's creation. Some areas were not suitable for human habitation, which was fine by me as long as the mess hall stayed the center of the complex and they kept the oxygen flowing.

The thing about the SMC was that it was a fairly recent entity in galactic history. The War had started about two and a half centuries ago, spanning generations of combatants. It looked like it would be a perpetual conflict as the Skrangs refused to negotiate or even think about a peace treaty. Once they brought the B'clo'nos into it, pretty much all hope was lost that the War would ever end.

It didn't take long for resources to become scarce despite the millions of planets, asteroid fields, rogue comets, and other celestial bodies that made up the galaxy. Once our side, the Galactic Fleet, realized they were going to run out of materials needed to keep the War fueled and going, they put out a call for solutions.

An enterprising ex-general in the Fleet decided to put some discharged ex-Marines to work and the Salvage Merc Corps was born. That ex-general, a Mr. Bon Chattslan, had the foresight to insist that the SMC be a neutral entity in the War and somehow managed to work out an agreement with not just the brass of the Galactic Fleet, but also with the leaders of the Skrang Alliance.

If a salvage merc had a ticket to claim then they would be allowed free passage and not be interfered with by either side. Whatever resources were salvaged would be offered at auction and each side could bid on them. It made Chattslan a very wealthy man.

But I have to give credit to the guy, he didn't sit on his riches. He built up SMC headquarters and branched out from just salvaging materials to taking on any job that someone, or something, was willing to pay for up front and avoid the auction all together. People, creatures, a lost wallet, he didn't care. If the SMC was neutral then that meant the tickets were neutral as well.

Salvage mercs don't pass judgement and don't quit a ticket because it might be morally questionable. Morals are for the Galactic Fleet and the Skrangs to figure out. Tickets are tickets, is a salvage merc's unofficial motto. We've got a lot more of those, mottos, but that's the big one.

You'd think with the War over, there'd be less demand for the SMC, but you'd be so wrong that I wouldn't even look in your direction. Thousands of inhabited planets needed some serious rebuilding. Resources after the War were thinner than during. The SMC was bringing in new recruits by the shipload each week.

Unfortunately, new also meant inexperienced. There were nearly as many merc deaths each week as recruits could be found. We had all started joking that our next tickets were only going to be finding recruits.

Not that some of our tickets weren't that way already. Hopsheer seemed to be entirely tasked with tracking down unique recruits that the bosses found of interest. Not that she talked about that much. I only knew because I had been one of those tickets six months earlier.

"You gonna fondle that tap or pour a beer?" a voice asked from my left elbow.

I shook my head and realized I'd just been standing by the tap wall, thinking.

"Hey, Scott," I said, glancing down at the half-man, half-rollerball next to me.

Scott had been a medic in the War. He saved guys like me when their limbs had been blown off and insides were dangling over their belts. Eventually the odds caught up with him and he'd been on the receiving end of some bad luck. The bad luck wasn't the explosion that took his bottom half, but the fact that the medic that treated him had been barely in the field for a week and botched the patch job he did on Scott.

The guy wasn't eligible for battle legs like me, or even just normal legs, because he didn't have enough left to attach to. Instead he ended up plopped into a rollerball which doubled as not only his mode of transportation, but also helped keep him alive by filtering all his bodily fluids and making sure he didn't go toxic by eating too many Jesperian tacos. That and the rollerball also housed enough diagnostic equipment to make Scott a one man hospital on wheels. Or on ball. Whatever you'd call it.

"Maybe take it easy," Scott said as he eyed me closely. "Your adrenals will still be taxed from your salvage mission and alcohol, even the tame human kind in that ale you're pounding, will only stress your system more."

"If you're going to play doctor with me, Scott, then I'm going to need a few more pints," I laughed. He didn't. Scott's a nice guy, but he takes the health thing very seriously. I cleared my throat, filled my mug, and patted it with my other hand. "Last one, I promise. Just going to finish a story then go pass out for a couple days and let my body recharge. That cool with you, Doc?"

"I am not a doctor, Joe," Scott said. "Not officially."

"SMC would have to pay you more if you were," I said and sipped from my mug.

He pointed to his upper lip and I felt my own, gave it a wipe, and cleared the foam from under my nose.

"You are not wrong there," he said. "Come by my office when you wake up. If I don't hear from you in two days then I'll come looking for you myself. Don't make me do that, Joe. I have real work to do around here with all the recruits coming in every Friday."

"What's today?" I asked and saw him frown. "No, really, I'm not sure. I hit two wormholes on the way to my last ticket which meant two on the way back. My sense of time is crap right now."

"It's a Tuesday," Scott said.

"Cool," I responded, sipping again. "See you Thursday, at the very latest, okay?"

"Okay," Scott said and pointed to the row of taps. "Care to pour me a spring ale? I'm off shift for the next eight hours, so I thought I'd indulge myself for a change before I get back to immunizations and cavity searches."

"Cavity searches? Yikes," I said as I took the mug he offered and poured him a fresh beer. "You deserve to have your own keg tucked inside that rollerball of yours."

"I plan to when I retire in a couple decades," he said, taking the mug from me. "Thank you."

"My pleasure, man," I said and nodded at the table of mercs waiting anxiously for my return. Okay, maybe not anxiously since it looked like Hopsheer had started telling a story of her own. "Gotta get back. See you on Thursday."

"Thursday," Scott said as he rolled one way and I walked the other. "I'm holding you to that."

Everyone at the table burst out laughing just as I got there and I gave them my most hurt-looking face.

"What'd I miss?" I asked, grabbing my seat and plopping down as I watched tears roll down Hopsheer's stoney cheeks. Damn she was beautiful.

"Hoppy was telling us about that time she was training you and you fell into a nest of baby gumps," Ig said. "Did you really get six down your uniform?"

"Oh, fo, I'd forgotten about that," I said and gave everyone a smile. "And it wasn't six, it was ten, and yeah, they got down my uniform and became attached in places no one should have a gump attached to."

"It wasn't ten," Hopsheer said, shaking her head. "It was six."

"Now hold on," I said raising a hand. "It was ten, trust me. I remember every single one of those claws that clamped onto me." I took a long drink and settled in. "I can see that Hoppy has butchered a great story. How about I tell it from the beginning so you know what really went down?"

There were some groans, but I could see everyone was ready to hear my version. Even Hopsheer as she gave me that sly smile of hers.

I'd gone through the baby gumps story, a rehashing of the latest ticket adventure since new mercs had shown up so I needed to start at the beginning, and then a weird tale about when I was a kid and an older cousin decided to see if I could fit in the cook unit and still breathe when he turned it on. I had half the table gasping for breath from laughing and the other half shocked as all hell that I didn't die and my cousin hadn't been sent to a reeducation planet for treatment.

It was four in the morning before I was able to stumble back to my quarters, which was on the far port side of the SMC headquarters, and fall drunkenly into bed. Alone. Always alone.

Well, not quite alone since mercs had to share their quarters with their assistants due to space issues with all the new recruits.

We didn't have to share bunks, praise the Eight Million Gods, but I'm not a small man and Mgurn is a foing Leforian and seven feet tall, so the cabin felt cramped anytime both of us were in it at the same time.

"Talked to Scott," Mgurn said as I tried to slip my boots off my battle legs.

"Did you?" I asked

Technically, I could have had my feet hardened and not needed boots, but the ladies of the galaxy prefer my synthetic skin to cold metal, so I wear boots to keep the synth skin intact. That and you can hide stuff in combat boots. That stuff, such as a couple of steel blades, a stun strip, two containers of stimulant gel, and a pack of multi-species condoms, came tumbling out when I finally kicked my boots onto the metal floor.

"Your uniform has pockets, you know," Mgurn said.

"I know," I said. "Old Marine habit. If your CO shouts for you to empty your pockets, you don't want to be caught with stim gel and alien porn on your person. That's just asking for an ass reaming."

"I am glad I never enlisted in the Marines," Mgurn said. "But speaking of, Scott wanted me to make sure you weren't pushing yourself too hard."

"I'm not," I said.

"That's what I told him, but he does have a point," Mgurn said.

The big Leforian rolled over on his bunk that sat directly across the cabin from mine. His four eyes centered on me and I knew he'd been waiting up just to give me a talking to. The "Mom" nickname for Leforians wasn't for nothing.

"You joined six months ago," Mgurn said. "We've been partners for five of those months. In those five months, you have accepted every ticket handed to you without a single break. I love the chits being racked up in my account, but I'm Leforian, I can handle the exertion and constant work. You are human, you cannot."

"I have battle legs," I said and smacked my calves. "Six nuclear cells per. They never get tired."

"The rest of you does," Mgurn said. "I have put in a request with the bosses that we work on training for the next couple of weeks and not take any tickets."

"You what?" I snapped and sat upright, my face hot with anger.

The world spun about me as the alcohol in my system danced in my brain. I put out a hand to steady myself and missed my bunk frame completely. I was on the floor in a heap before I knew it.

"That right there," Mgurn said.

"I'm drunk, not exhausted," I said.

I lied. I was fairly exhausted. But that's because it was four in the morning! I wasn't too exhausted to keep working. Marines don't quit even if we get kicked out of the service.

"I know what you are thinking," Mgurn said.

"No, you don't," I replied.

"You're thinking that Marines don't quit," Mgurn said. "You're thinking that if you prove yourself hard enough in the SMC then maybe the Fleet will take you back."

"Wrong," I sneered. "On the last part. Shut up on the first part."

"They won't take you back," Mgurn said. "The Fleet doesn't need more Marines, they need less now that the War is over. And why would you want to go back?"

"I don't want to go back," I said. "Why are you harping on this? I love being a merc and working for the SMC. Pays better and I have way more freedom and control over my life."

"Good," Mgurn said. "That's what I was hoping you'd say. I was worried the announcement would change your mind and you'd go back."

"The announcement?" I asked. "What announcement?"

I'd managed to untangle myself from the heap on the floor and pulled myself back onto my bunk.

"Mgurn? What announcement?" I asked.

"You didn't hear?" he said and his eyes went wide. "Damn. I should have kept my jaws closed."

"Spit it out, dammit," I snapped.

"There was an announcement on the galactic vid just before midnight," Mgurn said. "You know how they do that because of the time differential in the many systems."

"Yes, I know how they do that because of the time differential in the many systems," I mocked. "Get on with it, already."

"The Fleet made an announcement that Admiral Xvltndg is stepping down and his replacement has already been named," Mgurn said.

"Xvltndg is stepping down?" I asked, shocked. "I thought they'd have to bury him in that admiral's chair of his."

"The War is over," Mgurn said. "Two years of transition and now it's time for a new leader in peace time."

"Yeah, I guess that makes sense," I replied. "Still, hard to imagine Xvltndg stepping down."

I thought back to all the times I'd seen that angry, scarred, scale-covered face barking on giant vid screens before a big battle. The guy had scared the holy crud out of me, but damn if he didn't know how to rally troops to action.

"Wait a minute," I said as something occurred to me. "What does Xvltndg have to do with me wanting to re-up with the Fleet? I'm not seeing the connection."

"You will," Mgurn said. "Bring up your news feed."

I eyed him warily then tapped at my wrist a couple times until the holo of the galactic news feed started streaming before my eyes. I watched it scroll through a few special interest stories, mostly about orphans and widows and huggy feely stuff like that, then stopped it when the news of Xvltndg showed up.

My world dropped out from under me as I saw the name of the man that would be replacing him. It was a human, which was rare since we only made up ten percent of the Fleet's population. But that wasn't what had me stunned. It was the name of the specific human that would become the new admiral of the Fleet.

Crawford Helms.

My old Marine battle mate.

"Crawford?" I asked out loud. "How is this possible?"

"A lot of organizations are asking the same thing," Mgurn said. "He's not the youngest to become Admiral of the Fleet, but he's close. It seems like a strange choice to me."

"Crawford?" I asked again. "He was a sergeant when I left the Fleet. He'd always said he had no desire to become an officer, let alone to become admiral. He liked being a sergeant, liked being where the action was."

"Not as much action with the War over," Mgurn said. "Maybe he's thinking about galactic politics. Admiral of the Fleet is a direct road to that career."

"Crawford hates politics," I said. "He hates everything about it. I'd never met any man that was more gung ho about killing Skrangs and B'clo'nos than him. I just always thought he'd get bored with the Fleet once he couldn't blast the enemy to pieces anymore."

"Yes, well, it looks like he decided to stay," Mgurn said. "I hope that means you won't be trying to join back up with the Fleet. You now have a direct line to the admiral. I bet you could call in a favor and he'd reinstate you by next week."

"Well, yeah, I guess he would," I said.

That was when Mgurn's concern about me going back to being a Marine really sunk in. I loved being a number, living the life of a salvage merc. The chits were great, the work was great, I got to have an H16 again. I flew around the galaxy and killed stuff or saved stuff. Sometimes I did both to do both. It makes sense if you think about it.

But here was an opportunity that I had never thought I'd see. Mgurn was so right. I could call up Crawford and there isn't a question in the galaxy about whether or not he'd let me be a Marine again.

"Now you're thinking about it," Mgurn sighed before rolling over and turning his armored back to me. "Great. Wonderful. Just lovely. Do me a favor and give me a heads up if you do quit the SMC, okay? Don't make me find out in the weekly newsletter, alright? That wouldn't be cool, Joe."

"No, right, yeah, not cool," I said, my mind reeling. "No newsletter heads up. I tell you first."

"Close enough," Mgurn said. "Try to get some sleep."

He clapped his hands together and the lights blinked out.

I lay there for another hour, my eyes wide open and staring at the pitch black of the room, all the possibilities racing through my head until I finally started to doze. Just before sleep took me, I had a weird moment of clarity, though. It wasn't so much a thought as a memory.

The last time I'd spoken to Crawford, just before I became a salvage merc, he'd sounded off. Same smart ass as always, but the humor was forced. I thought it was because he didn't know how to talk to me since I'd become just another civilian. But thinking back on it, I began to believe that maybe he wanted to tell me something but couldn't. Not uncommon when dealing with the Fleet, but it was Crawford. We never kept anything from each other.

I made myself a promise to call him in the morning. Wish him congratulations and all that. And listen closely to see if I could hear that same forced humor and offness from before.

FOUR

I was on hold for close to an hour before I was put through to the admiralty office.

"Admiral Helms's office, please hold," said the cute brunette Slinghasp in my holo. She had those iridescent scales that all Slinghasps have, making it hard to look directly at her as the artificial light of the transmission amplified everything.

"Wait, wait," I cried out. "I've been on hold for an hour already. Can you tell Crawford that Joe Laribeau is calling? I promise not to take too much of his time."

"The *admiral* is very busy today, Mr. Laribeau," the Slinghasp replied. That slit of a mouth of hers was smiling, but it never reached her reptilian eyes. "I will tell him you are on the line, but it could be a while before he is available."

"I totally understand," I said. "Thanks."

"You are very welcome," she said, making it known that I was not welcome at all.

I tuned out the Galactic Fleet propaganda that streamed on my holo and surfed the Grid on my wall unit in my quarters while I waited for Crawford to come on.

Mgurn had vacated the quarters as soon as he woke up and saw me staring up at the ceiling. He grumbled something about training, but I wasn't listening. The idea that Crawford Helms could become an admiral only two and a half years after the War didn't sit right at all. I'm pretty sure Mgurn saw that on my face and got out of there before he got stuck in a room with me bitching.

I'd have bailed too if I were him.

I had just come across an interesting article about a mining colony that had been treated for some rare disease that only gumps get when a loud chime rang out from my wrist and Crawford appeared.

"Joe," he said and smiled. His smile didn't reach is eyes any more than his secretary's had. "Man, it has been a while. I hear you're with the Salvage Merc Corp now. Good for you. You have too many useful skills to be stuck as a security guard at a station mall or as some bouncer for one of the taverns on Xippeee."

"Don't think Xippeee would take me," I said and waved him off before he could ask why. "Forget about me, brother, let's talk about you."

"Yeah, well, things have been moving fast," Crawford chuckled. "Maybe too fast."

His face blanched and he looked around. He coughed and tried to widen his smile, but his cheeks weren't obeying.

He was an average-looking guy. Brown hair, brown eyes, nice smile, dark red skin. Human as the rest of us that are human. You probably could have passed Crawford in a crowded market or stood by him on a shuttle platform and never really noticed him. He was average.

But I noticed him. I noticed how the skin at the corner of his eyes twitched and looked tight. I noticed how his hairline had started to recede. I noticed how he was wearing makeup to hide the black shadows under his eyes. Makeup. Make and up. I noticed.

"Fast? That's an understatement," I said and laughed. It was my nervous laugh, the one I used to use right before we dropped into battle with the Skrang Alliance. "Hey, brother, listen, I don't want to take up your time today since I know every politician and planetary leader in the galaxy is probably calling you."

"You have no idea," he said and gave me a worried, but thankful smile.

"Can we meet for lunch or dinner or maybe a few pitchers of beer sometime soon?" I asked. "Just two friends shooting the crud about the good old days? It would be great to hear how you got this new job straight from your mouth and not over a holo."

"I...uh...yeah," he replied. "Give Ssssssgerfernssssss a few dates that work for you and she'll schedule a time for us. I'll call you back as soon as I can so you know I'm not foing with you. Cool?"

"Cool, brother," I said. "Take care of yourself, alright?"

"Will do, man," he said. "Gotta go. This place is insane and I'm just trying to keep my head above water."

"You've got this, Marine," I barked. "Hooah!"

He laughed and gave me a wink. "Hooah!"

Then the holo flickered and Sssssgerfernsssss came back on.

"What dates work for you, Mr. Laribeau?" she asked. "Give me a few so I can schedule a couple of backups, just in case."

"In case of what?" I asked.

"Just in case," she replied. "The admiral is a very busy man."

I hadn't been given a new ticket assignment yet, so I told her my days were open and she could pick what would work best. We set a time for a week from then on a nice little station that orbited the burning planet of Caga over in the Relic System. I'd eaten in their top cafe once and the view of the planet was spectacular as Hell. Literally, since Caga was a burning planet like its very own tiny version of Hell.

After the call was done, I showered quickly and decided I'd get the exam with Scott out of the way. It occurred to me as I gave him a quick holo call to make sure he was in that I had no idea what his last name was. Maybe Scott was his last name? I'd have to ask him during the exam.

Of course, I totally forgot once the exam got started because I absolutely hate needles. This is what? The 32nd century? Why are there still needles? Has no one invented a better delivery system for inoculations and vitamin regimens? Even the subcutaneous injector guns use needles. They just shoot in and out really fast, so you don't feel it, but they're still needles.

"Relax," Scott said for the eighth time. "We're done with the shots."

"Right, sure, liar," I said as I sat on the cold metal of the exam table in his office. Every few seconds, a wave of static electricity surged under me, killing every germ and microbe my ass may have had, then winked back out before I could even twitch. "You always save an extra shot for the very last just to mess with me."

"Since when have I ever done that?" Scott asked.

"Not you, doctors in general," I said.

"I'm not a doctor, Joe," Scot sighed. "I'm a trained medical professional recruited into the SMC because of my specific physical condition and experience with treating battle wounds."

"You say you aren't a doctor, but you're a doctor," I replied, making him grit his teeth and roll away across his office. He returned with a long rod that gleamed brightly under the exam room lights. "What's that? That a shot? It is! Damn you, Scott! I knew it!"

"Not a shot," he growled as he placed the tip of the rod against the top of my left foot.

All feeling from that foot ceased and the synthetic skin split wide open to reveal a smooth, polished metal finish underneath. He tapped the metal with the rod and the top of my foot split open just as fast as the synth skin had. It was a trip to see the insides of my foot, all fiberoptic cables and whirling nano-machines working in synchronicity.

"Any issues at all with mobility? Speed? Response time?" he asked.

"Response time?" I replied. "What do you mean?"

"Are your legs acting like legs?" he asked as he stuck the end of the rod deep inside my foot. "Do they respond like legs should or is there a pause sometimes? Maybe just a split-second, but long enough for you to notice?"

"Nope," I said. "My legs have been working perfectly. If anything, they respond before I want them to like they know what I'm thinking."

"That's probably a side effect of your gift," Scott said as he withdrew the rod and tapped my foot until the metal closed, followed by the skin. "Your brain is processing the request faster than your conscious mind can track. Most of us never notice those issues, but with your clarity, I can see why you would."

He repeated the same process with my right foot then closed it all up and gave me a pat on the knee with the rod.

"You are in perfect health," Scott said. "Even your adrenals are in the clear. You are as fine as you said you were last night."

"Gotta trust your patients more, Scott," I said and grinned.

"Probably not," he replied.

I hopped off the table and grabbed my uniform from a hook on the wall. I was dressed and about to step out of his office when something occurred to me.

"Hey, Scott? Twitching around the skin at the corners of the eyes is just a sign of stress, right?" I asked.

"More than likely," he replied as he entered my exam results into a terminal on the wall. He glanced over at me and frowned. "Why do you ask?"

"No reason," I said. "Just a friend I'm kind of worried about. I'd hate for his ticker to blow before we could get together again."

"There would be bigger signs if his heart is failing," Scott said. "This wouldn't be Admiral Crawford Helms you're asking about, would it?"

He laughed before I could respond and tapped at the terminal.

"I have your whole history here, from school up through the Marines," he said. "Admiral Helms's name pops up a lot. I am sure the twitches you are seeing are due to an immense amount of stress. Does he have a history of heart troubles?"

"No, not at all," I said. "Just a weird feeling I have."

"Huh," Scott said and gave me a very serious look. "I don't have much pull with any of the medical department in the Fleet, but I do have a couple of friends from my service days. Want me to send word through back channels that maybe Admiral Helms is due for a complete work-up if he hasn't already received one recently?"

"Can you do that?" I asked.

"I can try," he said.

"Yeah, that would be great," I said. "I know Crawford and he'll never go see the doctors on his own."

"Yes, I am well aware of the behavior," Scott said and turned back to his terminal. "I'll send you a message when I've reached out to my friends."

"Thanks," I said and left his office feeling a little better about Crawford's sudden situation.

The mess hall was almost deserted when I stepped through the swinging doors and took a look around. A couple of techs and a few mercs were seated at various tables, but no one I usually shot the crud with. I grabbed a tray and went down the line, grabbing up a mountain of food for breakfast. The cook at the end that scanned my wrist stared at the tray and shook his head.

"You're gonna toss half of that," he said. "What a waste."

"It all gets tossed at the end of the breakfast shift anyway," I said.

"Nope," he replied. "We recycle."

"Do I want to know?" I asked as I looked down at the food on my tray.

"Probably not," the cook replied and laughed. "Bon appétit."

"Yeah, thanks," I said.

I turned and found a spot by the far wall that I'd discovered when I first came to the SMC headquarters. It allowed me views of every entrance to the mess hall while also giving me a wall to put my back up against. Not that I worried about an attack happening in the headquarters, but it's best to be safe instead of sorry. My mom used to say that and she was known to keep her back to the wall most meals.

My parents settled on a rough world. Resource colony on a swamp planet. They took the job because it paid triple what other jobs paid and was a good distance from the front. The War was everywhere in the galaxy, but some places were safer than others. Bax wasn't one of those planets. Swamp planets have their issues. Gas pockets, bog traps, fauna, and flora, that would snatch you up in a second, brutal weather conditions.

The real problem were the settlers. All of them were there for the chits. They were paid a stipend plus a percentage of resources they found. Not much in the way of minerals, but it was a gas rich planet, not to mention the depth of organic material available. My parents did pretty well.

Until they were butchered in their sleep while I was off camping with friends in one of the hummock tree canopies. Their bodies were the first things I saw when I got home. Strung up outside our house, skin flayed off them, rotting in the humid air.

Jirks.

They'd killed a dozen other settlers before someone realized they were dealing with skintakers. I was too late to get my revenge, a mob had already hanged them and then set the bodies on fire. I got there just as what used to be my parents' faces melted off a couple of the Jirk bodies.

Not a fan of Jirks, if you can guess.

"This seat taken?" Hopsheer asked as she held a tray just above the table, her body poised to sit, but not quite taking the seat. "Joe?"

"Huh? Yeah, yeah, sit," I said. "Sorry. Talked to an old friend today and it's bringing up memories I thought I'd buried."

"Want to tell me about it?" she asked as she dug into the pile of food on her tray that was easily as big as mine. "I'm a good listener."

"I know you are," I replied and smiled. "But I'd rather let the dirt settle on these memories. Maybe some other time."

She shrugged and took a huge bite.

We ate in silence for a couple minutes then she leaned back and belched loud enough to make one of the mess hall attendants jump.

"Sorry," she said and laughed.

A couple more minutes of eating and I could tell she was dying to say something. Gwreqs are horrible liars. Despite their stone bodies, they wear their emotions on their faces. Add human behavior into that mix and you get one easy to read halfer.

"Come on, say it," I said as I set my fork down and picked up my drink. It was some cold tea, but I couldn't tell what kind. Fruity, but not sweet. "You either have something to tell me or something to ask."

"That obvious?" Hopsheer laughed.

"Yeah," I said. "So?"

"The new admiral, Crawford Helms, he's your old Marine buddy?" she asked.

"Yep," I said. "We fought side by side through six systems and eight campaigns. Saved each other's lives more times than I can count. Crud, I'd have lost a lot more than just my legs if it wasn't for him."

"You trust him?" she asked.

"Was I not talking out loud?" I responded. "I trust him with my life."

"Good to know," she said.

I waited, but she didn't offer any more.

"You're gonna have to fill me in here, Hoppy," I said. "Why do you want to know if I trust Crawford?"

"He's the new Admiral of the Fleet," she said and shrugged. "He has the power to get the War started again if he wants."

"He doesn't want," I said.

"How can you be sure?" she countered.

"Because he hated the War," I said. "He was a great marine. Dedicated, skilled, determined. He would have died for the Fleet, but he didn't like to kill for it. He comes from a pacifist culture."

"Yeah, I saw the red skin," Hopsheer said. "Saldt sect?"

"Yep," I replied. "He was kind of a disgrace to his family when he didn't fight being drafted by claiming a religious exemption. Saldts were basically an automatic pass. But he wanted to fight for the Fleet and prove himself as more than a follower."

"So he became a Marine?" Hopsheer chuckled. "There are better ways to prove you're not a follower."

"Oh, I razzed him about that constantly, especially around the holidays," I said.

"You think his Saldt standing is why he was chosen? A figurehead from an anti-War culture?" she asked. "Helps to sell peace."

"Could be," I said. "But I doubt it. There is something more going on. No way Crawford is qualified to be Admiral of the Fleet. Not having been only a sergeant less than three years ago."

"Sounds like you're working on a conspiracy theory," Hopsheer said and gave me that warm smile of hers. "Want to share?"

"Nah," I said. "I don't have any theories. I do have a lunch date with Crawford next week. I'm reserving all judgment until after that. I'll know what's up just by sitting down across from him."

"Mmm hmm," she replied.

"What does that mmm hmm mean?" I snapped. "You know something and you're just foing with me."

"Huh? What? No, no, I don't know anything," she said.

"You're Salvage Merc Eight," I said. "You have access to intel that I don't. What have you heard?"

"Number isn't rank," she said, quoting straight from the SMC manual.

She was right. In the SMC, a number is just a number. Seniority is all about time served, not what your merc number is. Mercs die all the time, so numbers get recycled. But, in Hopsheer's case, she's only the third Salvage Merc Eight and has been with the SMC for quite a few years. Her number almost equaled her seniority rank.

"Don't fo with me," I growled. "You know something and you're dying to tell me or you wouldn't even be sitting here. Tell me what it is or get the hell out of the mess."

"Damn," she sighed. "You're grumpy."

"I had to get shots," I said. "And my best friend looks like he's going to die of a stress-induced stroke before I can have lunch with him next week. Plus, that smile of yours always gets me all confused, so just be out with it."

"My smile?" she asked, looking stunned.

Crud. Fo. Damn. That shouldn't have been out loud.

"You know, uh, your, uh, I got a secret smile," I said, trying to recover. "It's what gave you away."

She eyed me closely then shook her head.

"Whatever, Joe," she said. "Smile or not, what I'm going to tell you stays between us, got it?"

"Yeah, of course," I said.

She pushed her tray aside and leaned across the table. I pushed mine aside and met her halfway.

"The bosses got word that something big is about to go down," she said. "They don't know what, but they are 100% sure it has to do with the admiral's office. Sources in the Fleet, as well as those close to the Skrang Alliance, think maybe Admiral Xvltndg's retirement wasn't exactly voluntary. Your friend might be being set up as a patsy."

"Patsy? For what?" I asked.

"What do you think?" she responded.

"I don't know, you tell me," I said. I knew. I'd had a brief bit of clarity as I spoke with Crawford over the holo line, but I'd ignored it then because I thought it was just nervousness due to my buddy being one of the most powerful people in the galaxy all of a sudden. My gut said Crawford didn't have long to live. But my head and my heart didn't want to believe it.

"I can see by the look on your face you know exactly what I'm talking about," Hopsheer insisted.

"War," I whispered. "Someone wants to start the War back up."

"Lots of someones want that," Hopsheer said and shrugged as she leaned back. "They always have. But the galaxy is exhausted, so it'll take something very big to get both sides back to the fight."

I leaned back also and watched her closely. She gave me that smile. My gut clenched.

"The bosses monitored my holo, didn't they?" I asked. "Then they put you up to coming and questioning me because they know I... Uh... You gave me that smile on purpose."

I stood up and my chair fell back with a loud clang. The few people in the mess hall all turned to stare then turned back again as they saw the look on my face. I grabbed up my tray and shook my head.

"Low," I said to Hopsheer. "You know I... We've had this... Low, Hoppy. You stepped over a line."

"Joe, wait," she called as I stalked to the trash slot.

I slid my tray through the slot and stared at the bright flash that always happens. At least they don't recycle food from the trays.

"Joe!" Hopsheer yelled as I kept my back to her and walked out of the mess hall. "Joe!"

I balled my fists and just started walking. An hour, two hours, three. I walked the halls of the SMC headquarters, going from one side to the other, navigating the chaotic wings of the complex, my feet on autopilot.

Mgurn found me eventually and took me to the target range. He knew that shooting a few thousand blasts from my H16 would calm me down. He was right. Two hours of target practice and I was able to think again. I was still pissed as hell, but I wasn't do something stupid and get my ass jettisoned into space pissed anymore.

"Beers?" he asked as we turned in our weapons and left the range.

"Nah," I said. "I'm going back to our quarters."

"Beers," he said and I knew he would use his Leforian strength to force the issue if I tried to balk again.

"Fine. Beers," I said. "But not in the mess. I can't even look at Hoppy if she's in there."

"We'll go sit up in the observation sphere," he said. "They just put sixty-four taps in."

"They did?" I asked. "When did they do that?"

"Last week," he said. "I never told you because I knew you'd end up passed out in the sphere every night."

"Yeah, I would," I replied. "Beers with a view? Lead on, Mgurn. Lead on."

FIVE

A week later I was in my ship and on my way to the Relic System. Caga was only a few clicks from the wormhole portal, but I decided to take the scenic route since I was a few hours early.

"Why are we adjusting course?" Mgurn asked from the co-pilot's seat.

My ship was a Hamershacht Whip-wing 409. Standard SMC issue. Not the fastest of its class, but agile as fo. I'd rather have maneuverability than speed any day. Simply put: you'll never outrun a full fire barrage from a Skrang destroyer, but you can outfly one.

"Joe? Where are we going?" Mgurn asked.

"I want to check something," I replied, heading for a cluster of moons that orbited Caga's sister planet, Gaca. It's a water planet, but uninhabited. Maybe some plankton-like critters down there, but nothing even close to sentience. "Keep an eye on our scanners, will ya? Make sure no one is following us."

"Who would follow us?" he asked.

"One of those ships that was in the jump queue back at the wormhole portal," I said. "I recognized a few as SMC, more as civilian transports, but there were at least three that looked out of place. They had an Edge look to them."

"Edge? Like edge of the galaxy?" Mgurn asked. "What would Edgers be doing by the SMC port?"

"I don't know," I said. "I could totally be wrong, but my gut says I'm not."

"Why not dock at the Caga station and alert the security detail there?" he asked. "They can handle things, I'm sure."

"I bet they can," I replied. "But do you want to risk our security to a bunch of hourly employees that make barely above minimum chits? I don't."

"You have a pessimistic view of galactic society, Joe," Mgurn said. "The War is over. Perhaps you should think of being more inclusive instead of—"

"Just watch the scanners," I snapped and pointed us towards the smaller of the moons.

I don't know why I was so irritable that day. It may have been emotional residue from my feeling of betrayal by Hopsheer. It could have been that I was nervous about lunch with Crawford. Could have been that Mgurn was just rubbing me the wrong way, which was certainly known to happen. All I do know is that I was not in the best of moods when I woke up that day and that mood just got worse as the hours wore on.

Once we were around the shadowed side of the moon, I spun the ship about so we could face the wormhole portal. I wanted to see who came popping out after us. If it was one of those Edge ships then I'd call it in to SMC headquarters and request backup. They'd pass it on to the Fleet and probably get my lunch with Crawford cancelled. But at least we wouldn't be blasted to Hell while in the middle of slurping overpriced soup.

No one came out of the wormhole portal except for two cargo ships that were obviously foodservice suppliers. No Edger ships. Not even a civilian buggy or two out sightseeing.

"You will be late to lunch if we don't go soon," Mgurn said as he tapped the console in front of him showing a holo appointment reminder. "Getting through security is going to take longer because of the admiral's presence on the station."

"I know," I said, but kept the ship were it was.

"Joe? We need to leave," Mgurn insisted. "If anyone was following us, they would have arrived in the system by now."

"I know," I said again, but still refused to turn the ship about and head for the Caga station.

Mgurn let out one of his patented sighs and crossed his arms over his armored chest. He drummed his fingertips against his biceps over and over, knowing full well that noise drove me insane. But I ignored it. I kept my eyes on the portal and waited until the very last second to leave.

When the holo on the console started to beep and flash bright red, I swung the ship about and punched it towards the Caga station. A speed warning came over the com as the station detected our approach and I slowed us just before they started to yell.

Mgurn was a nervous wreck and barely said a word to me as I docked the ship and got off, leaving him to watch over things while I met Crawford. He grunted a couple of reluctant well wishes, because Leforians can't help themselves, then I closed the hatch and presented myself for a full-body security scan.

"Clean," the security officer said as he finished sweeping my battle legs. "Nice hardware. Aftermarket or did you get those directly from the Fleet?"

"Fleet made and Fleet assigned," I said. "But I preferred my originals. The flesh ones I was born with."

The security officer rolled up his sleeve and split the skin on the inside of his forearm. Bright metal gleamed out from the slit.

"Rago Prime," he said. "My H16 went thermo after a B'clo'no slimed it."

"That must have been the 3184 model," I replied. "They fixed that glitch the next year."

"A year late for me," he said, but shook it off and gave me a grin. "Hooah."

"Hooah," I replied.

I moved on as a hatch opened and a team of Fleet guards waited for me inside the station proper. They didn't say a word to me, just gestured for me to follow. I did.

A fast ride on a stuffy elevator and I was walking out into the domed dining room of the Caga station cafe. The place was packed with diners, but it didn't take a genius to figure out that the vast majority were planted there by the Fleet. It was a lot of protection for a new admiral, especially one overseeing peace time.

The planet far below cast a red glow that gave the cafe a warm yet sinister ambience. I'd never noticed the sinister part before, but all the Fleet plants had me kind of jumpy. Not to mention that as I got closer to Crawford, I could see that the stress of life was getting to him even more than when we'd spoken a week before. The skin around his eyes was messed up.

"Joe," Crawford said and I was glad to see him crack a smile as he stood up and offered me his hand.

Normally, we would have done the man hug thing and slapped each other on the back, but his guards looked like a handshake was about as much of a violation of Crawford's personal space they'd allow.

"Craw," I said as I took a seat across from him. "So, what's new?"

He chuckled, but it wasn't a happy one. I probably shouldn't have led with the joke question.

"Nothing much," he replied. "Just running the Fleet."

"Is that what you do now? I thought there was a council for that?" I said.

"There is," Crawford sighed. "But they're all appointed politicians. They wouldn't know the difference between a destroyer and an asteroid breaker. I gave a report two days ago and slipped in the words 'regimented baffling' and not one of them even raised an eyebrow."

"What's regimented baffling?" I asked.

"Nothing, that's the point," he said. "I made it up just to see if they were paying attention. No one noticed. I'm sure some analyst will when they go back over the transcript later, but not one of the council members even asked me what that was. They all pretended like they knew."

"Eight Million Gods," I said. "That's gotta be a pain in the ass to deal with."

"That's one of the lesser pains," Crawford said. He spread his arms. "Getting to this cafe was more complicated than planning a battalion assault."

"Sorry, man," I said. "I should have just had you come to SMC headquarters. It's already vetted by Fleet security."

"Don't bet on it," Crawford said low enough that only I could hear him.

I gave him a quizzical look, but he shook his head and waved me off.

"Don't listen to me," he said. "I haven't slept in days."

I pointed to the corners of my eyes.

"That why you're twitching so much?" I asked.

He put a fingertip to the corner of his left eye and rubbed for a second then shook his head.

"How's things at the SMC?" he asked, changing the subject abruptly. "You making good chits with your claims?"

"I've punched a few lucrative tickets since I started," I said. "But I've also screwed up a few. You remember that time we thought we were going to take out a nest of B'clo'nos, but turned out to be B'flo'dos instead? That was about how well my last ticket went. Pretty much foed the whole thing up and had to have some other numbers come rescue my ass."

"Numbers?" he asked.

"Mercs," I said. "That's what we call each other."

"Oh, because you all have numbers," he said and nodded. "What's yours?"

"I'm One Eighty-Four," I replied.

"That good or bad?" He asked.

"Doesn't really matter," I said, acting like I hadn't just been reminded of that the other day. "It's only a number."

"Oh," he said and looked over at the waiter that was hovering a few feet from us, trying not to look like he wanted to take our order and get the hell out of there. "I think we're ready."

"We are?" I said as I looked down at the menu I hadn't even touched. "Come on, brother, give a guy a chance to choose a sandwich."

I saw a strange pained look sweep over Crawford's face and started to apologize for whatever it was that caused the look, but I never got the chance. The second I opened my mouth there was an explosion from the kitchen strong enough to shake the dining room tables and make the dome shudder. Screams filled the room as the diners that weren't Fleet panicked and ran for the exit while the diners that were Fleet pulled various and assorted weapons and rushed towards our table.

Most of them never made it more than a couple steps.

Turns out that our waiter wasn't looking nervous because he had to serve the Admiral of the Fleet, he looked nervous because he was strapped with half a hover tank's worth of explosives.

He went off like a flesh-filled bomb and I was simultaneously thrown from my chair and covered in his guts and gunk. My ears began to ring so loud I thought an alarm was going off in my head as I pushed up to my hands and knees. I wiped the waiter blood from my eyes and went for my pistol, but of course it was back on my ship with Mgurn because I couldn't bring a pistol to a lunch with the Admiral.

Men and women of all races ran this way and that. Many of them were engulfed in flames while others were busy firing randomly into the smoke that was filling the dining room. A blast scorched the carpet by my side and I rolled to the right, putting my half-demolished table between myself and the chaotic violence.

A hand grabbed my leg and I almost turned and started wailing on the owner with my upraised fist, but I saw it was Crawford that had grabbed me and all the strength went out of my body in an instant. He was coated in blood from head to toe and it was obvious it wasn't waiter blood. Part of his face was missing. Just gone. Nothing but splintered bone and dripping blood was left.

"Craw!" I yelled and to my damaged ears it sounded like a weak whisper. "Craw!"

I grabbed him up and pulled his body into my lap. He struggled to breathe, his chest hitching with every inhale and locking tight on the exhale. I looked around for something I could wrap his face in and saw the scorched end of a table cloth by my boot. I reached down and yanked it free from the burning debris that surrounded us and pressed the cleanest part I could find over Crawford's gaping hole of a face.

His eyes met mine and I knew right then that he had expected this. He almost looked like he welcomed it. That having his face blown off by a terrorist waiter was preferable than life as Admiral of the Fleet. His hand sought mine and I took it. I gave him a reassuring squeeze. He squeezed back and something hard pressed into my palm.

I pulled my hand back and saw he'd given me a data crystal. It was black. My blood went cold at the sight of it. No one used black data crystals unless they needed something beyond important encrypted and protected. They were the most reliable way to keep data safe, but a dozen miners died for every crystal found. One black data crystal was worth more than my ship.

I held the crystal in my palm and looked back at Crawford, but his eye was empty. He'd died before I'd even registered he'd handed me something.

I didn't know what to do. My attention was drawn between the crystal and my dead friend. I kept looking back and forth between the two. Then clarity hit me and everything slowed to a pace that I had never experienced before.

The first thing I did was jam the crystal into a small pocket on the inside of my boot. As soon as I inserted it there, the pocket sealed itself and I knew the crystal was safe. Or safer than in my hand, at least.

The second thing I did was focus on the pistol grip sticking out from under Crawford's Fleet jacket. I yanked it free and prayed it was universal and not locked to Crawford's biometrics. When the thing started to hum in my palm, I knew I was in business.

I didn't have time to gently set Crawford on the dining room carpet. It wasn't one of those days. So I shoved his corpse aside and jumped up to my feet, pistol out and hot. I fired five times before my brain caught up with my body. Five targets dropped fast and I dove to the left as a barrage of blasts came flying at me.

I rolled to a knee and fired again, taking down three more targets. I'll be honest, I wasn't entirely sure I was shooting the people responsible for blowing everything to hell or if I was killing Fleet agents by accident. At that moment, I didn't really care. If a weapon was aimed at me then I took down the person on the other end of that weapon.

And my gift made sure I did it all with perfectly clear precision.

Through the smoke and flames, I saw a man standing against the opposite wall. He didn't have a weapon, he didn't look injured, and he didn't seem to care about the nightmare happening around him. He was solely focused on me, his eyes drilling a path across the room and into mine.

I stood and took aim, because he freaked me the hell out, then blinked, and he was gone. Just like that. For a millisecond, I thought I'd imagined him, but the way he stared at me was etched into my brain. He'd been there, I was certain. I wracked my brain for what he looked like, but the only feature I could recall were those eyes.

Pitch black eyes.

Stone eyes.

A halfer like Hopsheer? Part Gwreq and part human? Or had he been all Gwreq? I didn't notice four arms or stone skin even, but like I said, it was his eyes that my memory locked onto.

All of that happened in the space of a terpig's fart. Clarity kept me from dwelling too long on the mystery man and I instinctively ducked as a heavy blade was swung at my neck.

I went low and put two blasts in the belly of the man that had come at me. Well, not really a man as much as a scarred-up Jesperian. He certainly wasn't Fleet by the way he was dressed. And smelled. I think he was leaking taco drippings from every orifice, including the two new ones I gave him as he attacked me. Not cool.

Even with a belly full of plasma blasts, he kept coming. I avoided his blade, as well as his taco leakage, by leaping backwards and grabbing up a fallen chair. The blade slashed through the chair, splitting it down the middle easily, but that gave me time enough to take aim with my pistol and put a couple more blasts in him. That time they were directly between his eyes.

The Jesperian's head exploded and I nearly gagged as the smell of tacos increased exponentially. That guy was hopped up on Tacos, man. Tacos with a capitol T. No wonder a couple of shots to the belly hadn't stopped him.

I grabbed up his blade, thinking that an extra weapon wouldn't hurt, and moved towards the exit. The panicked diners had already escaped. Or most of them had. I was forced to step over a few corpses on my way to the exit. When I reached the doors, I looked over my shoulder at the insanity behind me.

It was Edgers for sure. The way they were dressed, the variety of species and races that were attacking the Fleet agents and guards, and the suicidal way they fought, hellbent on killing instead of surviving, told me as much.

A blast scorched the wall by my head and I quit my study of the combatants, more than ready to get the hell back to my ship and off the station.

I made it three hallways over before the world exploded around me again. Half a wall ripped open, sending shards of metal everywhere, and six Skrang troopers stepped into the hallway. *Skrang troopers.* Not Edgers, but Skrangs. They saw me and lifted their heavy rifles to their shoulders. I balanced the pistol in my palm, knowing that gift or not, I wasn't going to slow down what was about to happen in time to defend myself.

Luckily, I have a really good assistant.

"Frag out!" I heard Mgurn call from behind the Skrangs and I dropped to the floor faster than a Lipian whore's panties during Fleet week.

More world exploding, more ringing in my ears, and more plasma fire. Life was in the sucky category that day.

I felt hands tugging at me and I had the presence of mind to know they weren't enemy hands. Enemy hands wouldn't tug, they'd hit. Or shoot. Which meant I wouldn't have felt tugging, but a hot, burning pain then nothing but the black void that comes after we depart this realm. Or something like that.

"Joe! Get up!" Mgurn yelled into my face. I read his jaw movements more than I heard his words.

I got up and he helped me limp my way down the hall, past the obliterated bodies of the Skrangs, and towards the docking area.

We didn't slow once on our way even when we heard people screaming for help and the evacuation claxons started to ring out. Technically, being part of the SMC meant we were required to assist civilians in need during an emergency. But even Mgurn, Mr. By The Book himself, didn't pause as we rushed through hatch after hatch until we were in the docking bay.

He coded us into our ship and locked the door as fast as he could before setting me down on the floor so he could get the engines started up. I just sat there, my back against the cool metal wall, the lunch events swirling in my brain. Clarity was over and everything was just a jumble of stimuli.

It wasn't until I felt the lurch of the ship and the pressure in my temples from takeoff that I pushed up to my feet and hobbled my way to the small bridge. I collapsed into my chair and started to reach for the controls, but Mgurn slapped my hands away so I just relaxed back into the chair's netting and looked out at the Relic System as Mgurn got us out of there as fast as possible.

Alarms rang out and Mgurn said something about the Caga station exploding, but I wasn't listening. I was too busy watching a ship duck into the wormhole portal and blink out of sight.

"Did you see that?" I asked. "That was an Edge ship."

"Yes," Mgurn said, his voice a muffled grunt in my ears.

"Good," I said. I turned and smiled at him then closed my eyes and let sweet, sweet unconsciousness take me away.

SIX

Grogginess was no excuse to be late to a meeting with the SMC bosses. So I didn't bother saying a damn thing as I walked into the conference room, pulled back a chair, and plopped down at the table.

The thing about the SMC bosses is that no one knows who they are. It's some handy stealth tech they employ to stay anonymous. No facial recognition, no voice recognition, nothing. As soon as you leave the meeting, all you can remember is the substance and most of the content of the discussion, but not the identities of the people you just had a conversation with.

I asked Hopsheer why that is and she just shrugged in that way she does. I asked other mercs and heard a lot of theories, but none that were convincing. Except for Mgurn's.

"Maybe they are still working in the field," Mgurn said. "They'd become targets themselves if their identities were known. We'd end up salvaging the bosses instead of being assigned tickets by them."

Interesting theory. Could be right. At that moment, only a few hours after I watched my best friend die, I could care less who they were. I just wanted authorization to go kill some Edgers and get revenge.

"There will be no revenge," Boss One said.

They gave themselves their own numbers, just like mercs. Didn't help a whole lot since you had to relearn the numbers every time you met with them, but it kept them straight in your head while they were talking.

"We are not a military organization," Boss Two said.

"There are other mercenary outfits that handle that sort of thing," Boss Three said.

"We salvage. That is our job," Boss Four said.

"It is how we stay neutral and are allowed access to any part of the galaxy without threat of harm," Boss Five said.

"Are you foing crudding me?" I snapped.

"Threat of harm from the Fleet or the Skrang Alliance," Boss Six clarified. "Our job is a dangerous one, so the potential for personal harm is always present."

"You don't have to tell me twice," I said as I leaned back in my chair and tried to study the faces in front of me.

No go. As soon as I stopped looking at a face, all memory of its features vanished from my mind.

"If I can't go hunt some Edgers to kill then why am I here?" I asked.

"You were given something," Boss One said.

"Your friend was dying, but he still managed to get it to you," Boss Two said.

"We believe he would have given it to you anyway, even without the attack," Boss Three said.

"It was why he agreed to lunch with you despite his schedule," Boss Four said. "What did you have for lunch, by the way?"

"What?" I asked.

"The Fleet council was not happy he was meeting with a number," Boss Five said, pushing the grilling forward.

"Even if you were old friends and had fought together in the Marines," Boss Six said.

"How the hell do you know he gave me something?" I asked.

I wasn't mad, despite my tone. I was actually curious how they knew Crawford had slipped me the crystal. The crystal that was still in my boot at that moment.

The wall behind the bosses was usually an open view of the spacescape outside SMC headquarters. Clusters of stars, the far off nebulas of Golan and Gonal, merc ships coming and going. I believe it was meant to be an added distraction and keep a person from focusing on the bosses. That wall had never really mattered to me before.

But when the wall solidified, and a full-scale holo of my meeting with Crawford was projected, it started to matter. I leaned forward and focused past the bosses, my eyes locked onto the scene, studying it, looking for every single possible clue I could find.

"You hacked the Caga station's security feeds?" I asked.

"We did better than that," Boss One said.

"We inserted one of our own into the cafe," Boss Two said.

"We were watching in real time via a trans-space signal," Boss Three said.

"That man," I said. "The one that disappeared. He's one of us?"

"Yes," they all said.

"Then why the hell didn't he help me?" I asked. "The foing coward ran off as soon as things went bad."

"It wasn't his job to help you," Boss Six said.

"It was his job to observe you without being observed," Boss Five said.

"Well, since I'm talking about him, I guess he failed," I said.

"He did not fail," Boss Three said.

"He made his presence known after the attack began," Boss Two said.

"His job was finished since there was nothing more to observe," Boss One said.

There was a long pause.

"What? My turn?" Boss Four said. "Crud. Why do we have to talk like this?"

There were hisses and grunts from the other bosses.

"Alright, calm down," Boss Four said and cleared his (?) throat. "He had faith that you would extricate yourself from the situation."

"Although he did take a risk considering that Admiral Helms gave you something of obvious importance," Boss Five said.

"We would like to see it now," they said together.

"Sure," I replied.

I reached into my boot and the small pocket opened at my touch. I fished out the data crystal and held it up for them to see.

"But I need a few assurances before I hand this over," I said.

The crystal was snatched from my fingers before I could blink. I looked about and didn't see anyone else in the conference room with us. Despite the weirdness of the bosses, I was 100% sure they hadn't snagged it from me. My gut started to flip flop and I had to take a couple of deep breaths to calm down.

"Our meeting is done," Boss One said.

"You may leave now, One Eighty-Four," Boss Two said.

"It would be in your best interest not to see what is on this crystal," Boss Three said.

"That would make you a target," Boss Four said.

"We do not say this lightly," Boss Five said.

"Who was the guy with the black eyes?" I asked. "He wasn't a normal merc. Tell me."

"Good bye," Boss Six said.

I didn't move. Pretty sure they expected that reaction from me because the next thing I knew I was waking up from my bunk with a worried Mgurn sitting across from me.

"You have been asleep for two days," Mgurn said. "Another few hours and I would have been concerned."

"Those bastards knocked me out, kicked me out, and have shut me out," I said.

I sat up expecting a whopper of a hangover, but I felt surprisingly good. I felt rested and refreshed. It was the best I'd felt in a long time.

"I never got to give you my condolences on the loss of your friend," Mgurn said. "I am sorry that Crawford Helms died. Is there anything I can do for you in your time of grief?"

"Find out when the funeral service is being held," I said.

"It has already been held," Mgurn said. "It was broadcast on all channels. The Fleet issued a statement that Edger separatists were responsible and they retaliated swiftly, destroying several Edger outposts outside of Skrang Alliance territory."

"Skrangs!" I exclaimed. "There were Skrangs on the station!"

Mgurn waved his hands at me and looked around in a panic.

"Quiet!" he hissed. "I left that out of my official report."

"You what?" I asked, totally shocked. "Mgurn left out vital information in a report? Why the hell would you do that?"

"Because... Well... I am not sure, to be honest," Mgurn replied. "The fact that the Skrangs were not in military uniform made me wonder if they were acting on their own. Perhaps a splinter cell working with the Edgers. I didn't want to cause a galactic incident when things are so confusing."

"Good reasons," I said.

"That and they were skintakers," Mgurn said. "I could smell the Jirks as soon as I stepped into the hallway."

"Eight Million Gods dammit," I growled. "Mgurn, we've talked about the order in which you give me information. Please lead with the Jirks part next time. That right there is the nugget of intel I need to know first."

"I know," Mgurn said. "But that is not how I communicate. I say what is most pressing in my mind then work my way to the rest."

"Okay, fine, whatever," I said. "I don't want to argue with you about this. Just tell me how you know they were Jirks."

"I saw two shrivel after I killed them," Mgurn said. "So, I assume the rest were Jirks. Maybe they were not. I did not see them shrivel since I was busy rescuing you."

"Thank you for that," I said.

"You are welcome, Joe," Mgurn said. "It is why numbers have assistants."

My stomach growled and I glanced at our door.

"Let's eat," I said. "Then we can return and talk this all out."

"There is no need," Mgurn said. "Secrets never last in SMC headquarters. Every number on board knows about as much as we do."

"Not quite," I said. "I may know a few things the others don't."

"Such as?" Mgurn asked.

"Eat first," I said as my stomach stopped growling and started shouting. "And beer. Lots of beer. Then we get a few of our most trusted colleagues and we make a plan."

"Oh, Joe, that is not a good idea," Mgurn said.

"Why's that?" I asked.

"You'll see," Mgurn sighed and stood up. "Come on. Let's feed you and get you some beer."

I didn't like the way his carapace slouched as he opened the hatch and stepped out of our quarters. A slouching carapace was never a good sign on a Leforian.

Didn't take me long to find out what the "You'll see" statement was about.

"We are all under strict orders from the bosses directly not to assist you in any way with a revenge plan," Hopsheer said as I stuffed my face with a gump burger.

Yes, the little buggers are annoying pests, but they do make one hell of a burger.

"Fo va," I said.

"Chew your food, man," Tarr said. He winced as I opened my mouth wide and gave him a show. "You are disgusting."

"Fo that," I said as I swallowed. "Edgers killed my friend. I don't care if the Fleet went and wasted some of their outposts. I want to make those bastards pay."

"Sure you do," Ig said. "No one blames you for that. But we have orders. Every single number has orders. No one is allowed to help you unless they want to be kicked out of the SMC."

"That's terpigcrud," I said. "What ever happened to loyalty amongst comrades?"

"It died with the War," Tarr said.

"Looks like I know who I can and can't trust," I said.

"It's not about trust, Joe," Hopsheer said. "And you can trust every one of us. It's about the fact that the bosses already have something going and we'll probably screw it up if we get involved."

"Something going? What?" I asked.

"Not a clue," Tarr said. "It's all rumor at this point."

"So, what's the rumor?" I asked.

The three mercs looked at each other then looked at me. I waited. Then cleared my throat. Then started to get pissed.

"Tell me or I swear one of you will learn what a size eleven battle foot feels like shoved up whatever orifices you have," I snapped.

Ig gulped some air and inflated to full size. "We heard they sent the Big Guy in."

"The big guy?" I asked.

"No, not big guy. Big Guy," Tarr said. "Him."

"Salvage Merc One," Hopsheer said. "The best of all of us."

"Salvage Merc One," I snorted. "That guy is a myth. Everyone knows that when Bon Chattslan died, the merc number One was retired."

"Everyone who?" Hopsheer asked. "Because I never heard that."

"That's a thing?" Ig asked.

"Isn't it?" I replied. "I thought it was. I know someone said that to me."

"You were probably drunk and misunderstood what was being said," Tarr said.

"No, pretty sure that's what I heard," I said. I looked around the mess hall. "Where'd Mgurn go? He always knows this stuff."

"He's getting pitchers," Hopsheer said, cocking her head towards the taps.

I saw him over there chatting with a couple of assistants as he held eight pitchers, two in each hand. I gave a loud whistle and Mgurn almost dropped two of the pitchers. He juggled successfully, said his goodbye to the assistants, and hurried back to our table.

"Sorry," Mgurn said. "I just heard the most interesting rumor. You will never believe—"

"They sent Salvage Merc One to go do whatever the bosses want done," I interrupted.

It was a mean thing to do. Mgurn had just gotten us all beer and I stole his thunder. At that moment, I didn't care.

"Forget about Salvage Merc One being real," I said as I poured pints for everyone.

"Oh, he is real," Mgurn said.

I got several "see?" looks from the mercs.

"Whatever," I said as I shoved pints across the table. "One is real, good for him. But where is he going and what is he doing? That's what I want to know."

On that I got several shrugs, but zero answers.

"Then we need to find out," I said. "Because I don't care who the bosses send, if the mission isn't to wipe out every last Edger from the galaxy then the mission is wrong."

"Interesting way to look at it," Hopsheer said. "But Edgers aren't organized enough for every single one to be guilty."

"And there is the issue of the skintakers," Mgurn said. His armor went grey and he looked down at the table. "Oh, fo. I shouldn't have said that out loud."

"Good one," I said as I studied the faces of the other mercs. Surprised doesn't describe their looks. "Yeah, there were some Jirks disguised as Skrangs on the Caga station. They nearly took me out, but Mgurn saved my butt and got me out of there."

"You told this to the bosses, right?" Hopsheer asked.

"Maybe," I said and shrugged.

"That means he didn't," Tarr said.

"His discussion with the bosses is privileged," Mgurn said. "He cannot divulge what he did or did not discuss."

"They already know everything," I said as I finished off my gump burger. I pounded a pint of beer and gave a loud belch before leaning back from the table. "The whole headquarters knows everything. Except for the Jirks part."

"It doesn't change a thing," Tarr said. "We can't help you."

"You can, but you won't," I said. "Big difference."

"Listen, Joe, look at us," Hopsheer said. "We are veteran mercs. We have been at the number game for a long time. None of us have assistants anymore. We don't need them. You do. Why? Because you need that extra voice in your ear to help second guess your decisions. You need someone around that can stop you from making a bad decision. So, listen up. All of us are acting as your assistants right now. Drop the revenge plan. It's a losing mission."

"And there are no chits in revenge," Ig said. "You will bankrupt your account just getting to the Havlov System."

I grinned. Everyone else frowned.

"Crud," Ig said. "He didn't know."

"I do now," I said. "Havlov System? The separatists are hiding in a system of gas planets? Good choice. Messes with long and short-range scans. No indigenous races, or any life, to get in the way. Plenty of places to hide if you have the right habitat tech."

"Joe," Hopsheer said softly. "Stop this. The bosses will kick you out. They might kick us all out for letting you jabber on like this."

"They are certainly going to kick out Ig for telling him about the Havlov System," Tarr said.

"Hey, it was a simple mistake," Ig said. She took a deep breath and puffed up to twice her normal size. "Someone would have slipped eventually. Mercs can't keep their mouths shut. Everyone knows that."

"I don't think they'll care," Tarr said.

I poured a third pint, having downed my second as Tarr and Ig bickered, and focused my attention on Hopsheer.

"Are Gwreqs the only race that can turn their eyes to stone?" I asked.

"What? Why do you want to know that?" she replied.

"Just something I saw on the Caga station," I said. "I think the bosses sent him. Maybe. Hard to remember what they said about that part. Might have been a halfer like you. His eyes turned to black stone."

"Black stone?" Hopsheer echoed.

"That's what I said," I replied. "Black stone. Not grey like yours, but black. Glassy like obsidian."

"I haven't heard of any Gwreqs having black eyes," Hopsheer said. "Variations on grey. Some have dark, charcoal eyes, but never obsidian black. Not even the halfers I know."

Tarr and Ig continued to bicker and Hopsheer reached over and slapped both of them upside their heads.

"Shut up," she snapped and poured herself more beer. "Have either of you children heard of a race with obsidian black eyes?"

"The eyes weren't black all the time," I said. "They changed from normal to black like Hoppy's do when she's itching for a fight."

"Black eyes?" Ig asked. "Only Maglors and Bverns. Both are primitive races. They wouldn't be involved in an assault on the Caga station. They barely know how to dig a hole and cover their feces up."

"This guy looked human," I said. "He wasn't a rat thing like a Bvern or a monkey bird like the Maglors. Everything about him was normal except for the eyes."

"Did you get any vid of him?" Hopsheer asked. "You had to have had your camera recording."

"No," I said. "It was just supposed to be a lunch with Crawford. I didn't wear a micro. The Fleet guards would have taken it off me anyway."

"But the station would have vid," Mgurn said.

"Yeah, it would," I said. "If it was still intact. The station was obliterated."

"Yes, but not the security feed," Mgurn said. "That would have been transmitted via trans-space to an off-station data storage facility. It's an automated protocol in case of a catastrophic accident."

"Being blown up by Edgers is pretty catastrophic," I said and leaned forward. I played with the condensation on my pint glass then looked over at Mgurn. "Where is this facility?"

"There are quite a few," Mgurn said. "Hard to know exactly which one the Caga station used."

"Can we narrow it down?" I asked.

"Joe," Hopsheer warned.

I held up a finger and I didn't need to turn my head to know she was glaring at me. I could feel those eyes of hers go stone cold. Not obsidian black, but that frigid grey they become.

"How do we narrow it down?" I asked.

"Distance to the station," Mgurn replied, looking very uncomfortable with the way the conversation had turned. But he was my assistant and sworn to aid me. "Also, facility capacity and security level. Caga station didn't need Fleet-level security, but it is visited by many holo stars and galactic dignitaries. That means the data storage would have to be secure enough for those visitors not to worry that their private meetings are being sold to news outlets."

"Just tell me how many facilities," I snapped.

"Six, maybe seven or eight," Mgurn said.

"I'm out of this," Ig said.

"Yeah, me too," Tarr said as they both stood up. "Unless you have a ticket in hand, what you are thinking of doing is breaking and entering. The SMC can't protect you if you're caught. Your credentials will mean nothing. You'll end up in prison and we all know what happens to numbers in prison."

"They are rehabilitated?" Mgurn asked.

"In the butt," Ig said. "They are rehabilitated in the butt. Or similar orifice."

I looked across the table at Hopsheer.

"You bailing on me too?" I asked.

"I haven't decided," Hopsheer said.

"Hoppy, come on!" Tarr exclaimed. "If you help him, you'll be kicked out of the SMC. You heard what the bosses ordered."

"They ordered us not to help Joe with any revenge plans against the Edgers," Hopsheer responded. "They didn't say anything about helping Joe figure out who the obsidian-eyed person was on that station."

"She does have a point," Ig said.

"So you'll help too?" I asked.

"Oh, not a chance in Hell," Ig replied. "Sounds like a stupid risk with almost no payoff."

"I wouldn't even add the almost part," Tarr said. "This has no payoff at all."

"Unless you count pertinent information into an ongoing investigation of the murder of the Admiral of the Fleet," Mgurn said. "There is a certain patriotic payoff."

"Patriotism doesn't pay for ship fuel," Tarr said. "Good luck, Joe. Try not to die, alright?"

"What he said," Ig said and nodded her bulbous head at me then turned and hurried away from the table on her eight legs while Tarr just shook his head.

"Hoppy, walk away," Tarr said, clapping her on the shoulder as he turned and followed Ig.

"You can, you know," I said. "This is a data retrieval mission. I've handled those before. I doubt I need backup."

"You always need backup," Hopsheer said.

"I don't always need backup," I said, probably with a little more pout in my voice than I wanted.

Hopsheer looked at the pitchers on the table and shook her head.

"That's a lot of beer left," she said. "How about we finish it and then I decide whether or not I'm helping you?"

"I was going to finish it all anyway," I said and shrugged. "But you can help if you want."

"I said we'd finish the beer first before I decide to help," she replied.

"No, I mean you can help with the beer," I said and grinned. "I know you'll help with the mission too, but beer first."

"Don't call it a mission," Hopsheer said, filling both our pints. "It's not a mission. It's a heist at the very least."

"I've always wanted to pull a heist," I said and raised my glass. "To the heist."

Hopsheer didn't echo the toast, but she did raise her glass.

"I am not comfortable with any of this," Mgurn said, fidgeting next to me. "I have had no desire in my life to pull off a heist. This is not why I joined the SMC."

"Don't worry, buddy," I said. "We are going to do this the smart way, all the way."

I finished off my pint and went back for more. I needed fuel to help me think.

SEVEN

Not that much thinking happened after the fifteenth pitcher was emptied.

I can say that for a fact since I woke up the next morning with my head on a very comfortable pillow and my naked body nestled into some very expensive sheets.

Needless to say, I did not wake up in my own bed.

"Oh no," I heard a voice say. "No, no, no, no, no."

That was my feeling too once I recognized the voice.

I opened an eye, which was not an easy task since it felt like an entire pitcher of beer was resting on my eyelid. The first thing I saw was a ceiling that was the perfect holo depiction of the Krjia nebula. It was absolutely gorgeous and I would have kept staring at it if the bed hadn't started shaking violently.

"Get up and get out," Hopsheer said. "This shouldn't have happened. No. No, no, no. Get up, Joe."

It hurt to turn my head, it hurt to move everything really, but I forced myself to look at the enraged halfer that was standing naked by her bed, her hands pushing and pulling at her unbelievably plush mattress. I realized that seniority in the SMC had its perks.

Hopsheer was an incredibly beautiful woman with her SMC uniform on. Without it, she was beyond stunning and it was all I could do to remember to breathe.

"Get up!" she snapped and yanked hard enough on the mattress to flip me out the other side.

I landed hard on the floor and just barely managed not to brain myself. I got my hands underneath me and pushed up, peeking over the edge of the bed at the really pissed off halfer that was pacing back and forth. Mesmerizing couldn't begin to describe it.

"How did this happen?" she was asking herself. "We were drinking and talking. That was all. We'd finished those pitchers then you went back for more since Mgurn had already gone back to your quarters for the night. Did you get wubloov? Was that what we drank next? Crud. You brought back the pitchers and... And..."

"And we came back here and got it on," I said.

The boot hit me right between the eyes and I found myself on my back, staring up at the Krjia nebula once more.

"Ow," I said as I rubbed my face. "Where'd that boot come from? You weren't holding it."

"I'm fast," she said as she stalked around the bed and stood over me, her hands on her hips, her everything right there for me to see. "Get up. Get out. That is your boot."

I rolled my head and saw that it was.

I grabbed it and sat up then slowly got to my feet.

"Can I ask a question?" I asked.

"No," she said.

"Oh, come on," I said.

"What?" she snapped. "What's your question?"

"Were we any good?" I asked then pointed to the bed. "At that? Were we good together?"

"I have no idea," she said. "Luckily, I don't remember a damn thing about it. Foing wubloov beer..."

"Me neither," I said which was the truth. I didn't even remember going back for more pitchers of beer. "Too bad. If we did remember then maybe you wouldn't be so mad about this."

"I'd be mad no matter what," she growled. "A merc doesn't fo where she works. I can get it anytime I want out in the galaxy. Anytime. Keeps things simple, easy. But this makes things so complicated that I can't even begin to think of the repercussions."

"Repercussions?" I asked as I hunted around for my clothes.

I found my boxers and slid those on then found my pants. I hunted and hunted for my t-shirt, but it was nowhere. I did find Hopsheer's underwear hanging from a lamp on the wall. There was also a good-sized dent in the metal finish of the same wall. There were a few dents. I looked down at myself and noticed I had more than a couple of bruises blooming on my chest and arms.

"Damn," I said as I finally found my t-shirt and slipped it on. I plucked her underwear from the lamp and tossed them to her. "What do you mean by repercussions?"

She stomped towards me, still naked, still mesmerizing, but I tried to play it cool. I did a good job until she lifted my shirt and put a couple of cool, stone-skinned fingers on the largest bruise on the left side of my torso.

"Sorry," she said. "Gwreq mating can be rough."

"Yeah, I'll probably really figure that out later when I fully sober up," I said. "I'm still a little numb from the beer."

"The repercussions are that things will now be strained between us which could compromise our professional fortitude in the field," she said.

"Professional fortitude," I laughed. "You must really be freaked out to sound like a Fleet bureaucrat all of a sudden."

Her fingers were still lightly tracing my bruised torso. I could see a pink flush begin to spread across her skin. It turned the grey of her stone into a rose color that made me more than a little weak in the knees. It was a good thing I'd already put my pants on or she'd have really seen a repercussion.

Hopsheer snatched her hand back and took a few steps away. She started to speak then closed her mouth and looked about her room.

"I need to shower and get dressed," she said as she found a robe and draped it around her body. She didn't cinch it tight which made me smile. "Stop that."

"What? Smiling?" I asked.

"Get out, Joe," she said, but without quite the same aggression as before.

"Okay, okay," I said and snatched up my boots. No idea where my socks disappeared to. "I'm getting, I'm getting."

I made it to the door before I realized something.

"Hey, did we ever decide if you were going to help me or not?" I asked. I waved a boot-heavy hand at her quarters, which was really, really nice, and raised an eyebrow. "I know this has repercussions, but is one of those you not helping me get the security data?"

"Let me shower, sober up, and get some food in my belly," she said as she ducked into the bathroom.

I waited, but she didn't say anything else from the bathroom.

"Okay, see ya later, Hoppy," I called to her then quietly closed the door as I left.

Not sure why I quietly closed the door. Wasn't like I was sneaking out on her or anything.

And there certainly wouldn't be any sneaking of any sort as three mercs I knew in passing watched me try to walk away from her quarters as casually as possible, barefoot, with boots in my hand. The smirks were not held back.

My head cleared some on my way to my quarters, which was halfway across the headquarters from Hopsheer's. I could vaguely remember arm wrestling Hopsheer at one point the night before as a way to decide something. No idea what we were deciding or who won, but considering the strange pain in my right shoulder, I wouldn't have been surprised if Hopsheer won.

"Look who's rocking the walk of shame," Tarr said as he leaned against the wall next to the door to my quarters. "Who was the lucky gump? That secretary on level sixteen? Or the girl that works that snack bar over in the hangar? Yeah, I bet it was her. She's always had an eye for you."

"She has?" I asked as I pushed past him and keyed myself into my quarters. "Wait, which one? The redhead or the chartreuse head?"

"Chartreuse, of course," Tarr said, following me into my quarters. "That redhead is crazy. Stay away from her."

"You sound like you'd know," I said then stopped in my tracks as I saw Ig sitting at my table playing cards with Mgurn. "Howdy. What's up?"

I looked over my shoulder at Tarr and raised my eyebrows.

"Not sure why squishy is here, but I'm here because I changed my mind," Tarr said. "After that message you left me last night, I couldn't exactly turn my back on you, now could I?"

"He left you a message as well?" Ig asked. "He left me one, but I ignored it. It was the message from Hopsheer that changed my mind."

"What messages?" I asked. "I don't remember leaving any messages."

"Hopsheer?" Tarr asked then looked me up and down. "Oh, no way. No, no way. It wasn't snack bar girl at all, it was Hoppy."

"What was Hoppy?" Ig asked.

Mgurn lifted his head and sniffed.

"Sex," Mgurn said. "Joe and Hopsheer had sex."

"Yeah they did," Tarr laughed.

"Back off guys," I said. "Nothing happened. I had way too much to drink and Hopsheer let me crash on her floor last night. That's all that happened."

"Really?" Tarr asked as he pointed at my neck. "Her rug give you those hickeys?"

I grumbled and tossed my boots on the floor.

"Hopsheer and I finished all that beer you guys left us with," I said. "Then we may have gotten more. That's all I really know." I rolled my right shoulder. "And at some point we arm wrestled."

"Yeah you did," Tarr laughed again. "You arm wrestled all over each other."

"This conversation is bordering on disrespectful," Mgurn said. "Could we change the subject? Human sexuality is not a topic I enjoy."

"Hopsheer is a halfer," Tarr said. "So it's only three quarters human sexuality and one quarter Gwreq sexuality. That's the part I want to hear about. Does every part of her turn to stone? Huh?"

"Do you want to get hit?" I asked him. "Because I'm still just drunk enough to deck you and have no regrets."

"You'd deck me and have no regrets sober," Tarr said, holding up his hands. "But I'll stop. I was just playing with you. It's good you two finally got that out of your systems. It's been really annoying watching you guys flirt and pretend you are aren't."

"Really annoying," Ig said then laid her cards on the table. "Gin."

"That is annoying right there," Mgurn said and showed his cards. There wasn't a match in his hand.

"Do you know how to play Gin?" I asked him.

"Were we playing Gin?" he replied and looked at Ig. "I thought we were playing Klav cribbage."

"You don't have a bowl of pudding," Tarr said and plopped down on my bunk. "You can't play Klav cribbage without a bowl of pudding."

"I'm not one for cards," Mgurn said and pushed back from the table. He smiled at me in his quad-jawed way. "It appears you now have a sufficient team to pull off your heist."

"It appears so," I said. I stood there for a couple seconds. "So now what?"

"You tell us, man," Tarr said.

"This is your thing," Ig said. "You tell us what the plan is."

"I don't have one," I said. "I just woke up like twenty minutes ago. We don't even know which data storage facility the security feed is being held in."

"That is not entirely correct," Mgurn said. "After leaving you and Hopsheer to your drinking binge last night, I came back here and did some research. It took me most of the night, but I have the possibilities narrowed down to two facilities."

"That's great, Mgurn," I said. "Good work."

"Yes, well, you may not thank me after I tell you the names of the two facilities," Mgurn said. His quad-jawed smile turned upside down fast. "The first is Mlo Station. The bottom half is entirely taken up with data crystals. Trillions of them, grown on the premises and never harvested. They can house a nearly infinite amount of information since they are still alive."

"Mlo? That's the black hole system, right?" I asked.

"Yeah, that's the one," Tarr said.

"The station is on the very edge of the system because of the black hole," Ig said. "It is in a constant struggle to maintain its position."

"I bet it is," I said. "What's the problem with that station?"

"There is no wormhole portal," Mgurn said. "The closest is two systems away. That would mean a week to get there and two weeks to get back because of what the black hole's gravitational pull does to time."

"If that is where the data is, it could take us days to find it," Ig said. "Black hole time is not easy to navigate. Spend too long there and black hole madness sets in."

"Then how do people work on the station?" I asked.

"They don't," Ig said. "It is maintained by androids."

"Oh," I said and looked at Mgurn. "The black hole isn't the bad part, it's the androids, right?"

"Yes," Mgurn said. "No living being has set foot on that station in decades."

"That makes things tricky," I said.

"Yes, it does," Mgurn said. His frown deepened which is creepy as hell on a Leforian.

"What?" I asked. "Don't tell me the second possibility is worse."

"Is that a direct order?" Mgurn asked.

"Is what a direct order?" I replied.

"Not to tell you the second possibility is worse," he said.

"Just tell me," I snapped.

"Earth," Mgurn said.

Both Tarr and Ig gasped. And they weren't tough guy gasps, but more like someone squeezed a baby gump too hard gasps.

"Is it too late to take back my offer to help?" Tarr asked.

"I would also like to put in a request to rescind my assistance," Ig said.

"Guys, guys, relax," I said. "Maybe the data is on the android station. No need to panic now."

Earth. Yikes.

"Yes, well, I am not so sure that is how it will turn out," Mgurn said. "My research is leaning towards Earth as our target."

"Why is that?" I asked.

Mgurn shifted uncomfortably.

"Mgurn? Why do you think Earth is the target?" I asked.

"Because I tasked SMC surveillance probes to go take a look," Mgurn admitted. "Two Edger ships just arrived in the Sol System less than an hour ago."

"Oh," I said.

"Yeah, that's a bit of a giveaway," Tarr said.

"How armed are they?" Ig asked.

"Heavily," Mgurn said.

"It would appear they are after the same data we are after," Ig said.

"Or some Edgers decided to take a vacation on a radiation-laden, mutant-populated, cesspool of a planet," I said. "You never know with Edgers."

"You believe that?" Tarr laughed.

"No," I admitted. I thought for a couple of seconds then shook my head. "If it is Earth then there is no way I can ask you guys to help me. The SMC doesn't even take tickets for Earth jobs."

"It would be best to forget the idea of retrieving the data altogether," Mgurn said. "But I know you will not do that."

"We are still in," Ig said. "Right, Tarr?"

"Yeah, I was kidding about taking back my offer," Tarr said. He smirked. "We do have one advantage, though."

"What's that?" I asked.

"We all know someone that's actually punched a ticket on Earth before the SMC stopped taking them," he replied. "I believe you now know her intimately."

"Hopsheer? She's been to Earth?" I exclaimed. "No way."

"Way," was what she said when we were all sitting down in her lounge.

Yeah, her quarters has a lounge. I was starting to wonder just how many lucrative tickets Hopsheer had punched before I joined the SMC. To have a lounge off of her main room was a serious luxury.

"It was a long time ago," Hopsheer said. "I was still apprenticing with Salvage Merc Fourteen. That was when the SMC had the mentor/mentee thing going. Now they assign assistants to rookies and cross their fingers."

"Lucky you," I said. "So, what's Earth like? Is it as bad as everyone says?"

"No," Hopsheer said as she shook her head.

It took all of my willpower not to just stare at her while she did that. She caught me looking and pursed her lips. I smiled and cleared my throat.

"It's not as bad as everyone says," Hopsheer continued. "It's a thousand times worse. There are creatures on that planet that would make a B'flo'do turn around and flee."

"That would be due to the radiation levels," Mgurn said, sipping some thick, black tea that Hopsheer had offered us. He looked like the only one that was enjoying it. "The B'flo'dos cannot feed off of energy in that spectrum. They would become just as sick as any species would. Probably more so since they would process the radiation immediately. It would be a death sentence the second they left the protection of their ship."

"Then how the hell do we survive?" Tarr asked.

"There are ways," Hopsheer said. "We triple our personal shields while wearing containment suits. We keep an eye on our meters and the second they hit yellow, we hightail it back to our ship and decontaminate. We'll have to wait twenty-four hours before going back down, but that's just how Earth is. You take it in shifts, not all at once."

"How long does it take for our meters to hit yellow?" I asked.

"No more than eighteen hours," Mgurn answered. "Ig could handle more since Groshnels have a higher tolerance for radiation, but even she would need to return to the ship within thirty hours."

"Who the hell would put a data storage facility on Earth?" I grumbled.

"That is the bad part," Mgurn said.

"Oh, brother," Tarr said and rubbed his face with both hands. "Who is it?"

"The Fleet," Mgurn said. "The data storage facility there is controlled by the Galactic Fleet."

Ig raised six of her eight arms. "May I ask why it is so important that we find this data? Is it all to see some obsidian-eyed mystery man? Because there are plenty of mysteries in the universe that I can do without solving."

"Again, I can't ask you guys to come with," I said. "I'm doing this because I need to know why my best friend was murdered. And why Jirks with Skrang skins were on that station. My gut is telling me that the black-eyed son of a bitch can answer those questions."

"Joe, you realize that even if you get the security data, all of this could just lead to more questions, right? You may not get the answers you are looking for," Hopsheer said. Her voice was firm yet kind. She knew my mind was made up, but she cared enough to try to get me to back off.

"I know," I said. "But there have to be some answers there or why would two Edger ships even be in the Sol System."

"Earth," Tarr said.

"Earth," Ig echoed.

"Yes, Earth," Mgurn agreed and nodded his head up and down.

I met Hopsheer's eyes and she gave me a half-embarrassed smile. The other half was honest concern. It was at that moment I knew the night before hadn't been a complete mistake.

No, the complete mistake was to involve my friends and comrades in my personal business. But they were grown mercs and could make their own damn decisions. Can't blame me that the decision involved Earth, right?

Right?

Right…

EIGHT

Once Mgurn got us the schematics of the data storage facility, planning our heist wasn't too hard. The place had great security, but not anything too high level to give us any worries. It was obvious that the Fleet expected the location on Earth to be deterrent enough for would-be thieves and hackers.

Which was brought up.

"Why not just hack the facility?" Tarr asked. "We establish a link and suck that data right out of there."

"We can't," Mgurn explained. "It is a one way pipeline. Not that it is a literal pipeline, but the transmission can only be received. The facility has no way to transmit data. Once information is stored there, it is locked down and can only be accessed by a local interface."

"Not a very efficient system," I said. "How does a ship's captain access his cat pictures?"

"Cat pictures were outlawed three centuries ago when the Cervile race was discovered," Mgurn said.

"Unless you count Cervile porn," Tarr said.

"Do we?" Ig asked.

"I do," Tarr said.

"Can we focus, please?" Hopsheer sighed.

"I'm focusing," Tarr said and gave her a wink. He tapped his head. "Focusing on some hot and heavy—"

"Yes, we get it," Hopsheer said and swiped at her tablet, bringing up the full schematics of the data storage facility. "We keep the ships in orbit and pod down here."

She pointed to a spot by a ridge about one click to the east of the facility.

"Once on the ground, we hustle to the facility and Mgurn gets us inside," Hopsheer said.

"You all have the skills to gain access," Mgurn said. "Like I said before, the facility itself is not that hard to break into."

"True, but we'll be watching your back while you get us in," Hopsheer said. "This is Earth we're talking about. The second we touch ground, we'll be hunted. Everything on that planet hunts or kills."

"There is a difference?" Ig asked.

"On Earth there is," Hopsheer replied. "Hope you're killed if something gets you. The ones that hunt, do so for pleasure, not food."

"Oh," Ig replied and her squishy body turned bright blue.

"It's good, it's good," Tarr said. "You have eight arms for a reason. Those reasons are called H16 Carbines, my friend."

"We watch Mgurn's back and he gets us in," Hopsheer continued. "Once inside, we lock it back down and move as fast as possible to the first extraction terminal. Mgurn hacks the data, we copy it onto crystals that we'll each carry so we have multiple copies, just in case, then we get the hell off that planet and back here."

"There might be other steps in that plan," I said. "Steps that involve shooting things."

"Probably, but we won't know until we get there," Hopsheer said.

"What about the Edgers?" Ig asked. "They will have already arrived."

"That's the shooting part," I said.

"No, I have confidence in my fighting skills to take on some Edgers," Ig said. "But what if they are after the same data we are and get to it first?"

"This is the good news," Mgurn said. "I have studied the storage facility interface extensively in the brief time I've had and it looks like data can be extracted, but not deleted. Even if they get the data for themselves, they cannot prevent us from getting it as well. They will only have it first."

"Why do they want to know who this obsidian-eyed feller is?" Tarr asked.

"They may not," Mgurn said. "The data is from the entire Caga station's security system. They may be after some other component we know nothing about."

"I guess we'll find out," I said. "But let's focus on finding out who the black-eyed bastard is. You guys didn't see him, I did. There was something very, very off about him."

"Yeah, we get that," Tarr said. "Are we done here? I could use a nap before we hit the wormhole portal."

"One hour," Hopsheer said. "Then we each start leaving."

That was the hard part, getting away from SMC headquarters without raising flags. Everyone had to take their own ship or it would look suspicious. We also had to log in different destinations with the SMC controllers. That meant some serious misdirection to go from SMC headquarters to Earth via several wormhole portal detours.

And it's not like we worked for an organization that wasn't good at figuring stuff out. It's the foing SMC. They specialize in figuring stuff out. Organizations hire them for that specific reason. Salvage is the main part, yes, but how you get that salvage is really like solving a puzzle.

So, yeah, we had to be careful or the bosses would smack us down big time.

"Have you ever thought of putting a Cervile and Bvern in the same room together?" I asked Mgurn as we launched from headquarters. "One is feline and the other is whatever rat things are called."

"Murine," Mgurn replied.

"Yeah, that," I said as I steered us away from headquarters and put us on a course for the closest wormhole portal. "That would be something, right? Cat and a rat in a room."

"That would not be something except for a recipe for bloody disaster," Mgurn said. "The Bvern would win. They outweigh the Verviles by a good hundred pounds."

"But those claws that Cerviles have," I said. "They could slice a Bvern up in a snap."

"Why?" Mgurn asked.

"What?" I replied.

"Why would you think up something like that? What purpose does it serve?" he asked. "Why hypothesize the outcome of a death match between races?"

"Because that's what my brain does," I answered. "I think up things like that. Probably because I'm bored. Flying this ship is boring. It pretty much does all the work for you."

"Then let me fly," Mgurn said.

"No, no, then I'd be even more bored," I said. "I'm an action guy. I like being in the field. I like the adventure of hunting down a salvage and fighting off bad guys to claim it. I hate the getting to it part."

"Most of life is the getting to it part," Mgurn said. "So, in essence, you hate most of life."

"Hmmm," I replied. What he said actually made sense. "I hadn't thought of it that way. You see, Mgurn, this is why we make a good team. I'd probably be lost if the bosses ever assigned you to a new number. I'd end up flying directly into a sun or try and navigate an asteroid field blindfolded."

"Why in the Eight Million Gods would you do that?" Mgurn exclaimed. "That's just insanity."

"But not boring," I said as we approached the wormhole portal.

I waited for the all clear signal to be transmitted to my navigation system. And waited. And waited.

"This isn't good," I said.

"We have an incoming transmission from the SMC," Mgurn said. I could smell the nervousness on him. "Would you like me to respond or should you take this call?"

"I'll take it," I said and activated the holo com.

Boss Four popped up in front of me, busy eating a sandwich and chewing with his mouth wide open. Or I think it was a he. Hard to remember at the time.

"Where are you going, One Eighty-Four?" he asked.

"Out for a stroll," I replied. "I can't stay cooped up in the headquarters forever and you lot aren't going to assign me a ticket anytime soon, so I'm heading to the Klatu System to see what nightmares have been thought up by that dreamer race that lives there. Mgurn has adjusted the blaster so we can shoot monsters."

"The Klatu System is a non-weaponry system, One Eighty-Four," Boss Four said then shrugged. "But do what you have to to stay out of trouble with us and the Fleet. You are going to stay out of trouble with the Fleet, correct?"

"Cross my heart and hope to die," I said.

"That is an awful saying," Mgurn muttered.

"I've approved your portal jump," Boss Four said. "But if you screw me on this, One Eighty-Four, then you will be in a universe of hurt when you get back."

"I'm kind of there now," I said. "Dead best friend and all that."

"Which is the only reason we don't tractor beam your butt back here," Boss Four said. A huge clump of something yellowish fell from his sandwich onto his uniform or whatever he was wearing. I can't remember. "Dammit! I gotta go. This stuff stains something fierce."

The holo cut out and I gave Mgurn a smile.

"Let's blow this place and go get us some illicit data," I said as I hit the thrusters and sent us flying through the wormhole portal.

I wasn't kidding about the Klatu System. We hit there first, saw some very, very messed up things, then jetted it to the next wormhole portal and started our circuitous route to Earth. It took us a while, especially with the traffic jam in the Javitz System due to everyone stopping there to get food or drink or whatever at one of the dozen drive-thru planets, but we eventually blinked into existence in the Sol System.

"Plutonians." Mgurn shivered. "They freak me out."

"Says the bug dog," I said. "What do you have against Plutonians?"

"Nothing against them, it's just that they are made entirely of mercury," he replied. "Which makes no scientific sense. Why is their mercury sentient and other mercury isn't?"

"I want to know why a race on Pluto is made of mercury, but there's no race on Mercury made of plutonium," I said. "Think on that for a second."

"No," Mgurn said. "It'll make my head hurt."

"Doesn't matter," I said as we raced by Saturn, having already passed the other planets in the Sol System. "We'll be at Earth in about twenty minutes. You want to take over while I double check the gear?"

"Gladly," Mgurn said.

I didn't really need to double check the gear since I'd triple checked it back at headquarters and I know Mgurn checked it at least as many times. But I needed a moment to get my head together. There were a lot of emotions running through me and I had to be sure they weren't completely ruling my thinking.

I know Hopsheer and the other mercs were worried and they did have some good points. But, as I went over my containment suit and checked the charge on my personal shield, I knew deep in my gut that I was doing the right thing. Crawford's death wasn't just an assassination. It wasn't just some Edger separatist terror attack. It wasn't me being in the wrong place at the wrong time.

Too many things didn't add up.

One of those things was the twitching at the corners of Crawford's eyes. What was that about?

Another was the presence of the Jirks looking like a Skrang kill squad.

There was more than that, but those two things were what jumped out at me.

So why go hunt down the black-eyed stranger? Why risk my life, and the lives of my friends, on Earth to find security data that may or may not give me any more information than I already had?

Simple: my gut was telling me it was the right move.

I wasn't having full-blown clarity, nothing like that, but it was like the butterflies I get right before my gift kicks in. It was as if the answer was just out of reach, like by a fingertip, and all I had to do was take one small step and I'd have it.

Yeah, I know, going to Earth is not even close to being considered a "small step." It's more a nightmarish leap off the tallest building you can find and insisting that you only do up one strap of your parachute. Or something like that.

"Joe? We're here," Mgurn called over the com. "Looks like Hopsheer and Ig have arrived ahead of us. Still waiting for Tarr."

"Be right there," I replied.

I set my gear aside, making sure it was packed for a one-handed grab, if need be. I looked up at the grey metal ceiling of the ship's hold and said a quick prayer to the Eight Million Gods. Not that I'm much of a religious man, never have been. But one thing a Marine learns fast: always take your luck/help/divine intervention where you can get it.

Like they say, "There are no atheists in the belly of a cweatt dragon."

When I reached the bridge, Tarr had arrived. We went over the plan again, double checked from orbit that our drop zone was clear, made sure the Edger ships weren't in close proximity (which they weren't), set security systems to full defense, and loaded up in our respective drop pods.

Mgurn and I had to share a pod since we couldn't afford to drop both pods and end up stranded if something went wrong. Which, let's face it, we all knew would happen.

It was Earth. Everything goes wrong on Earth.

Dropping from orbit in a pod is a lot like someone tying a string to your nuts and pulling that string really hard up through your gut, your chest, your throat, and right out the top of your head. Not the greatest feeling, but not the worst either.

The worst feeling is when the pod lands and gravity hits you full on. And Earth gravity is a bitch, let me tell you.

Yes, I'm human, so I should have been genetically ready for Earth gravity, but I wasn't. The pod split open and I came out with my H16 up and swinging back and forth. I took my steps carefully as my body adjusted to the weight. It pressed on me like I had six more containment suits and a pack full of lead.

In the galaxy, there are lots of high-gravity planets. Many races build muscles on top of muscles on top of muscles because of the force of their homeworld's gravity. Then they go off planet and can rip steel apart with their bare hands. It's scary to watch.

But, Earth? Earth has a gravity that isn't so much about the force that presses down on you as much as it is the heaviness of everything around you. I've staggered under gravity ten times worse, but never had to deal with how the gravity on Earth seems to seep into your pores. It just gets in you and everything is heavy.

Your thoughts, the light streaming into your eyes, the air you breathe even though it's filtered, even the words you speak. All of it is just foing heavy.

"I am not enjoying this sensation," Mgurn said. "It feels as if my insides want to be outside and my outside wants to be inside."

"That is a damn fine description, Mgurn," I said. "I'm feeling the exact same way."

We hustled over to the other three pods and knelt down, keeping the drop zone covered while Hopsheer, Ig, and Tarr all exited their pods and acclimated to the messed up planet that is Earth.

"Any sign of hostiles?" Hopsheer asked.

"Nothing so far," I said. "Mgurn?"

"Zero presence of lifeforms within our immediate vicinity," Mgurn said. "That could change quickly."

"Storage facility is over this ridge," Hopsheer said. "I'll take point. Fall in behind and keep your eyes peeled."

"I only peel my eyes for that someone special," Tarr replied. "And that's only for special occasions."

"Please tell me that's not literal," I said.

"Oh, you know it is," Tarr said. "I'm all about the literal."

"You have something wrong in your head, Tarr," Ig said. "I like it, but don't let it get us killed."

"It's the wrong that fuels me, Ig, my woman," Tarr said. "I ever tell you the story about the Neffernian girl with the six arms and four legs? Talk about a long night of wrong. You know only one of their orifices is for reproduction, right? The rest are strictly for pleasure."

"Can it, Tarr," Hopsheer said. "Save it for the mess hall later when we can enjoy the story over some pitchers of beer."

"Roger that," Tarr said.

We crested the ridge and stared down at the valley below us. We probably stood there staring for far too long, but it was really the best option at the time. None of us wanted to take another step towards the data storage facility that was smack dab in the center of the valley.

"What are those?" Ig asked, his voice low and measured. "Were they some type of livestock?"

"At some point," Mgurn said. "That would have been at least ten, maybe twenty, evolutionary cycles ago."

The valley was small, maybe a kilometer across at the most and two long. But in that valley were things that may have been cows at one point in their ancestry. But they sure weren't like cows I'd seen on other terra-like planets. These things had horns that curved out and down around their heads, the tips gleaming and sharp. I'd worry about the horns, and maybe the massive tusks that stuck out of their thick, powerful-looking jaws, but they had one feature that was way more worrisome than their dental mutations.

"Are their tails shooting barbs?" Tarr asked. "They are, aren't they?"

"Yeah," I replied.

We watched as a small group of cows in the herd turned at once and began firing up into the air with their tails. Shiny barbed darts flew high into the sky, cutting down the flock of birds that had attempted to fly over the open valley. The birds were about as nasty looking as the cows, but apparently had not developed a defense against the bovine projectiles.

"How do we do this?" Ig asked. "Guns blazing? Or skirt around and find a stealth way in?"

"The facility is in the middle of the valley," Hopsheer said. "There is no stealth way in. We'll have to blast ourselves a path and hold it until we can get inside."

"We can set up a laser perimeter close to the facility once we hit the entrance," I said. "It won't stop the barbs, but it'll keep the cows from stampeding and trampling us."

We all looked at each other and shook our heads. None of us expected what we saw down in the valley. Giant mutant lizard things and maybe some humanoid cannibal tribes, but not barb-shooting cows that were obviously not herbivores any longer.

"Man, they're really tearing into those birds," Tarr said as we skirted the edge of the valley, looking for an easy path down. "You can hear the crunching all the way up here."

We found our path, but it wasn't an easy one. The bowl of the valley was pretty much just loose shale, so going straight down was not an option. Even with our combat boots on, we would have spent most of our time falling on our asses.

So we followed the switchback trail that was barely wide enough for us to go single file. Ig had a better go of it because of her many limbs, but the rest of us barely kept our footing on the way down. That meant there was plenty of slippage. And with slippage comes noise as shale shards slid halfway down the valley wall, alerting the mutant herd to our presence.

By the time we reached the bottom, most of the cows were more than a little curious as to what we were. They made that very clear by rushing at us, mouths wide open, barb-shooting tails raised and firing away.

"This way!" Hopsheer yelled as she led us along a small stream that was choked with brown weeds and looked like it was mostly filled with cow poop instead of water.

I was right behind her with Mgurn behind me and Tarr and Ig following in that order. Ig started tossing grenades at the herd as the rest of us laid down a blanket of H16 fire. Cows began to fall fast, their black and white hides smoldering from all the blasts we sent their way. Bovine parts filled the air as grenade after grenade detonated, sending the cows flying in every direction.

Half the herd was ten kinds of pissed off at us and the other half was fleeing as fast as their hoofed legs could carry them. The fleeing ones weren't much of a concern. The ten kinds of pissed ones were.

They came at us like demons from Hell. Their horns looked a lot sharper up close than they did from up on the valley ridge. One of those horns could easily pierce our containment suits. They'd get a shock from our personal shields that would probably drop them dead on the spot, but that wouldn't matter much as Earth's radiation cooked us crispy.

Yeah, our containment suits were durable, but not rage-pissed demon cow durable. What was?

Hopsheer led us around the main part of the herd then cut in towards the facility. We passed skeletons of various sizes and species, not to mention more than a couple stock tanks and feeding troughs which told us maybe the cows weren't feral and had been placed in that valley for the strict purpose of guarding the facility.

Hopsheer pointed ahead and then off to the right and the left. She kept moving straight while Mgurn and I spread out to the left and Ig and Tarr spread out to the right, giving us all some more room to work with. We dropped cow after cow, barely keeping them back long enough to throw in new plasma magazines as ours ran out. It didn't take a math genius to realize were spending all of our ammo and explosives on the trip to the facility.

What the hell were we going to foing do to get back out?

"Coming fast on our three!" Hopsheer yelled.

Ig spun about, producing two more H16s from Eight Million Gods knows where and started firing. She took down three cows before a fourth nearly trampled her. Luckily, the gal is pretty much made of air and flesh and was able to roll with the hit without getting gored to death. She tumbled across the ground as the cow sent barb after barb down at her.

Until Tarr put three blasts between the thing's horns, sending its brains flying out across its broad back.

Ig was up and double checking her suit before the next wave came for us. None of them were firing barbs directly at us which made me think that they were conditioned not to shoot towards the facility. That was a very good thing. It gave us time to concentrate on keeping moving while dropping as many as possible. Not that they needed barbs to scare the living hell out of all of us.

"Three!" Hopsheer yelled. "Six! On our six! Eight Million Gods dammit, Joe! Watch our six!"

"I didn't know I was watching our six!" I yelled back. "Next time tell me if you're going to act like our squad leader!"

"No whining in battle!" she shouted. "So shut up and kill cows!"

The absurdity of that order was not lost me.

NINE

For every step we each took, ten times that many cows converged on us. They seemed to sprout from the ground. I know that wasn't what happened, but damn if it didn't feel like it as we fought for every inch forward.

Finally, we hit the wall of the facility and were able to put something up against our backs. We fanned out on the wall and side-stepped our way around to the entrance, keeping our H16s hot and firing the entire way. My carbine powered down and I ejected the tenth magazine then slapped in a new one. My mental inventory told me I had six magazines left. That was not good math for the escape.

"Mgurn!" Hopsheer shouted as she reached the entrance. "Do your stuff!"

Mgurn moved away from my side and crouched low to the entrance's thick, heavy door. He studied it for a couple of seconds then pulled out his tablet, cracked open the entrance keypad, and began to hack our way in.

It took him about thirty cows to crack the code before the door slide open and we were able to hurry inside. The second we were all in, Mgurn locked that entrance down tight and we slumped against the wall, desperate to catch our breath. But relaxing was not in the cards as we kept our weapons up and scanned our new environment.

"Air is clean," Mgurn said. "No radiation or toxicity detected. We can take off our suits, if we like."

"I like, but not doing it," Tarr said, patting his chest. "This is all that's keeping me from freaking out and running back to my pod. Earth sucks gump nuts."

"It does," Ig agreed.

"Suits stay on," Hopsheer said. "Be ready to bug out at the first sign of trouble. We don't have the ammo for a firefight inside here and still be able to shoot our way out of this valley and back to the pods. Conserve your plasma, watch your targets, don't get stupid."

"Joe's already failed that last one," Tarr said. "Or we wouldn't be here."

"That would mean we all failed the last one," Ig said.

"Very true, woman," Tarr said. "Very true."

"Cut the chatter, you two," Hopsheer said as she moved away from the wall and took a few cautious steps down the dark corridor we faced. "Eyes and ears open. Mgurn? Which way?"

"Straight ahead," Mgurn said. "It's all straight ahead. Data banks are in the center of the facility. Everything around the data banks seems to be insulation from the outside environment. This is a heavy duty bunker."

"Bunker?" I asked. "Are we going below ground?"

"We will be," Mgurn said. "There is a ten percent grade to this corridor. The data banks would be able to survive quite the direct hit from above if a ship began firing down on the facility."

"Good to know," I said. "That means we won't get a missile in our butts while we search the banks for the Caga station data."

"I could say so many things about missiles in butts right now," Tarr said. "But I won't."

"You're a giver," I said.

"I know," he replied.

"Quiet," Hopsheer hissed.

We shut up and listened. That wasn't her in charge hiss, that was her she heard something and we need to shut our pie holes hiss.

She took point again and led us down the corridor. The air in the corridor was dry and thin. More like being at a high elevation than being on a valley floor. I could hear the ventilation system running at full blast, keeping the Earth's abundant moisture out of the facility. The planet may have been a toxic dump, but it was still an ocean planet primarily. They were nasty, scary oceans, yes, probably crawling with behemoths I never wanted to see, but still oceans. The atmosphere was a moist one and data banks are not a fan of moisture.

We made it down the corridor and were faced with a set of double doors. As far as I could see, there were no handles nor any sign of a keypad for entry.

"Mgurn?" Hopsheer asked. "This is not basic."

"Actually, it is," Mgurn said as he stepped up to the doors and pressed on them.

The right one swung open on squeaky hinges. The left one stayed put until Hopsheer pressed on it and opened it as wide as the right.

"No locks," she said as she inspected the door jambs as well as the edges of the doors themselves. "The Fleet has a lot of confidence in those cows."

"Or they have confidence in something else we don't know about," I said.

"Bringing us down as always," Tarr responded, but I could tell by the tone in his voice he was thinking the exact same thing.

It was all too easy.

"This way," Mgurn said as he took lead and walked us through the next corridor and the next, all separated by only those swinging double doors. "We are almost to the banks."

My ears popped and I wondered just how far down we were. A ten percent grade wasn't much, but it added up when you kept walking through corridor after corridor. I almost had to wonder also if we hadn't just walked ourselves out of the valley by then.

A final set of double doors stood closed before us and those had a keypad on each side.

"Why two?" Mgurn asked.

None of us answered because we knew he was talking to himself. Plus none of us had an answer.

He tapped at his tablet for a couple of minutes then turned and looked at us.

"This wasn't part of the schematics," Mgurn said, spinning the tablet around so we could all see what he saw. "There shouldn't be two keypads. I'm afraid that only one of them is legitimate and the other is a decoy."

"What happens if you access the decoy?" I asked.

"Nothing good would be my guess," Mgurn replied.

I could see the worry on his face. It was different than his usual worry.

"Flip a coin?" I suggested.

"That would not be wise," Mgurn said. "Let me continue my scans for a few minutes. I may be able to detect a difference between the two interfaces."

"Five minutes," Hopsheer said. "Then we either risk it or we turn around and go back empty handed." She checked a readout on the holo display projecting from her wrist. "We have three hours until sundown. I do not want to find out what nocturnal fauna lives around here."

"The cows seem to be able to take care of themselves," Tarr said.

"True, but we also left a lot of dead meat out in that valley," Hopsheer said. "That is going to be hard for any predator or scavenger to resist."

"This really was not a well thought out mission," Ig said. "I believe we may have been rash and rushed into this."

"Story of my life, Ig," I said. "Mgurn? Get your bug butt to work."

"I am already working," Mgurn said. "So please do not interrupt."

We waited as he studied the interfaces. Despite looking like simple keypads, they were considerably more complicated. Not only did you need to enter in a numeric code, but they also scanned your biometrics, including heart rate and brain waves, making sure no one that wasn't supposed to get in did.

That meant Mgurn didn't just need to figure out the code, but also the parameters that would satisfy the scans and keep us from getting blasted to hell by the facility's defenses. We couldn't see any gun turrets or laser grid bases, but we were all sure they were there waiting, ready to slice us and dice us if the wrong info went into the system.

"I believe it is the right keypad," Mgurn said.

"Right is right?" I asked.

"It would appear so," Mgurn said.

"It would appear so or it is so?" Hopsheer asked.

"I cannot be for certain," Mgurn said. "This part of the security system is vastly more complex than the rest. I do find it strange that the schematics are up to date on all other aspects of the facility except for these doors here."

"Probably a recent upgrade that some bureaucrat forgot to enter because he was too busy thinking about what he was gonna do over the weekend," Tarr said. "I hate pencil pushers."

"I hate pencils," Ig said. "I'm allergic to the living graphite they use in them now."

"You get stabbed with one of those and that mark travels all through your skin before it wears itself out," I said. "I dated a teacher once and it was wild to see where those graphite marks would go."

"Spare us the description," Hopsheer said a little sharper than was needed.

Ig and Tarr gave me a look. I shrugged.

"Code is easy enough," Mgurn muttered. "Biometrics can be overridden, but it's the theta waves I'm having a hard time getting past."

"Theta waves?" Tarr asked. "Not beta waves?"

"No. Theta," Mgurn said. "I almost missed it, but it looks like you have to be in a calm, relaxed state before these doors will open."

"Makes sense," Hopsheer said. "That way no one can be forced to open the doors under duress."

"It also makes it tough to hack," Mgurn said. "I'm not complaining, just explaining why it is taking me so long."

There was a loud clang and thump from far off in the facility and we all turned in that direction.

"No life forms detected," Ig said as he studied his holo scans. "That was either mechanical or the Edgers are wearing stealth tech."

"Or neither," Tarr said. "This is a Fleet facility. We could have tripped a trans-space alarm. Mgurn is good, but he may not have covered all bases."

"I covered all bases," Mgurn replied. "There is no evidence of a trans-space signal being sent. Nor any evidence of a local signal being sent. Your insults are not helping me figure out how to get around the theta wave dilemma, Tarr."

"Slow jams," I said.

"What?" Mgurn asked. He turned and looked at me then shook his head. "No."

"Come on, Mgurn," I said. "Slow jams is the way to relax."

"Slow jams?" Ig asked.

"You'll see," I said.

Mgurn turned on the speakers on his tablet and the sweet, sweet sounds of Ella Htzgrbs and the Mood Swingers began to play.

"Ah, yeah," I said and slowly moved back and forth. Even with my containment suit on, it was pretty smooth. "That's the sound of sexy, right there."

Mgurn shook his head and everyone else looked at me like I was insane. But after a minute, Mgurn got into the groove and he figured out how to fake the theta waves. It only took about a minute longer before he got the doors open.

"Oh," I said quietly as we stared at the barrels of several rifles, carbines, and various other weapons that were aimed right at us by the dirty, nasty Edgers holding them. "Hey there."

"That him?" one of the Edgers asked, glancing over his shoulder at an insanely tall woman with ebony hair and dark, dark blue skin. "The stupid looking one that was dancing?"

"That is him," the tall woman said. "The others are not needed."

"But we're worth a lot!" Tarr shouted. "The SMC has no problem paying ransom for its mercs!"

"He's got a point, Midnight," the first Edger said. "We could get a few thousand chits out of this."

"We're not here for the chits," Midnight said, her grey eyes locked onto mine. "We are here for the human and that is all."

"You are?" I asked. "What makes me so special?"

"That is not your concern," Midnight replied. "I have been hired to retrieve you and that is what I shall do."

"Hired? Who the hell would hire you to retrieve Joe?" Tarr asked. "He's still wet behind the ears. If you're looking for a real merc, then take me, blue lady. I've got skills you can't even imagine."

"My job is clear," Midnight said. "I will leave it up to my crew to decide whether they take the rest of you or leave your corpses here to rot."

There was another clang from far off in the facility. Most of the Edgers looked wary of the noise, but Midnight didn't flinch, she just kept her eyes locked onto mine.

"Crew?" she asked.

"I vote we take them," the first Edger said. "The split is crud on this gig. We can use the extra chits."

The rest of the Edgers agreed and the first one waved his carbine in our direction.

"All of you up against that wall except for this guy here," the first Edger said, indicating me. "He comes inside."

"I get separation anxiety," I said. "Can my assistant at least come with?"

"Thanks, pal," Tarr muttered.

"Your assistant is a useless Leforian," the first Edger said, apparently the spokesperson for Midnight's minions. "He's just a Mom that will get in the way."

"I do not appreciate being called a Mom," Mgurn grumbled.

"Maybe this will make you appreciate it," First Edger said as he pulled the trigger and a bright blast of plasma nailed Mgurn right in the chest.

"Nooooooo!" I yelled and dove for Mgurn, but Edger hands were all over me and dragging me into the data bank room before I could get two steps.

There was plenty of shouting and even some slapping, but luckily no more shooting, as I was held in place by five Edgers. Not that it took five to control me. The muzzles against my head and back kept me in check pretty well.

"Mgurn?" I whispered. "Come on, buddy, wake up."

"I'm awake," Mgurn muttered as he lay face down on the facility floor. "I just can't move. That blast hit a nerve center. I'm paralyzed.

"I don't know what you want with me," I said to Midnight. "But I am guessing your employer wants me alive, right?"

"Client, not employer. And good guess," Midnight replied. "What gave it away? The fact you're still alive?"

"Yeah. That," I said. "But if you don't let my friends go, and I mean go go, not just into the hands of your underlings, I will off myself before you get a chance to deliver me. Understand what I'm selling here, sister?"

"I have transported plenty of marks to plenty of paying clients," Midnight said. "I know how to keep you from committing suicide."

"You ever transported a really, really, really pissed off salvage merc before?" I asked.

"Yes," she said and sneered. She moved close to me and leaned in against the face plate of my environmental suit. "They all lived."

"Oh," I said. "But did they have a cyanide capsule instead of a back right molar?"

Midnight took a step back and studied me. Then she snapped her fingers and one of her goons handed her a tablet. She swiped through it for a few seconds then shook her head.

"Fo," she cursed as she gave the tablet back to the goon. "No dental records."

"They were purged from my file when the capsule was installed," I said. "For just this reason."

Midnight glared at me then looked out of the data bank room at Hopsheer, Tarr, and Ig.

"Come on, Midnight," First Edger whined. "Don't force us to let a solid payday go."

"I am not forcing you to do anything," she said and pointed at me. "He is."

I didn't see the blow coming. First Edger slammed the butt of his carbine into my solar plexus and all the breath left me in one big whoosh. I was down on my knees, coughing and gasping, as the next blow hit me in the back of the neck. My life turned into swirling stars and flashing lights. Plus, pain. Plenty of that.

"Stop," I gasped "Or I chomp hard."

"Let him be," Midnight said and I was helped to my feet.

It was hard to focus, but I was able to see Midnight give a nod at Mgurn then at the others.

"Get," she said. "Now. Before I change my mind."

Hopsheer, Tarr, and Ig rushed in and picked Mgurn up. Hopsheer started to say something to me, but I shook my head, which hurt like hell to do. She nodded and watched their backs as Tarr and Ig carried Mgurn out of the data bank room and into the corridor. With a last look from Hopsheer, they fled and I was left alone with the Edgers.

"So… Where we headed?" I asked.

"That is not your business," Midnight said. Her grey eyes drilled into me. "But it will be when we arrive."

"I figured that," I said and looked about at the data storage banks that filled the immense room. "You mind if I ask a favor?"

"Is this guy for real?" First Edger asked.

"I am," I said. "I came here for a reason. How you knew I'd come here, I'm not sure, but I'm here now. I need some data from the Caga station. I just need to look it over before you give me to your client."

She laughed hard. Like really hard.

It kind of pissed me off, but I let her laugh, waiting patiently until she was done, her hands holding her belly. It must have been a seriously fit belly because I didn't see a single jiggle while she was busy larfing it up. Yes, I was checking her out. She was extremely good looking. If I had to guess, I'd say she started off using her looks to climb her way up the Edger gang ladder until she was done being taken for granted and had built enough of a following to make a move.

It may have been the 32nd century, but the ladies still get a raw deal in the galaxy. Too many macho planets with macho races that were afraid their little dingles would fall off if the females of their species were allowed some equality. Except for the female-only planets. Those planets had it reversed and eliminated men as soon as their duties were done.

However it was, there was no way I would take Midnight for granted. She'd beaten me to the data storage facility and knew exactly when I'd show up.

Midnight held up her wrist and projected a holo in front of my face. It was the scene at the Caga station cafe just before things got ugly.

"Why do you have that?" I asked.

"Because I was told you'd be looking for it," she replied. "My client was very thorough in their research."

"They?" I asked.

"I speak in the unisex singular," Midnight said. "Not the collective."

"Ah," I said and nodded. Then something occurred to me. "Did you watch it?"

"Yes," she said.

"There's a guy in there," I said. "Black eyes."

"Like obsidian," she said. "Yes, I saw him. Is he why you're here? I thought it was to erase the footage of the Admiral of the Fleet handing you the data crystal."

"That's on there?" I asked. "Crap."

"That's not why you wanted this?" Midnight asked. "You were just looking for the black-eyed man? That is ridiculous. All the Edgers know him. He walks amongst us as if he's the owner of everything."

"He does? He is?" I asked. "Who is he? Does he own you?"

"What? No, he does not own anything," Midnight replied. "Edgers are a free people. No one owns us."

"That's nice," I said. "Maybe work on quitting the raiding and murdering and raping thing and start going with the not being a pestilence on society thing. Less pirate, more person."

"Fine advice from a salvage merc," Midnight scoffed. "Useless, ignorant advice, but fun to hear."

"Some of us like being pirates," First Edger said.

"Shut up," Midnight snapped.

"Who is he?" I asked again. "The black-eyed man? What's his name?"

"He doesn't know his name!" First Edger exclaimed. "What an idiot!"

I ignored the others as they laughed and I focused on Midnight.

"Tell me his name and I promise I won't make trouble while you transport me," I said.

"I have no reason to trust you will keep that promise," Midnight said. "And now that I have something you want, I believe you'll behave anyway. If you want any chance of getting answers to your many stupid questions."

Before I could respond, the distinct sound of a plasma blast echoed down the corridor outside. Midnight growled and motioned for her men to go see what it was. They stepped into the corridor and I watched their eyes go wide. Before they could raise their weapons and fire, Hopsheer, Tarr, Ig, and the still wobbly Mgurn, all came rushing into the data banks room.

"How many of you are there?" Hopsheer shouted at Midnight. "Because you need to tell them we had a deal! Call them off so we can get away from here!"

"What?" Midnight exclaimed. "All of my men are accounted for! There shouldn't be anyone...else... Dammit. Dammit all to Hell."

"I'm guessing your contract wasn't exclusive," I said. "Sounds like the competition has arrived."

"No, that's not it," Midnight said.

There were more blasts and the couple of Edgers that didn't dive back into the room were vaporized before our eyes.

"Lock it down!" Midnight said. "Lock the room down and call the ship! NOW!"

TEN

"Call the ship?" I asked. "What does that have anything to do with this?"

"None of your business, mark," Midnight spat.

"My name is Joe, not Mark," I said.

"Not that kind of mark!" she roared. "You are my mark! The mark my client wants me to retrieve!"

"Oh, sheesh, chill," I said.

More blasts and the wall by the doors began to smolder as a heavy duty plasma stream nailed it.

"They have canons," I said. "You might want to take my friends up on their offer to help fight."

"Not a chance in Hell," Midnight said and pointed at Hopsheer. "Keep yourself and your people under control and out of my way and things may go right for you when this is over."

"If those aren't your men then you are seriously outgunned," Hopsheer said. "Give us our H16s back and we'll get you and your men out of here alive. That's what we do."

"The SMC is not the only skilled organization in the galaxy!" Midnight shouted. "Edgers are more than capable of handling their own fights! And I am more capable than most Edgers!"

"I am not feeling so well," Mgurn said and slumped down against one of the data banks. The crystalline machine began to hum and Mgurn scooted away to lie on the floor. "I'll just rest here."

"Where is the ship?" Midnight growled as she pushed First Edger forward. "Cover the corridor and be ready!"

First Edger and the rest of Midnight's men rushed to the room's doors. They peeked out then jumped back as a heavy plasma blast melted half the wall where they had been standing.

"Over a dozen," First Edger said. "And they aren't what we thought they were."

"What in Hell did I think they were?" Midnight snapped, making First Edger flinch. "Tell me. You seem to be able to read my mind."

"Skrangs," First Edger said. "That's what they are."

"Just like on the Caga station," I said as I crouched down next to Mgurn. "Hey, buddy, how are you doing?"

"I am resting," Mgurn said. "I do not believe my injuries are life threatening, but I will not be of any assistance to you or the other numbers anytime soon. My body can repair, but it will need time."

"Time you do not have," Midnight said as she shoved me out of the way and reached down to yank Mgurn to his feet. "But you will buy us some time."

She walked him to the doorway and then threw him out into the corridor.

"NO!" I yelled and rushed at them, but two Edgers slammed the butts of their rifles into my sides, dropping me fast. "MGURN!"

I stared in horror as Mgurn tried to scramble back into the room. But he was too late. A plasma blast ripped through the air and then there was no Mgurn.

Clarity hit me and everything slowed down.

I kicked out with my left foot and snapped the leg of the Edger next to me. I kicked out with my right foot and made a nice pair of matching cripples by my sides. The two Edgers fell hard and I was on them before they could even open their mouths and cry out. I ripped out the throat of one with my bare hands then grabbed up his rifle and put two blasts into the head of the other one.

"Stop!" Midnight yelled. "What are you doing?"

I whirled about and fired without even aiming. She was fast. Surprisingly fast for a woman her size. The plasma blast I sent her way just missed her shoulder as she dove to the ground and came at me in a tight roll.

In my peripheral vision, I could see Hopsheer and the others jump into action. Edgers began shouting and screaming as they were taken down. Blood flew everywhere as we all buried our grief in a healthy dose of brutal violence and revenge.

Midnight clocked me across my chin and I almost lost my clarity. My head began to ring and I had to tumble backwards to avoid the second shot coming at me. Midnight yelled something again, but I didn't make out the words as I got to my feet and centered the rifle on her chest. Her face was nothing but dark blue fury then I saw her eyes go wide and look past me.

Barely able to spin in time, I started firing, knowing the Skrangs had reached the doorway. One dropped, his head nothing but a smoldering stump of flesh. A second one fell as he met the same fate.

Then they both went poof and their bodies deflated.

"Jirks!" I yelled as I continued firing, keeping the rest of the skintakers away from the doorway and pinned down in the corridor. "What the fo?"

I felt a hand grab my shoulder and I started to turn, but the world around me did the turning for me. Everything became a kaleidoscope of colors and shapes. Then I was on my hands and knees throwing up, my stomach still turning even though everything else had become still.

Or almost still. I could feel the thrust of engines and knew I was on a ship as it was accelerating through space. Then the tell-tale whump and thump of a wormhole portal told me we'd just left the Sol system. How, I had no idea.

"Get up," Midnight growled close by. Her boot hit my ribs for emphasis. "I said get up."

I wiped the puke drool from my mouth and got to my shaky feet. I could see we were in a modified ship's hold. Modified because there was a heavy platform under my feet that was humming a high pitched noise that made my teeth hurt.

"You are an idiot," Midnight said as she picked up the rifle at my feet. "There was no need to kill my men."

"No need?" I coughed as I tried to take a swing at her, but stopped before I lost the little bit of balance I had managed to recover. "You killed my friend!"

"That is not entirely correct," Mgurn said from a spot by the wall where he was lying on a med cot, watched over by four Edgers as a medic tended to his wounds. "It appears that Ms. Midnight has acquired a rare molecular transporter and used it to send me to her ship."

"I wanted it to look like he had been vaporized," Midnight said. "That way when the Skrangs attacked us in the data banks room, we could do the same thing and they would think we are all dead. That would give us a head start back to the Edge."

"They weren't Skrangs," I said. "They were skintakers. Jirks."

"Yes, I saw that as well," Midnight said. "All the more reason for them to think we, especially you, are dead. Now they not only know we are still alive, but that I have a moltrans device on my ship. That makes me and my men targets because once word spreads about what we have, this ship will be almost as valuable a mark as you."

"Why would Jirks look like Skrangs?" Hopsheer asked from within a circle of heavily armed Edgers. Tarr and Ig were next to her, both looking like they were ready to just give up and go home.

I didn't blame them.

"This is like those Skrangs you saw on the Caga station," Hopsheer continued. "That means Jirks are killing Skrangs to take their forms. Whatever they are after, it must be incredibly valuable to risk starting a war with the Skrangs."

"Are none of you paying attention?" Midnight asked as she stepped off the moltrans platform and took a bottle of liquid offered to her from one of her men. She drank long and deep then tossed the bottle over at Hopsheer. "How can you be salvage mercs and be so clueless?"

Hopsheer caught the bottle easily, studied it, then took a swig. She coughed lightly and handed it over to Tarr. He took a longer swig, didn't cough, and reluctantly handed it to Ig who just waved her arms, refusing the bottle.

"Those Jirks weren't on the Caga station to kill Admiral Helms, were they?" Hopsheer asked, grabbing the bottle from Tarr and taking another drink. "They were there to grab Joe."

"Do you require breadcrumbs to follow for every mission you undertake?" Midnight sneered. "Yes, Salvage Merc One Eighty-Four was their mark. Just as he is my mark."

"Fo me," I said and held my hand out. Everyone looked at me like I'd lost a few marbles. I probably had, but that wasn't the point. "Drink! I want a drink too!"

Hopsheer threw the bottle at me and I caught it with only a slight bobble. I drank half the liquid, which burned all the way through my soul, before Midnight yanked the bottle from my lips.

"This does not grow on trees," she snapped.

"Actually, that specific spirit does come from the fruit of a— AAAAH!" Mgurn started to explain then stopped as he had to scream from the pain of having his carapace fused together by a nanotorch.

"Joe? You look like you had a thought," Hopsheer said.

"It's a rare enough occurrence to warrant special attention," Tarr said then gave me an apologetic look. "Sorry. Too easy to pass up and I'm stressed to the balls here."

I looked over at Midnight and tilted my head.

"What exactly have you been hired to do with me?" I asked.

"Why does it matter?" she replied.

"Really? It matters a lot if I end up being killed at the end of this trip," I said. "Tell me what your client wants and maybe I can help us all."

"My client has paid for anonymity as well as discretion," Midnight said. "If I were to tell you anything about my client then I would never be hired for another job again. Not in the Edge or anywhere in this useless galaxy."

"Was this an exclusive job?" I asked.

"Yes," Midnight said. "But that doesn't matter. Why do you need to know this?"

"I don't think I ever had lunch with my best friend," I said. "The wrinkling around Crawford's eyes. It's bugged me. I think he was a Jirk."

"A Jirk?" Hopsheer asked. "But wrinkling around the eyes is not a sign of a skintaker."

"No, it's not," I said. "But I think I have a theory about why he looked strange."

"Is that so?" Midnight asked. She waved at her men and they grabbed onto Hopsheer, Tarr, and Ig. "Take them to the brig. I'll decide their fate later."

"Oh, knock it off," I said. "You got me. I'm not going anywhere since I'm stuck on your ship. Leave my friends alone and I promise I'll cooperate the whole trip."

"Do you now?" Midnight laughed. "Well then, I'll just let three salvage mercs run free on my ship." She nodded to her men again. "The brig."

"We'll be fine," Hopsheer said. "Just try not to talk yourself into getting killed."

"Me?" I smirked.

"Be safe, Joe," Hopsheer said.

"I will," I replied.

We held each other's gaze for as long as we could until the three of them were yanked from the ship's hold and into a corridor beyond.

"We shall go eat," Midnight said. "I want to hear this theory of yours. It sounds entertaining, if nothing else, and will be a welcome distraction while we travel to the Morigun System."

"Morigun System? Not the Edge?" I asked.

"Why would we be going to the Edge?" Midnight responded. "That is not where my client wants you delivered. The Morigun System, specifically the planet of C."

"C? I hate C," I said. "Have you ever been on C? The whole place is a planet of meadows filled with wildflowers. It drives my allergies crazy."

"I have been to C, but I do not plan to stick around long enough to enjoy the scenery," Midnight said. "I drop you off, collect my pay, and I leave. What my client does with you is entirely up to them."

"Them?" I asked.

"The unisex singular," Midnight sighed. "Pay attention, merc."

"Oh, I'm paying attention," I said. "Don't worry."

Mgurn moaned from his cot and the medic stood up and turned to look at Midnight.

"I've done what I can," the medic said. "He will live and he will heal, but I cannot say much beyond that."

"Living and healing will work," I said. "He getting tossed in the brig as well?"

"He is," Midnight said and snapped her fingers. "But I won't be so cruel as to have him actually tossed. He'll be set in there without further harm coming to him."

"What happens when I'm turned over to your client?" I asked. "With my friends. What will you do with them when I'm gone?"

"Squeeze whatever chits we can out of the SMC," Midnight said and shrugged. "But let's talk about that over food. I am starving to death. You?"

"I could eat," I said. I didn't want to, but it was a way to keep Midnight happy and talking. "Lead the way."

I studied as much of the ship as I could as we made our way through the corridors to her private quarters where a nice spread of food and drink was waiting for us. If I needed to, which I wasn't 100% sure I did, I could probably find my way back to that hold and get the hell out using the moltrans unit. Not that I knew how to work it, but how hard could it be?

"Don't bother thinking too hard about escape," Midnight said as she indicated for me to take a seat by the table of food. "There is no way off this ship."

"There's always a way off a ship," I said.

"Not mine," Midnight insisted. "I have made sure of that. You would not be the first to try and fail."

"But maybe I'd be the first to try and succeed," I replied.

"No," was all she said as she sat down and grabbed up a piece of fruit.

I assumed it was fruit. Could have been entrails. You never can tell without labels.

"You were saying that you did not believe that to be your friend Crawford that died?" Midnight asked as she popped bits of food into her mouth then poured us two very full glasses of wine. "You expect me to believe that a Jirk was able to impersonate your friend and fool the Fleet as well as you?"

"I don't expect you to believe that because I barely believe it myself," I said as I sipped at my wine. It was a good vintage, but my stomach was still not settled enough for me to enjoy it. I set the glass down and leaned my elbows on the table. "But it is the only explanation I can come up with."

"But you spoke to him," Midnight said. "I watched the holo. You sat down and had a whole conversation with your friend. Are you telling me you didn't notice then? That he knew things about you and he that had you convinced you were sitting with the real Crawford Helms?"

"He knew enough to convince me," I said. "But stories and information can be memorized. They can also be fed to someone via a com."

"Okay, let's say you are right," Midnight said. "Then why would a Jirk impersonator hand you a data crystal which you would obviously be handing right to the SMC bosses?"

"Misdirection?" I asked. "I never did see what was on the data crystal. Maybe it was given to me to lead the SMC in a specific direction."

"Such as?" Midnight asked.

"I don't know," I said. "I'm only guessing here." I pointed at her wrist and twirled my fingers. "Can I watch the security holo from the Caga station? Maybe that will help me figure things out."

"Get crazy," she said and projected the holo over the center of the table.

We sat there and watched it from start to finish at least three times before I told her to turn it off.

"The more I watch it the more I see I was duped," I said. "I don't know how they got me to believe that was Crawford I was having lunch with. Some of the gestures are right, but the majority of the body language is completely off. I think I chalked it up to him being nervous about his new position. I never even guessed that he was a Jirk."

"Again, why give you a data crystal?" Midnight asked.

"That is a good question," I replied. "Add to it, how did the Edger separatists choose that day and that location to attack? Who tipped them off?"

"Those were not Edger separatists," Midnight said. "They were an illusion as well."

"They were? How do you know?" I asked.

"I just know," Midnight replied.

"But the Jirks I ran into on the way out that looked like Skrangs were no illusion," I said. "Other than the skintaker thing. They were there to kill me."

"Were they?" Midnight asked.

"Yeah, they were," I said. "Just like today."

"We don't know they were there to kill you today," Midnight said. "They could have a capture and deliver order like I do."

"But deliver to who?" I muttered. "Why would Jirks all of a sudden want me...?"

"What?" Midnight asked. "You have thought of something."

"Not all of a sudden," I said, more to myself than to her. "There were other Jirks. Before. When Hopsheer found me."

I stood up and pointed at her closed quarter's door.

"I need to see my friends," I said. "I need to speak to Hopsheer."

"Tell me why and I'll consider it," Midnight said. She took a long drink of wine and fixed her gaze on me, waiting for my answer.

"Hopsheer recruited me for the SMC," I said. "I didn't know her then, so I had no idea she was acting strange. But now that I've worked with her, it makes sense."

"Not to me," Midnight said. "Request denied."

"The day Hopsheer found me, so did a pair of Jirk bounty hunters," I said. "Or I thought they were bounty hunters. Maybe they're part of all of this that's happening now. Hopsheer acted like it was a race to find me and she was beyond relieved when she did." I shook my head. "I don't know. There's just too much I don't know."

"Yes, I am more than certain of that," Midnight said. She finished her wine, sighed, and stood. "I'll take you to your friends. You can talk to them for as long as it takes to reach the Morigun System."

"Thank you," I said.

"Don't," she said. "This isn't me being nice, it's me giving a dead man a last request."

"You think I'm dead when you hand me over?" I asked.

"I honestly don't know," Midnight said. "But clients don't pay me what I was paid to hand over a new roommate."

"Whatever," I said. "Just take me to the brig."

"Can do," Midnight said and poured herself another glass of wine for the walk.

ELEVEN

Hopsheer squirmed as I waited for her answer. Tarr and Ig looked from her to me and back while Mgurn just moaned on the floor of the brig, his torso wrapped in heavy gauze. I stood outside the brig's energy cage, watching Hopsheer closely, looking for the lie I knew would come.

"I followed the ticket," Hopsheer said. "I made my claim. That's all, Joe."

"It's not," I said. "Why were those Jirks there? What did they want with me? Normally, I would have been all over that slight hiccup, seeing it for what it was, but everything moved way too fast once you took me to SMC headquarters. I was a new number and out in the field in record time."

"And doing a piss poor job of it," Tarr said. He held up his hands. "Hey, man, no offense, but you're not the greatest merc the SMC's ever had."

"Yeah, I know I'm not the greatest," I said. "I've been doing this for less than a year. Cut me a break."

"Joe, I punched the ticket, made the claim, and the rest was your decision," Hopsheer said.

That got me. That right there.

"The rest was my decision," I said. "Eight Million Gods. Those Jirks were hired to scare me into joining the SMC."

"That is quite the intuitive leap, Joe," Ig said. "The galaxy is a dangerous place. I am sure they were there for some other reason."

"No, they weren't," I said and glared at Hopsheer. "Hoppy? Tell me I'm wrong. Tell me they weren't just some suckers hired by the SMC to manipulate me into agreeing to go with you and join the SMC?"

"I had a claim to make," Hopsheer replied. "I'm Salvage Merc Eight, Joe. There's a lot of responsibility with that number."

"I thought numbers didn't matter," I said.

"Yeah, they're just numbers," Tarr said.

"A number dies and a new merc takes his or her place," Ig added. "Just numbers."

"They aren't just numbers," Hopsheer said. "Each one has significance. Especially…"

"Especially?" I asked. "Especially what?"

"Especially Salvage Merc One," Hopsheer replied after a couple of seconds.

"I knew it," Midnight said as she leaned against the wall behind me, her arms crossed, a knowing smirk on her face. "This crud is all part of the foing legend."

"Legend?" I asked. "What legend? Can everyone stop being so damned secretive and just tell me what is going on? It'll be a lot faster than forcing me to work it out myself."

"Midnight?" a voice called over the intercom. "We have arrived."

"Time's up, Joe Laribeau," Midnight said. "I need to deliver you to my client."

"Hold on!" I snapped. "Just a couple more minutes!"

"The deal was you could talk to your friends until we arrived at the Morigun System," Midnight said. "We have arrived. Time to go. Fight me and I hurt your friends. Make it easy for me and I make it easy for them."

"You spare their lives," I growled.

"I already told you they are worth squeezing some chits out of the SMC," Midnight said. "They are worth more alive than dead. So relax."

"We'll be fine, man," Tarr said. "Not the first time I've been locked up by a blue-skinned babe."

I looked down at Mgurn and he gave me a slight nod. My gut was all twisted, but not in any soon to be clear way. In fact, other than the brief time down on Earth, I hadn't been feeling the clarity much at all since leaving SMC headquarters. That had me almost as worried as what I would find when Midnight gave me over to her client.

"Joe," Hopsheer said. "Trust yourself."

"I may be the only one I can trust," I said, giving her a pointed look that made her wince. "Except for Mgurn. I can always trust Mgurn."

"I am honored," Mgurn said.

"And you are a fool," Midnight said as she pulled me from the brig and shoved me down the corridor. "I am surprised you haven't figured out that trusting people is why you are in the mess you are in."

"There are a lot of reasons I'm in the mess I'm in," I replied. "That I can trust."

We made our way to the hold and the moltrans unit. Midnight indicated for me to step up onto the platform and I did. She followed right behind me and held my arm as she gave a thumbs up to a man standing by a control console. He tapped at the holo interface and before I could say anything we were no longer on Midnight's ship, but standing in a field of wildflowers.

I started to sneeze almost immediately.

"You weren't joking about the allergies," Midnight laughed. "Come on."

I was so busy sneezing that I didn't notice we'd materialized only a few meters from a beautiful estate house. It wasn't until Midnight led me through a gate, guarded by men and women that looked like they'd seen better days, that I realized the house looked familiar. The guards were rough looking, for sure, but the house was gorgeous.

"This way," Midnight said. "There is someone you need to meet."

"Your client, I know," I replied. But the familiarity of the house made me wonder if I already knew the client. But that couldn't be. Unless...

"You'll see," Midnight said and led me inside the estate house.

The moment I stepped through the doorway, my allergies began to subside. A few deep breaths and I was back to normal. Midnight smiled at me and gave me a wink.

"You are not the only one that has need of a clean space," Midnight chuckled. "The house is sealed and the air filtered to reduce the pollen exposure as well as getting rid of undesirable microbes."

"Lucky me," I said. She chuckled again which was disconcerting. It was like her personality had changed as soon as we were down on the planet.

Instead of leading me into what looked like a pretty well-stocked library, which is usually where secretive weirdos like to hold court before their big reveal, Midnight walked me to a small door that led into the kitchen. The second I was through that door I knew I'd been played yet again. And I knew I was right about the house and who was in it.

A man stood by the large stove, stirring a huge pot of gump stew. I knew it was gump stew because I'd know that smell anywhere. I can't even count how many times Crawford had made it for us while we were on some backwater planet fighting for the Fleet. It was an easy recipe and gumps are everywhere. He used to tweak the seasoning to fit what was available, but usually he could get it almost perfect every time.

By the smell filling the kitchen, the batch on the stove was going to be delicious.

"Nice house," I said. "A friend of mine used to show me holos of a house just like this. A place his grandparents owned when he was little."

"That was a fine house. This is only a replica, of course," the man stirring the stew said. "Sorry for all this secretive crap, brother. You can't imagine what my life has been like the past few months. I hope Midnight didn't hurt you or your friends too much. I told her to play it up, be authentic, but she can get carried away."

The man turned around and every inch of his skin not covered by clothing was wrapped in thick bandages. A shimmer of electricity pulsed across the bandages at two second intervals, making the man shiver slightly as he stood there watching me.

Watching me with eyes I knew very well.

"Crawford," I said. "You son of a bitch."

"I knew you'd recognize me," he said and held out his arms.

I started to step forward, but it was Midnight that moved in for the hug. Crawford pressed his bandaged face to hers and they stared at each other for a few seconds before Midnight turned around to face me, Crawford's arm draped across her shoulder.

"There's no client," I said.

"Sure there is," Crawford said. "Me. I just didn't have to pay this beautiful lady anything. Since, well, she is my wife."

"Oh," I said. "Congratulations? And, um, what the fo is going on!"

"He's handling this as well as you said he would," Midnight said. "You know your friend, love."

"Thanks, baby," Crawford said. "Joe, listen, I'm sorry for all of this. It's messed up and I shouldn't have had to drag you into it, but I did because I had no choice."

"Why the hell are you covered in electro-bandages?" I asked. "What's wrong with your...skin...? Oh. Crud."

"Figured it out yet?" Crawford asked.

"I knew that wasn't you on the Caga station," I replied. "The Jirk did a good job, but it was that twitching around the eyes."

"Side effect of getting things just right," Crawford said. "Normally, a Jirk consumes the lifeforce of their victim, takes their skin, and they become a perfect replica. Except for the teeth of the lower castes, of course."

"Of course," I grumbled.

He gestured to himself. "I couldn't really let Bacca take my lifeforce so we had to use chemical stimulants to boost his mimic abilities so his eyes looked like mine. I knew if the eyes weren't right, you'd figure it all out too fast before he could make the exchange."

"The data crystal," I said.

"Exactly," Crawford said. "I needed you to deliver that crystal to the SMC bosses so they knew what was going down."

"What is going down?" I snapped.

"Bacca, the Jirk you met, was part of the separatist movement," Crawford said. "As soon as we found out I was to be used as a figurehead admiral to lure you in, he volunteered to take my place. It was very brave of him."

"Not following," I said, my head feeling like it was full of bees. Angry, giant, man-eating bees. "Go slow. Give me details."

"I am part of the Edger separatists," Crawford said. "Have been since I met Midnight."

Midnight gave me a warm smile. Seriously. It was a genuine smile. Not the bloodthirsty grimace I'd first seen on Earth.

"The Fleet council wanted me as Admiral of the Fleet so that they could get to you," Crawford said. "You are a very important person. More than you know, brother."

"I'm starting to figure that out," I said. "But I don't know why."

"We'll get to that," he said. "What you need to know is Bacca died so he could get you that crystal. It has all of the files and intel on the Fleet's plans to kill you and make it look like the Skrangs were wanting war again. They don't. The Fleet does."

"All of that is on the crystal?" I asked.

"It is," Crawford said.

"Bacca used his brief position as admiral to hack the Fleet's covert data systems and obtain the evidence we needed to prove the Fleet council was staging it all," Midnight said. "He died to get you that intel."

"So I could get it to the SMC bosses?" I asked.

"Yes and no," Crawford said. "We wanted the SMC bosses to have it so they wouldn't be drawn into the Fleet's plan. The Fleet has never liked the neutrality of the SMC. There is too much power in not taking sides. They want the SMC to finally sign on with the Fleet, go back to war, and wipe out the Skrangs."

"Why?" I asked.

"Profit. Why else?" Crawford replied.

It was strange talking to my friend as he stood there in head-to-toe bandages with his arm around a woman that had recently tried to kill my friends. Maybe.

"This is making my head hurt," I said. "The guy I had lunch with was Bacca. He was a Jirk impersonating you, with your actual skin, so he could infiltrate the Fleet and get the evidence needed to expose them into my hands. Yeah?"

"Yeah," Crawford said and nodded.

"The Caga station was attacked by fake Skrangs to make it look like the Skrangs want war again," I said. "They also would have killed me, hopefully bringing the SMC into the fight. Yeah?"

"Yeah," Crawford said.

"So who were the separatists that attacked the cafe?" I asked.

"They weren't separatists," Midnight said. "We don't know who they were or why they were there. As far as we can tell, they were just some Edgers hired to kill Crawford."

"Hired by who?" I asked.

"We don't know," Midnight said. "Pay attention."

"Okay, okay, I get this so far," I said. "But what about the black-eyed man? The one that I saw in the cafe?"

"He wasn't supposed to be there," Crawford said. "We aren't completely sure why he was. Maybe to watch out for you. It was a strange move by the SMC."

"The SMC? What do they have to do with the guy?" I asked. Something in the back of my mind stirred. I thought I had the answer to my own question, but I couldn't grasp it.

"He doesn't know," Midnight said.

"Honestly?" Crawford asked.

"Honestly," Midnight said. "I don't think any of the salvage mercs know. Or some pretend not to."

"Just tell me who he is," I snapped. "This crud is getting old, Craw. Really old."

"The guy you saw was Salvage Merc One," Crawford said. "Or this version of him. Of course, there's no way he can be the original. But that was him. It really is weird the SMC sent him to watch over you like that. If they did. Salvage Merc One plays by his own rules most of the time."

"I think I'm sure the SMC knew he was there," I said.

"Why's that?" Crawford asked.

"I don't know," I said and patted my belly. "A gut feeling."

"Well, we both know to trust those," Crawford chuckled. "You still doing that clarity thing?"

"I am," I said. "But it hasn't been very reliable lately. Just brief flashes of it here and there. I should have gone full clear when Midnight came at us on Earth, but I didn't. I only touched on it for a couple of seconds when the Jirk Skrangs showed up."

I rubbed at my head. The pain wasn't bad, but it was annoying. Too much. All of it was too much.

"Why were the Jirk Skrangs at the data storage facility?" I asked. "Why would the Fleet need them to come after me again?"

"That had nothing to do with you," Midnight said. "They were there to stage an assault on the facility and bolster the Fleet's assertion that the Skrangs were wanting war again."

"And destroy any evidence from the Caga station's security feed," Crawford said. "Two birds, one stone scenario."

"So, why were you there?" I asked, my question directed at Midnight. "Just to bring me here?"

"We wanted the same security data, as well," Midnight said. "Then we found out you were going to be there so we waited around to make it look like a snatch and grab so no one suspects the SMC is working with the Edger separatists."

"Wait, are they? I mean, are you?" I asked.

"No," Crawford said. "The SMC is stubbornly neutral when it comes to everyone in this damn galaxy."

I took a couple of steps towards them and jabbed my finger at Midnight.

"Why the hell did you shoot Mgurn?" I snapped. "You could have grabbed me without having to shoot him!"

"That was unfortunate," Midnight said. "But it needed to look real. He will live, as my medic explained to you."

"And everyone else? My friends that are still up on your ship?" I asked.

"That is entirely up to you," Crawford said. "This is where things get foed up, brother. We want to let them go, we really do, but we need some assurances that the SMC won't try to go after the Edger separatists anymore. Even if they are hired to do so. It's tough enough dealing with the Fleet and the Skrangs, we can't be looking over our shoulder all the time to see if the SMC has a ticket on us and some salvage merc is coming to ruin one of our ops."

"So you are holding my friends hostage to force the SMC's hand?" I growled. "That's low, Craw. Real low."

"No, we are holding them to force your hand," Midnight said. "And we are holding you to force the SMC's hand. It's a long line of hand forcing."

"I'm still a rookie," I said. "The SMC won't sacrifice their neutrality to save me. There's nothing I can do to convince them to. You guys are crud out of luck."

"No, we aren't," Crawford said. "The SMC is very willing to sacrifice a lot to save you. You are their future."

"I am?" I asked. "I don't know what you two know, but have you seen my performance reviews? I'm mediocre at best."

"You are far from it," Crawford said. "In fact, you are the second most exceptional person at the SMC. They know it and they'll do a lot to protect you."

"Why? Just someone tell me why!" I yelled.

"Your gift," Crawford said, holding up his bandaged hands in a calming gesture. It did not calm me. "That stupid gift of yours. Clarity is only part of it. A small part that has shown itself. The rest will happen on its own when it is time."

"I give up," I said and walked over to a stool by a small island in the kitchen. I plopped down and put my head in my hands. "I should never have joined the SMC."

"Oh, don't say that, One Eighty-Four," a voice said from the kitchen doorway. It was sort of familiar, but I couldn't say why. "In fact, I really need you to take that back."

I looked up and the voice's familiarity came rushing back to me.

"Boss Four?" I asked. "What are you doing here?"

"Been following you the whole way," Boss Four said. He mimed using an old steering wheel. "Got my own ship and everything. Zooming across the galaxy." He gave Crawford and Midnight a little wave. "Stay put, please. I don't want to harm you if I can help it."

"How did you get in here?" Midnight asked. "How many of my people did you kill?"

"None," Boss Four said. "No need to kill anyone if they can't see me. I'm letting you three see me, but that is all. Your people could walk in here right now and they'd think you were talking to air. Oh, hey, is that gump stew?"

"Uh, yeah," Crawford said.

"Can I have a bowl of it? I've only had a sandwich today," he said and looked at me. "I got that stain out, by the way. Wasn't easy, but damn if I refuse to let a condiment beat me."

Crawford and Midnight turned their eyes on me and I shrugged.

"No idea what's going on," I said. "Just one more layer of what the fo."

TWELVE

Boss Four ladled out a bowl of stew then leaned back against the kitchen counter as he took bite after bite. No one said a word until he'd finished and set the bowl in the sink.

"You want me to rinse this out or can it go right in the washer?" he asked.

"You can leave it there," Crawford said.

"You sure? I don't mind putting it in the washer myself," Boss Four said.

"No, it's cool, thanks," Crawford said.

"Okey doke," Boss Four said and rubbed his hands together. "Alright. Down to business. I am going to need all of you to put your little plans on hold and help me out."

"Excuse me?" Midnight asked.

"Yes, I may have gotten the SMC in a bit of a pickle," Boss Four said. "I sent Salvage Merc One to the Skrang home planet with a copy of the black data crystal. The idea was that it would give the Skrangs evidence that a faction of the Fleet wants war again. They can use it to clear their names if more Jirks are sent out to frame them."

"That doesn't sound very neutral," I said.

"Oh, it's totally neutral," Boss Four replied. "We used to do this sort of thing during the War all the time to balance things out. Haven't you guys figured out that the SMC is why the War ended? If we came across intel that would bring balance back to the conflict then we shared it. The Fleet and the Skrangs not so quickly realized that a prolonged War wasn't going to be cost effective anymore because of what we were doing. Treaty, signed."

"That's why the Fleet wanted me dead, so the SMC would stop being neutral and go after the Skrangs," I said.

"Oh, you already told him that part?" Boss Four asked Crawford and Midnight. They nodded. "Good. Less for me to explain. It's also why the Skrangs staged the fake Edger attack on the station. They wanted the Fleet to attack the Edger separatists then swoop in and offer an alliance."

"In case the SMC joined with the Fleet," I said.

"What? Oh, no, they didn't have a clue about that," Boss Four said.

"You have this all figured out," Crawford said. "So why do you need the separatists' help?"

"No, no, you misunderstand," Boss Four said. "I want nothing to do with the separatists. The Edger rights movement is your own deal. I'm looking for your specific help. You, Mr. Crawford. And your wife's. I need you to assist One Eighty-Four here with the retrieval of Salvage Merc One. You see, we were late to the information about the Skrangs using fake Edgers. Didn't find that out until One was taken hostage by the Skrangs. Oops."

"Oh," I said. "You want me to do what now? Go rescue Salvage Merc One?"

"Yep," Boss Four said. "With some help from your old Marine friend and his highly skilled wife. And her people. But just her people. Not any of the other separatists, or it will look like we've joined forces and that would be bad."

"Why not send all your mercs in to get him?" Midnight asked. "You have way more skilled numbers than Joe here."

"Thanks," I said.

"No offense meant," Boss Four said. "But it's no secret you aren't our top number."

"Then why the hell did you recruit me?" I snapped.

"So you could become the next Salvage Merc One," he said. "We always have to be on the lookout for men and women with specific gifts. Number One isn't something that can be assigned like the other numbers. It is something that has to be passed on. It's far too complicated for you to understand, hell I barely do most of the time and I'm one of the bosses. But your friends here are right that the SMC would be willing to sacrifice a lot to keep you safe."

"So you're here to meet our demands?" Crawford asked.

"What? No, don't be daft," Boss Four said. "Your little freedom movement isn't even close to being on the same level as us. You never stood a chance against the SMC. That should be obvious since I'm standing right here with a belly full of gump stew. Which was delicious, by the way."

"And we hadn't made any demands yet, love," Midnight said.

"That too," Boss Four said. "Smart woman. It's why I need her help. If she wasn't already spoken for by your open ended plans to stick it to the man, I'd recruit her into the SMC. No lie."

"I need drinks. Lots of drinks," I said as I started to pace back and forth. "All the drinks. I need every drink that is in this house."

"It is a lot to take in," Boss Four said.

"No, it's not!" I yelled. "Because you haven't explained it at all! How the fo do I become the next Salvage Merc One? Why the fo would I want to?"

"Why wouldn't you?" Boss Four asked. "Being One is a pretty sweet gig. Power like you can't even imagine. All the privileges of the galaxy at your fingertips. Mad respect. Even the Edgers know not to mess with Salvage Merc One."

"That's true," Crawford said. "It's those eyes."

"So, what? I rescue this guy and then he hands me his badge? Is that it?" I asked.

"Oh, no, it's not like that at all," Boss Four said. "You have to kill him in hand to hand combat. Then all these lights start flashing and you are struck by lightning. Your eyes turn black and you become One."

"Oh, crud," I whispered. "That's messed up."

"Totally screwing with you," Boss Four laughed. "Yeah, he basically hands you his badge and we have HR make the change in our mainframe and then you're One."

I glare at him.

"What?" he asked. "Okay, yeah there's more to it than that. There is some training that goes with it, too. One was supposed to get back from this last ticket and then get to work teaching you how to take over his job. He thinks you're ready, especially after how you survived the Caga attack."

I threw up all over the nice tile floor.

"Yikes," Boss Four said. "We're gonna have to work on those nerves."

He handed me a towel and a glass of water.

"Still not sure why you don't send a different number to rescue One," I said. "Like Hopsheer. She's a way better salvage merc than me."

"True, but that's not how it works," Boss Four said and shrugged. "We need you because One told us it had to be you if he ever needed rescuing. Same thing happened to him when he was young. I wasn't involved with that transfer, since it was obviously Boss Six's deal, but I've read the report. I'd tell you what it said, but your small minds aren't capable of understanding. Mysteries of the universe and stuff."

I looked over at Crawford and Midnight. They each looked like they wanted to puke too.

"You guys up for this?" I asked.

"I'm not up for anything," Crawford said. "I can't leave this house until my skin grafts are done healing."

"And I am not leaving him alone here if there is a chance the Fleet knows what we have done," Midnight said. "I am sorry, Mr. SMC Boss, but you will need to find a different solution."

"It's Boss Four, no need to get formal with the mister part," Boss Four said. "And I had a feeling you'd say that. So, to sweeten the deal, I have authorized a protective detail of mercs around not just your estate, but the entire planet. It'll be logged as a salvage mission, of course, but with about two dozen SMC ships in orbit, the odds of the Fleet or the Skrangs making a move will be close to zero. Deal?"

"We are capable of protecting ourselves," Midnight replied.

"Tough customer, eh?" Boss Four laughed. "Then maybe, once this is all over and One is returned safely, we might be able to arrange for Mr. Helms here to take advantage of our skin growth tanks back at SMC headquarters. Months of healing done in only hours. How does that sound?"

"Why do I feel like I'm making a deal with the Seven Devils?" Crawford asked.

"You always feel that way when you talk to one of the bosses," I said.

"We didn't get the jobs by being pushovers and taking no for an answer," Boss Four said. "Speaking of, I need your answer now?"

"If we say no again, will you kill us?" Crawford asked.

"Yikes, why would I do that?" Boss Four asked. "If you say no again then I take One Eighty-Four with me and you two forget this meeting ever happened. You'll just think One Eighty-Four escaped and you're back to square one. Oh, and that maybe you'll have some Fleet destroyers or Skrang cruisers coming to knock on your orbit's door. Not as bad as dying, but that anxiety won't be fun."

"Baby?" Crawford asked Midnight. "This will be your ass at risk for no real reason that helps the cause."

"But it keeps the SMC in place as a neutral power," Midnight replied. "And they are all that stands between the Fleet or the Skrangs taking over the galaxy. Doing this may not directly help the cause, but it does keep the balance of power in check." She looked at Boss Four and squinted. "If I agree to help then I need one thing from you."

"Oh? Just the one? What is it?" Boss Four asked, looking amused.

"If the SMC needs outside help from now on then they hire me and my people to do it," Midnight answered. "It will be a way for us to profit and fund our movement without the SMC risking their neutrality. Everyone needs help now and again. If I do this under the table for nothing now then I expect other jobs to come up that actually pay."

"Deal," Boss Four said and crossed the kitchen with his hand out. He moved so fast that both Midnight and Crawford jumped, making the boss laugh. "Sorry. Sorry. I get enthusiastic when negotiations work out."

Midnight took his hand and shook. So did Crawford.

"Then, if that concludes the exposition portion of my duties, I'd like to return to SMC headquarters for a hot bath and a glass of sherry," Boss Four said. "It has been a long and tiring day."

"Wait, you're leaving?" I asked. "What about the planning? We need details on where Salvage Merc One is being held, what kind of resistance to expect, how we get on and off the planet, all of that stuff."

"What do you think I hired her for?" Boss Four said, hooking a thumb over his shoulder at Midnight. "I'm not dealing with any of that. Then it becomes collusion and neutrality is out the window. Keep up, One Eighty-Four. Don't make me regret this decision."

I had nothing to say to that.

"We done?" he asked. "Good. I will leave you with one bit of good news. All intel we are able to share on One's capture will be provided to Mgurn. He is your assistant so I expect him to be a part of this."

"What? He's blasted to crud," I said.

"Is he? Huh, I hadn't noticed," Boss Four said.

Then he was gone. Blink. Gone.

In his place was a very confused-looking Mgurn.

"I would like to ask what is going on, but I suspect by the looks on your faces that none of you can give me a solid answer," Mgurn said. He looked down at himself and patted his armor. "Well, it appears I am fully healed. How did that happen?"

"Who was that?" Crawford asked.

"What? That was Boss Four," I said and realized I remembered everything that Boss Four had said. I looked at Midnight. "What do you remember?"

"We are going to rescue Salvage Merc One," she said.

"We are?" Mgurn asked.

"We are?" Crawford asked.

"You aren't," Midnight said.

"Right, right, yeah, I sort of knew that," Crawford replied. "I think…"

"I have this pressure in my head," Midnight said to me. "Is that what it's always like?"

"Yeah," I said. "You get used to it. Any chance you remember what he looked like?"

"No," she admitted.

"Me neither," I said. "I remember his words, but not his face. Frustrating as hell."

"Excuse me, but I seem to have valuable information," Mgurn said, holding up one of his four hands to tap at his temple. "I cannot say how I have obtained this information, but it is lodged squarely in the front of my mind and refuses to move out of the way so I can think of anything else."

"Bosses are weird, man," I said.

"That they are," Mgurn agreed. "Now, in order not to go insane, I would like to start planning our mission as soon as possible in the hopes that this information will back off."

"Love? Would you contact my ship and make sure it is ready to go?" Midnight asked Crawford. "I would appreciate that. I will stay here and get a plan together with Joe and Mgurn."

"Yeah, sure," Crawford said, his eyes semi-glazed. "I'll be in the communications room if you need me."

"Thank you, love," Midnight said and gave him a quick kiss on his bandaged lips. We waited for Crawford to leave then Midnight pointed at Mgurn. "Tell us what you know."

"May I ask for a favor? If I say anything that gives you the urge to have me shot again, please let me know in advance," Mgurn said. "I will apologize immediately."

"No one is getting shot again," I said and glanced at Midnight. "But you probably should apologize to Mgurn if we're going to be working together."

"That is not necessary," Mgurn said.

"I think it is," I said. "Midnight? It would go a long way towards me trusting you."

She started to protest, as did Mgurn again, but I held up a hand.

"I am sorry that you were shot," Midnight said. "I did not intend for you to die, if that helps any."

"It does," Mgurn said. "And thank you for that. I did not require an apology, but it does show you are a person of character and that matters a lot with me."

"Mgurn likes people of character," I said. "He also likes Johnny Cash songs."

"I have recently discovered him," Mgurn said. "It is believed that all music leads back to him. Are you familiar?"

"No," Midnight said. "I don't listen to music."

"Oh, well, to each their own," Mgurn said. He coughed then activated his holos on his tablet. "Look at this. Much of the information has already been digitized. I believe we are looking at the Skrang home world, are we not?"

"That's it," I said. "Good ol' Skrang."

"Not very creative," Mgurn said. "But neither are the Skrangs."

"That there," Midnight said, pointing to the display of the planet as seen from half its system away. "That spot. Can you zoom in?"

"I believe so," Mgurn said and adjusted the view.

The spot grew and grew until we were staring at something none of us wanted to have to see.

"B'clo'no warship," I said.

"Actually, it is a cluster of eight warships," Mgurn said, zooming in even closer. "They have joined into a superstructure. For what purpose, I cannot say. During the War, they only did that if they were on the attack."

"You don't think the Skrangs and B'clo'nos have had a falling out, do you?" Midnight asked.

"Not that I've heard," I said. "Mgurn?"

"I am sorry, Joe, but I can't think past the immediate information," Mgurn said. "My apologies for not being able to remember anything that might clear that up."

"No worries, buddy," I said, clapping him on the shoulder. "We'll save it for later. If that info moves out of the way and you have any insight into the B'clo'no warship cluster, you go ahead and tell us. Don't wait to be asked."

"I certainly will," Mgurn said. "Now, after some quick analysis, I would say we'll want to approach the planet from the opposite side." He adjusted the view and the planet spun around. "Here would be safest. With the moltrans technology on your ship, Ms. Midnight, I believe we can orbit here and transport ourselves down to the planet's surface without detection."

"You're sure?" I asked. "They'll have to be expecting a ship to show up. Why won't they see us?"

"That I can't answer," Mgurn said. His faced scrunched up and he moaned slightly. "No. No matter how hard I try I cannot say why I believe this to be true."

"You ever think the bosses are just playing some weird practical joke on the galaxy?" I asked.

"If so then it is a painful joke," Mgurn said. "Speaking of painful, may we continue, please?"

"Yeah, let's," I said and we dove into the details of how we would take on a warrior race and rescue one guy that possibly could be held anywhere on said race's home planet.

Mgurn's head may have felt better afterwards, but mine sure hurt a hell of a lot worse.

"We sleep," Midnight said when we left the kitchen. "I'll show you where you can stay."

"Thanks," I replied. "I'm so tired I could curl up on the floor right here and sleep for a year."

"Don't do that," Midnight said. "Someone will step on you in the night."

I looked at her and saw she was smiling. It was obvious why Crawford had fallen for her.

"Thanks," I said. "That's good advice."

She showed me to my room and I was pleasantly surprised by the size of the bed.

"Last time I slept in a bed this size was at a whore house just after being discharged from the Marines," I said. "The woman had to kick me out of bed to get me to leave. I would have slept there forever."

"I'm sure if you paid her more she would have let you stay," Midnight said.

"Probably," I said and shrugged. "But I didn't exactly have a bankroll on me and she knew that. It's why she woke my ass up. She went through my things and found that I barely had enough to pay her for the night I stayed, let alone buy another night."

"Then you found gainful employment with the SMC," Midnight said.

I laughed. "Not even close. It would be over a year before Hopsheer found me. I spent a lot of time begging rides from planet to planet so that my pension wouldn't completely run out on me. I also did some jobs that I'm not exactly proud of."

"We've all been there," Midnight said. "Get some sleep, Joe. We leave at 0500."

"Not sure how well I'll sleep, even with this fancy bed," I replied. "I'm a little wired."

"Want a sedative? Crawford has plenty of injectors because of the skin grafts," she said. "I can get you a couple."

"Nah," I said and forced a smile despite the mention of the injectors. "I'll be fine."

"Well, goodnight then," she said and started to turn. "What about Mgurn?"

"He'll find me as soon as he's done going over our plan a few dozen more times," I said. "He always finds me. Looks like this room has a comfy couch, too, so he'll enjoy that."

"I can give him his own room," she said.

"He's my assistant," I said. "He'll sleep in here because those are the regulations even if we aren't back at SMC headquarters."

"Leforians," she chuckled.

"Leforians," I said. "Always the Moms."

"That they are," Midnight said. "Goodnight again."

"Goodnight," I replied and closed the door.

I listened at the wood for a couple of minutes. When I was sure she was gone I dragged a chair over and jammed it up under the door handle. Mgurn would have to knock to be let in, but I had no problem with that. I'd rather get up in the night than sleep with one eye open.

Not that I wouldn't be doing that anyway. Old habits die hard.

THIRTEEN

Somehow I wasn't surprised to see my ship in orbit around C when I stepped onto the bridge of Midnight's ship.

"Turns out your boss brought all the merc ships with him when he swung by yesterday," Midnight said, sitting in the captain's chair, her eyes studying a readout on her holo display. "Your friends disembarked a couple of hours ago, but your ship is still here. We didn't figure that into our plan."

"If you would like, I could fly it to Skrang," Mgurn offered. "It may be to our advantage to have another ship with us."

"No," I said. "Best we don't have an SMC ship show up in their system."

"Yes, of course, but I thought I would offer," Mgurn said.

"You want to leave it here?" Midnight asked. "I hate to be a killjoy, but it won't look good if a SMC ship is…"

Her words dried up as well over a dozen SMC ships popped into view, having just come through the local wormhole portal. They were moving at a fast clip and I actually cringed a couple of times thinking we'd be watching more than one collision. But, hey, they were numbers and knew how to fly, so no crashes.

"Your boss wasn't kidding when he said we'd be well protected," Midnight said. "I guess your ship won't be standing out."

"It'll look right at home," I said. "We ready to get going? The SMC ships are leaving an open corridor for us."

"Let's move," Midnight said.

She began barking orders at her crew and they jumped at every word. Not out of fear, but out of well-practiced obedience. I had no doubt any one of them would die for her if she asked them to.

Her ship was about five times the size of a number's SMC ship. Well-armed, fast, maneuverable, and equipped with some fun toys and gadgets that made her a formidable entity to come up against. It was a homemade job, but well-made and deadly looking. Even a Fleet ship would think twice before engaging.

"Portal time will be thirty minutes," Midnight said. "Then another thirty to get to Skrang. We have an hour to go back over everything. You up for it?"

"I am," I said. "Mgurn?"

"My mind would like nothing else," he said. "I am hoping that when we arrive at Skrang, I will be able to focus on the actions needed and this intel will fall away finally."

"I'm hoping so too, buddy," I said. "Because you're looking a little green around the gills."

"I do not have gills," Mgurn said. "And I always look a little green. I get that from my mother's side."

"Right," I said and gave Midnight a smile. "Gotta love this guy."

"If you say so," Midnight said. "Entering portal now."

I took a seat as the ship slipped into the wormhole portal and the usual disorientation hit us all for a split-second. Then things cleared up and I took a look around the bridge.

"Your ship have a name?" I asked.

"Gratuity," Midnight answered.

"Are you foing kidding me?" I laughed. "Gratuity? What kind of name is that?"

"It is a fitting name if you knew anything about me," Midnight said and her body language told me that the subject was closed.

"The SMC doesn't allow us to name our ships," Mgurn said. "That would imply possession and we work strictly on a lease system when it comes to transportation. It allows us to interchange vehicles as needed without dealing with ownership papers. And taxes. I believe it is mainly to avoid tax charges. Each system has its own tax percentage and having to constantly calculate—"

"I think your mind is allowing new info to come forward," I interrupted. "Yay for Mgurn's mind. Now shut up, buddy. No one wants to hear about galactic tax structures."

"Yes, I am thinking more clearly," Mgurn said, "and I apologize for the pedantic nature of my discourse. Taxes seem to be a subject that is of great interest to me right now. I cannot say why since I have never—"

"Mgurn? Man? Shut up," I said.

"Again, my apologies," Mgurn responded.

I could see he wanted to keep talking and it was about to drive him nuts.

"Sorry for this, folks," I said. A couple heads turned and gave me questioning looks. "I gotta take care of my assistant. Won't do if his brain starts leaking out of his head."

I looked at Mgurn.

"Your brain is in your head, right?" I asked.

"That is strange you should ask me that, Joe," Mgurn responded. "It brings up an interesting fact I just learned the other day about the hoocahna snakes that live on Rylia Five."

"Why would you invite him to continue?" Midnight asked, glaring at me.

"We need him sharp when we arrive," I said. "This will clear out the cobwebs and get him focused on the mission."

"It will make me homicidal, is what it will do," Midnight said.

"Fight the urge to kill," I said. "And it's not so bad. You'll tune him out after a couple of minutes."

"—after shedding their skin for the fifth time, the hoocahnas will then perform a series of dances," Mgurn was saying. "Not mating dances, but actual recreational dances. They are the only non-sentient, reptilian-like species in the galaxy that dances for pleasure. All of the others do it for mating or as part of their hunting process."

"What snake uses dance to hunt?" I asked. I quickly wished I hadn't. Hard to tune out someone when you engage them in conversation.

"Oh, that is another fascinating thing I have learned," Mgurn said. "Let me finish talking about the hoocahna snakes then we'll get into the disco lizards of Egthak. Now, where was I?"

He went on like that for the entire portal trip. There were some sidearms drawn after the first five minutes, but Midnight chilled her people out and no one was shot. I am pretty sure, though, that promises to shoot Mgurn after the mission may have been mentioned. Midnight didn't exactly order anyone not to act on those promises. That was troubling, but manageable compared to what was about to happen.

"We are in the Skrang System," Midnight's navigation officer stated as we left the wormhole portal. "Course set for Skrang."

"Bring us wide and well out of scanner range of that B'clo'no warship cluster," Midnight ordered. "I don't want them to even sniff out our exhaust."

"If your ship is giving off exhaust then there may be a malfunction in your fuel converter," Mgurn said. He did that weird Leforian grin when Midnight whipped her head about to glare at him. "That was a joke."

"He's smiling," I said. "Trust me."

"I know a Leforian smile," Midnight said. "I just don't need bad Leforian jokes right now."

"Understood," Mgurn said. "I did not mean to be distracting."

None of us could keep from smirking or snorting laughter at that.

"What?" Mgurn asked, looking hurt.

"Nothing, buddy," I said. "Let's get ready to hop on the moltrans train, okay? I want all gear accounted for and set."

"I have inventoried everything," Mgurn said.

"Yeah, but come do it again with me," I said. "Cool?"

"Cool..." Mgurn said, wary.

Midnight gave me a quizzical look, but I just smiled and gave her a wink.

I pulled Mgurn off the bridge and down a corridor. Once far enough away, I stopped him and tapped him dead center in his armored chest.

"What else did Boss Four plant in your brain?" I asked.

"Excuse me?" Mgurn replied. "I am unsure as to what you are referring to."

"Think," I said and moved my tapping to his hard forehead. "They had to put more than just basic intel inside your brainpan. Is there anything about Salvage Merc One and how I fit into all of this? Any hint at what I can expect if we save him and he starts training me? Anything else at all?"

"No, Joe, I am sorry," Mgurn replied. He looked genuinely hurt, so I know he wasn't ordered to deceive me or hold anything back. "I only have information pertinent to the rescue at hand."

"Okay, buddy," I said and patted him on the shoulder. "Let's go check out the gear and get ready to see the sights on Skrang."

"From what I have heard, there is not much to see," Mgurn said. "A lot of rocks for the Skrangs to sun themselves on when not on duty. Plenty of lakes that they live by and breed in."

"Breed in? They breed in the lakes?" I asked.

"Yes," Mgurn said. "They copulate and give birth in water. The young that pull themselves up onto shore after full development are considered worthy. Those that flounder are left to die and become nutrients for the other young still developing in the lake."

"Eight Million Gods, that's cold," I said.

"They are a cold-blooded race," Mgurn responded.

We reached the hold and started going through our gear. Midnight and her people had their own packs and weapons, but I left those piles alone. No one wants somebody else going through their stuff.

I checked my equipment then triple checked my two H16s. I wanted an extra since I always seemed to be coming up short in the weapons department more often than not. I also had two KL09 pistols and I strapped those onto my thighs, making sure the holsters were tight and secure. The H16s were my go-to weapons, but having the KL09s made me breathe just a hair easier.

Mgurn was busy strapping all kinds of stuff to his carapace. His own H16, a KL09, several energy blades of various lengths and thicknesses, a laser whip (that was new), and several somethings that looked like cans of beer.

"What's that?" I asked.

"Cans of beer," Mgurn said.

"Are you foing with me?" I exclaimed. "You're bringing beer?"

"The Skrangs detest beer," Mgurn said. "They have a deep-seeded aversion to the smell and will panic if they come in contact with the liquid."

"Never heard that before," I said. "That something the bosses told you?"

Mgurn thought for a second then shook his head. "No, no, I learned that from Nature Channel Two-Thousand. Fascinating documentary."

"I'll take your word for it," I said.

"We're here," Midnight announced as she walked into the hold with her team of Edger fighters. She stopped and looked at Mgurn. "Is that beer?"

"Yes, it is," Mgurn said. "Fascinating fact—"

"Save it," Midnight said. "I've had enough fascinating facts for today. Just don't drink on the job, alright?"

"Oh, I can assure you that is not what these are for," Mgurn said.

A few of Midnight's people mumbled about what a waste that was.

"Let me introduce you to who you'll be fighting alongside," Midnight said. "Some of them you recognize from the Earth incident."

"Calling it an incident, are we?" a woman snapped. "They killed—"

"Stow it, Nammy," Midnight barked. The woman shut up. "This is Nammy. She is our lock pick. I mean that literally. It's a skill she has. She can open any lock out there, whether physical or electrical."

"Oh, I am good with locks as well," Mgurn said.

"Great," Nammy said. "We can start a club and braid each other's hair."

That was funny coming from the woman since she didn't have a single hair on her body, let alone her head. She was tall, lithe and her fingers looked way too skinny for her hands. There was a reflective quality to her skin and it wasn't hard to tell she wasn't human.

"Juan," Midnight said, pointing to a man that was half brown and half bone white like someone had split him down the middle with a paint brush. "He is demolitions."

Juan gave me a smirk and then sneered at Mgurn.

"Don't like Leforians," Juan said. That was it. Just that he didn't like Leforians.

"Yes, well..." Mgurn muttered uncomfortably.

"That going to be a problem?" I asked.

"Not for me," Juan said.

"This is Mak and Kam," Midnight said, hooking a thumb towards two identical Cerviles.

Hairy, pointy ears, whiskers, oh, and six-inch claws that retract from their fingertips.

"Let me guess," I said. "Hand to hand is how they roll."

They flicked out their claws and each gave me a hissing smile as their whiskers twitched up and down.

"They don't like Leforians either," Juan said.

"Shut your gob," I snapped.

"Juan," Midnight warned. "Do as the merc says. Shut your gob."

Juan shut his gob.

"Barby is here and Grue is there," Midnight said.

A Slinghasp bowed and gave me a bright, snake-fanged smile.

"A pleasure," Barby said. "I look forward to working with you, Joe."

Slinghasps are just so damn helpful. And dead sexy. She had a figure that was all curves and not just because she was a snake race.

Grue was Gwreq. Not a halfer like Hopsheer, but a full-blooded Gwreq. He was easily eight feet tall and his skin looked like old, craggy granite.

"Move when I say move," Grue growled, his voice nothing but rumbling gravel.

"I'll do that," I said and nudged Mgurn.

"Yes, I as well," Mgurn said. "No need to become a squashed bug, now is there?"

She rattled off a few other names and people stepped forward to introduce themselves. Some were pleasant about it, some weren't, most seemed disinterested in even caring about who we were. They had eyes for Midnight only. She led them and they'd do anything for her.

Mgurn and Me? Not so much.

"Whatever gear you are bringing, make sure it is strapped on tight," Midnight said as she stepped onto the moltrans platform. "With the amount of people we are sending down to the planet, the system will be pushed to capacity. Anything that could come loose might end up being reintegrated inside your body, completely or partially, on arrival. Understood?"

"Understood," I said. Mgurn didn't answer. He was too busy double checking that everything he had strapped to his body was super tight.

I followed Midnight up onto the platform and Mgurn joined me. We were quickly shuffled aside as Midnight's team took their places. Apparently, they all had assigned spots and we were in them. Midnight didn't even glance our way as we were forced to the edge of the platform.

"Is there a molecular buffer zone we should be aware of?" Mgurn asked as he teetered on the edge of the platform.

No one replied as a man at the control console started working the holo display. One second later we were squinting into a bright sun and gasping for breath. Or some of us were gasping for breath. The races that didn't mind intense heat seemed to soak it up and sigh. Being human, I did not.

"Holy hell it's hot," I said and could feel the sweat forming in every crevice of my body. "Why would anyone live on a planet like this?"

"It is a welcome relief to the cold you humans prefer," Barby said. "But such are the differences in the races."

"You got that right," Nammy said. Not a drop of sweat beaded on her forehead, so it was safe to say her planet was pretty warm.

Midnight was immediately scanning the area, her wrist's holo display up for all of us to see.

"No hostiles in range," she said and pointed to the West. "Mgurn's intel said that One is possibly being held in a facility just over this ridge. We hike to the top and reassess there."

"You do not trust the intel I was given?" Mgurn asked.

"I don't trust much," Midnight said. "It helps keep me alive."

She started walking and her team fell in line. I took up the rear with Mgurn.

Skrang wasn't as desolate as I thought it would be. Yes, there were a lot of rocks. Plenty of rocks. Rocks on rocks on rocks. But there were also some really interesting plants. More than a few had flowers that would look mighty nice in Hopsheer's hair.

I reached down to pluck one and my hand was slapped away by two of Mgurn's hands.

"Ow?" I said, giving him a questioning look.

"Paralytic stamens," Mgurn said. "Any of the flowers with purple or bright blue have the same properties. They wait for insects to come collect the nectar then stun them and slowly wait for their bodies to dry out amongst the petals before devouring the husks."

"So not for weddings then," I said. "More like funeral arrangements."

"That would make for a messy reception party," Mgurn said.

We kept walking and it felt like the ridge we were aiming for wasn't getting any closer. But, it had to be because we were on that trail for close to an hour. Yet the ridge was the same height.

There was a very distinct reason for that optical illusion.

Three hours later, we stood at the base of the mountain that the ridge topped. There was a switchback trail carved into the mountain, and it certainly lived up to its name as it doubled back again and again for about three thousand feet almost straight up.

"We're going up that?" I asked. "You know, there's a reason the galactic races invented vehicles, right?"

"Do not worry," Midnight said. "We are going to make this easy. Grue?"

Grue grunted and placed all of his hands on the side of the mountain. His granite skin instantly changed to match the type of rock he was touching. I have no idea what type of rock it was. I'm not a galactic geologist. But it wasn't granite.

He took a deep breath then pressed his whole body against the rock and was gone. I gasped and Midnight gave me a sly smile. After a couple of minutes, he reappeared several meters up, clinging to the rock face above one of the switchbacks.

A power line dropped down to us as he hammered stakes into the rock. Then he was gone again only to reappear several meters above that position where he kept hammering more stakes. He did that over and over again until I could barely make him out.

"We are good to go," his voice said over the coms in our ears. "Line is secure. Grab on and hold tight."

Midnight grabbed the power line first and she was whisked up the side of the mountain in the blink of an eye. She was just a speck next to Grue as she sent the line back down.

"Ever used one of these?" Barby asked me.

"No," I said. "I didn't think people used power lines. I thought they were for hauling cargo out of mines and crud."

"That is what they were originally designed for," she said as person after person ascended the mountain in record time, the line dropping back over and over for the next person to grab onto. "The Edgers developed these to use in situations like this. They make for quick getaways when needed."

"If you have a Gwreq around to hammer in the stakes," I said.

"Cams," Mgurn corrected. "They would be called cams as this process is akin to mountain climbing. Cam is short for—"

"Cams. Got it," I said. "Doesn't look too hard."

"It isn't," Barby said just as her turn came up. "But make sure you hang on tight with both hands. The line needs a full circuit to work and not fry you."

"Wait, what?" I exclaimed as she grabbed on and was gone. "Mgurn? Did she say it could fry us?"

"Yes, she did," Mgurn said. "I believe the power line requires our bodies to complete the circuit and carry us to the last cam. Letting go with one hand may be the same as touching a live wire to your private parts."

"Nice," I said. "You first."

"Of course," Mgurn said and took his turn.

The bastard had four hands, so it was easy for him to hang on.

I was the last one and I craned my neck to see most of the team working their way up the last switchback to the top of the ridge. I almost preferred to just hike it than risk getting my privates cooked, but we didn't have that kind of time.

"You coming, Joe?" Midnight asked over the com.

"I'm coming," I said. "Just feels like cheating."

"Stop being a gump vent and grab the line," she snapped. "We do not have time for you to turn coward."

"I am many things, but coward is not one of them," I said as I grabbed the line.

It was like putting a battery on your tongue. Except my whole body was the tongue and the battery was constantly whipping side to side and trying to throw me off. Okay, bad analogy, but you get the idea.

I stopped right next to where Midnight was waiting. She took hold of the straps on my pack as I got my balance and steadied my footing on the thin switchback trail.

"Not so bad, was it?" Barby asked from Midnight's side

"Not so bad," I said. "But I feel like I need to pee."

"We all do," Midnight said. "The urge will go away in a few seconds. Just start moving and you'll be fine."

She was right. After walking a meter or two along the trail, the pressure in my bladder subsided and I didn't feel like I was going to burst. That's a strange side effect and one I made sure to remember. Good thing I'd peed up on the Gratuity before we'd moltransed down.

It was only another ten minutes before we reached the top of the ridge. I stood there, mouth agape, and looked out over the massive city that filled the rocky valley below. My mouth wasn't alone in its agapeness.

"Mgurn, please tell me you were given an address or maybe a street name where we'll find One," I said.

"I was given a sector, as you know," Mgurn said. He brought up his holo and everyone turned to watch as he scrolled through until he found the right location. "Here we go. Ah, it appears the sector is almost directly in the middle of the city. Let's see, let's see, yes, it is Sector Forty-One."

"Are they numbered from outside in?" I asked, fearing the answer.

"Yes, they are," Mgurn said. "Each sector is approximately eight square blocks so we will have about three hundred and twenty-eight blocks to move through undetected to arrive at the suspected location of Salvage Merc One."

"That's it? Only three hundred and twenty-eight?" I laughed. "No problem. Just a quick city stroll."

"We won't need to use the streets," Midnight said as she pointed at her own holo display. She swiped up and the city streets disappeared, replaced by a view of a massive tunnel network underneath. "Mak and Kam will lead us through the sewer. We should be able to travel the entire way underground."

"Great," I said. Not great. I lied. Sewer travel is not great at all.

"With Salvage Merc One on the planet, they will probably have patrols below," Juan said. "It will not be easy."

"We'll make do," Midnight said. "Everyone ready?"

"Ready," they replied.

"Barby? Show us the way down," Midnight ordered.

Barby nodded and her entire body seemed to shift. No longer was she a sexy snake-lady, but was almost full snake. She lowered herself to the ground and began to slither across the hot rock, finding the easy path through the many boulders, crevices, and cracks in the sloped side of the mountain valley that the city was situated in.

"This was once an old volcano," Mgurn stated.

"No science lesson, please," I said as we followed Midnight's team down. "I need to pay attention. Last thing I want is to fall on my ass and prove to everyone I'm a total fraud."

"You are far from a total fraud," Mgurn said. "Perhaps a five percent fraud. Maybe ten percent on a bad day."

"Funny, buddy," I said. "Just hilarious."

"I am learning," Mgurn said. "Careful of that loose gravel."

"Thanks," I said as I stepped lightly on the pile of gravel at my feet.

Stepping lightly didn't exactly seem to matter. My foot went out from under me and before I knew it I was tumbling head over heels down the slope, passing the entire team as they hurried to get out of my way or become a part of my accidental acrobatics.

One time, when I was little, and I mean little, like three or four, my grandmother took me to a planet called Ballyway. It was a planet that had nothing but arcades and amusement parks. I was one of the lucky ones because it fell to the Skrangs the next year and was turned into a sheet of slag.

But while I was there, I got to play a game called pinball. Silver ball, flippers, bumpers, lots of flashing lights.

I was the pinball as I went falling down the slope at an ever-increasing speed. There were no flippers at the bottom to stop me from falling into the very dark hole that waited down there just for morons like me.

When I finally stopped, I was fairly sure that every bone in my body was pulverized and I'd died and gone to Hell. I blinked a few time, expecting the Seven Devils to be standing over me and laughing, but there was just a pinprick of light above me.

Then the pinprick disappeared as a falling, screaming shape came right at me.

I discovered that my bones were not pulverized as I rolled to the side and avoided getting crushed by the falling shape. A shape that turned out to be Mgurn.

"You slipped too?" I gasped as I rolled onto my side and stared at my stunned assistant.

"No," Mgurn coughed.

He sat up slowly and patted himself down. Every beer can on him had broken open and the pit we were in smelled like a bar. He turned and looked at me, a serious look on his bug dog face.

"I followed you intentionally," Mgurn said. "Where you go, I go. I could not leave my number unattended."

"You're telling me you pinballed your armored ass down here on purpose?" I snapped as I struggled to my feet.

"I do not understand the reference," Mgurn said.

"Never mind," I replied as I winced. Everything hurt. I couldn't stop wincing. "You're an idiot."

"You have mentioned that before," Mgurn said. "But it was the right choice to make. Midnight will be able to rescue us from this pit and we will continue on with the mission. If you had been injured gravely then having me here would mean—"

He screamed as a flash of red light hit him square in the chest, sending him flying back against the pit's wall.

I tried to pull my H16 as I spun towards the source of the blast, but I didn't even get it unclipped from my pack before I was screaming and flying as well. If I thought the trip down Pinball Mountain was bad, the red blast was even worse. Every single nerve ending in my body decided to stand up and call attention to themselves.

I crumpled in agony against Mgurn and the last thing I saw was a troupe of Skrangs coming towards us with their rifles up. One of the Skrangs stepped out of the troupe and fired from a funny-looking gun. A gun that produced the red blasts.

More agony then it was night night.

FOURTEEN

Waking up was about as painful as getting knocked out by those blasts. On a pain scale for the day, my tumble down the slope was actually towards the bottom.

"They stink," Mgurn said from my side.

I opened my eyes, winced, and looked over at him.

All of his wrists were secured with glowing manacles, as were his legs. He was being held upright and in place by two very large Skrangs. I noticed that I was in the same boat as him, but only had the one pair of glowing manacles since I only had the one pair of wrists.

"They stink like the Seven Devils' piss," Mgurn said.

"What the hell are you talking about?" I asked, my voice a weak rasp.

"I am translating for you," Mgurn said. "The Skrangs are speaking their native language, not common."

That's when I heard the other voices and looked around at the room I was being held upright in. It was quite the room.

There were several rows of seats that stretched from one end of the room down to the other on both sides. At the far end was a wide platform with a small dais on it. Do I need to say there was a throne on the dais? There was. And one pissed-off-looking Skrang sat in that throne.

I wanted to keep my eyes on the throne sitter, but my attention was drawn to the many Skrangs that occupied the rows of seats. Most of them were on their feet, yelling curses and spitting at us as we were dragged down the center of the room towards the dais. Those not yelling and spitting were glaring, their eyes like accusatory daggers of open hatred. I'll be honest, some of them started spitting too once we were close enough.

"Their orifices will be filled with gump claws," Mgurn said. "I pray they are impregnated by a—"

"Stop," I said. "You aren't helping."

"You do not want to know what they are saying about us?" Mgurn asked.

"I'm getting the gist," I said as large glop of Skrang snot splattered across my cheek. "They aren't exactly being subtle."

The Skrang on my right barked something at me.

"What did he say?" I asked.

My already pained face took a hard hit under my right eye and I cried out.

"Eight Million Gods! What was that for?" I shouted. My answer was another shot just below the eye.

"She said to shut up," Mgurn said. "I would have told you that, but you said to stop translating."

"You're a dick," I replied and waited for the third pop, but it didn't come.

Instead, we were thrown to our knees at the foot of the platform. The back of my neck was grabbed and I was forced to look up at the throne on the dais. The Skrang that sat there wasn't dressed in robes or wearing a crown. He was adorned in quite a few battle scars, all of which were enhanced by glowing streaks of make-up that traced the outlines of each scar.

"You're pretty," I said before I could stop myself.

That's when the third pop happened as my head was yanked back further and the hit-happy Skrang on my right gave me a good one that closed my eye in a swell time of swelling flesh.

"Ow," I muttered as I was held in place and forced to face the scarred Skrang.

"Be quiet," the Skrang hissed in common. "Your jokes will not save you. Your fear will be real and not alleviated by levity."

I began to reply, since saying alleviated and levity in the same sentence was kind of redundant, but Mgurn barked at me the way Leforians do sometimes and I kept my mouth closed.

"That was a wise decision," the Skrang said. "The next time you speak out of turn I will have your tongue ripped out."

I just gave him a weak grin.

"Do not test me," the Skrang sneered.

He paced back and forth for a few seconds then stopped and stepped down from the dais.

"Do you know who I am?" he asked. "You may speak to answer without losing your tongue."

"I'm guessing you are the head honcho of these here parts," I said. "But I'll be honest, all of you Skrangs look alike to me."

Mgurn winced, but the Skrang before me only smiled at the insult.

"Yes, we do, don't we?" he replied and gestured to his face. "If you spend enough time around us, you learn the differences, but no human has spent the amount of time needed to accomplish that. We kill them too quickly."

There was laughter from the rows behind us. I chuckled softly just to go along with the bad joke.

"You find that funny?" he asked.

"I find a lot of things funny," I said and winced. "Crap. Was I supposed to answer?"

"We are now having a conversation, so yes, you were supposed to answer," he said. "What is your name?"

"My name? You don't know?" I replied.

"Why should I?" he said. "All of you humans look alike to me."

"Nice one," I said. "I'm, uh, Steve. Steve Nicholas. Just an average guy wandering the galaxy, looking for love and adventure while I help people in need."

"Do you believe I am stupid?" the Skrang asked.

"You're the guy that sits on the throne, so I'm guessing no," I replied.

"We get the galactic network broadcasts here as well, human," he said. "We know who Steve Nicholas is. He is the hero in the human drama called *Galactic Steve*."

There was some muttering from the rows behind me, most of it just repeating the name of one of the top shows on the vids. They kept saying *Galactic Steve* over and over until the head Skrang held up his hands for quiet.

"It is surprisingly popular on our planet," the Skrang said. "Now, what is your real name?"

"Kyle?" I said.

"Is that the name you want to die with?" the Skrang asked.

"No, not really," I said.

"It will be if you do not tell me your real name!" the Skrang shouted.

Spittle flew from his mouth and landed on my face, but my manacled hands were in no position to wipe it away. I cringed as I felt some of the tiny droplets come together into one single droplet and slide down my cheek to my jawline where it just hung there, unable to decide whether or not to take the plunge to the floor below.

"Can I get a little help here?" I asked. "I got some of you on me."

"Kill him," the Skrang said.

I was yanked to my feet and I felt the tip of a blade against my spine.

"Joe! My name is Joe Laribeau!" I yelled. "I was born on Bax, but I'm not a fan! Too many swamps! Way too many swamps! Don't get me wrong, I like a wet planet, who doesn't, but just too many swamps!"

"You like a wet planet?" the Skrang asked. He looked out at the rest of the room. "What does that mean? Is that a human thing? Do humans like wet planets?"

There was some lively discussion on the topic before the Skrang decided he was done and kicked me in the face. But he didn't get the spittle. It stayed put and was joined by a good amount of blood.

"I am Lord Messermeen," the Skrang said. "Have you heard of me?"

"I've heard of you," I mumbled as a guard set me up on my knees. "Every Marine in the Fleet has heard of you. You won the Battle of Heg and nearly defeated General Gossle in the Battle of Das."

"Gossle was a good general," Lord Messermeen said. "But not better than I. He got lucky with reinforcements just as I was pushing forward with a final assault. That day would have been mine if not for that."

"That's what all the textbooks say," I replied.

"Do they?" He asked. "I am mentioned in Fleet teachings?"

"Oh, yeah, totally," I said. "Right before how to wipe your ass and after how to avoid getting venereal diseases from non-compatible races."

"You are not funny," Lord Messermeen said. "I have told you this before. I will go back to the silence or lose your tongue rule if you do not stop with the jokes."

"Got it," I said and nodded. I'd say the nod hurt like hell, but I was so broken that everything hurt like hell so I couldn't really distinguish at the time.

"Why are you here, Joe Laribeau?" Lord Messermeen asked.

"That's classified," I said. "If I told you, I'd have to—"

"Joe!" Mgurn snapped. "Stop it!"

"The voice of reason speaks," Lord Messermeen responded. "You are his assistant?"

Mgurn did not answer.

"No need to confirm," Lord Messermeen said. "I already know you are. If this is Joe Laribeau then you would be Mgurn. I know all about you, Mgurn. I also know all about Salvage Merc One Eighty-Four. I have had the privilege of speaking with…"

He trailed off and cleared his throat several times. He started to speak again, but ended up coughing up a hunk of phlegm instead and spitting it right in front of me.

"To hell with talking like this," Lord Messermeen growled. "Trying to sound like an Eight Million Gods dammed nobleman. Skrangs don't talk like that. Skrangs talk with authority! With volume! With confidence! Pretty words are for weak-fleshed creatures like humans and Groshnels and Klavs! I am Skrang! I am Lord! I am strong, not weak!"

He thumped his chest and every Skrang in the room responded with an identical chest thump. He did it again and they did it again as well. It went on like that for a good five minutes. Long enough to wonder what he meant by pretty words. The guys sounded like a grunting terpig to me.

"Time to meet someone, Joe," Lord Messermeen said as he grabbed me by the throat and lifted me to my feet like I was made of nothing. My feet dangled a few inches off the floor as he carried me across the platform and threw me down by a concealed door. "Come out! Now!"

The door opened and out stepped a man that looked about like how I felt. His face was bruises and cuts and he only had one eye open, the other was swollen so badly that it looked like if you touched it, it would pop. Strips of flesh were missing from the back of his neck and I could see electrodes attached to the exposed vertebrae. The man walked a few paces past me, stopped, then spun on his heels and looked down.

"Hello, Joe," he said in a monotone voice. "It is good to meet you finally."

The one eye that wasn't swollen shut was bloodshot and the color of dusty blue. I had no idea who the guy was. He didn't look like the guy from the Caga cafe. He didn't look like a salvage merc at all. There was no way that was Salvage Merc One.

"You appear to be injured," the man said. "Do you need assistance?"

"He doesn't need assistance!" Lord Messermeen shouted. "He needs a good beating! One that will leave him in worse shape than you and more pliable to my needs!"

"Who are you?" I grunted as I tried to push myself up to my feet.

The strange man kicked me hard in the ribs and I doubled over, falling back to the ground in a ball of pain. I didn't get even a second to catch my breath as he closed on me, the tips of his boot nailing me over and over again as I lay there, unable to get the strength to curl up any tighter.

Through my own one eye, I could see Mgurn frozen in place where he knelt in front of Lord Messermeen. His head was down and he couldn't even look at me as I literally got the crud kicked out of me. Literally. I messed myself as the crazy man's boots obliterated my intestines. Honestly, I felt something give out inside me after about two minutes of constant pummeling.

I probably cried, I have no clue. I probably begged for him to stop. Again, no clue. That beating was a blur. My conscious mind took a backseat about the moment my poop met my pants.

Yet, unconsciousness wouldn't come. I prayed for it, I know. I'd had way nicer beatings before and passed right out. I'd fainted once when I saw a kid trip and break every tooth in his mouth as his face hit pavement. You would have fainted too if you saw that mess.

Sure, I had been a Marine. I'd witnessed horrors that no living being should witness. I'd watched buddies get vaporized right next to me, watched comrades in arms lose all arms as jacked up Skrangs ripped them from their sockets. I even witnessed the loss of my own legs.

But sometimes the mind just needs to check out.

Unfortunately, the beating Mr. Kicker gave me was not one of those times.

When he was done, or better yet, when he was told to be done, he stepped back casually and looked down at me like a child looks at a prized drawing they just made for their parents. He smiled with split lips and his one eye focused on me, boring into me, jabbing its sight straight through my own eye.

"Keep it together, Joe," a voice in my head said. It was warm and kind and filled with confidence and hope. I loved that voice. "Blink if you can understand me."

I blinked. Mr. Kicker above me blinked as well.

"Good job, Joe," his mental voice said. "Hang in there. Sorry for the beat down. It's the crap hooked to my spinal column that is making me do it. Luckily it only interferes with my willful motor control. All my other abilities are intact. Stay patient and we'll get out of this alive."

"We will?" I asked. "Good to know."

"What did he say?" Lord Messermeen growled as he shoved Mr. Kicker aside. "He dares to speak after that lesson! Start again!"

"Sorry," the voice in my head said. "I don't want to do this, but I can't stop it without revealing what I can do. We aren't at that point yet. Hang in there and keep it—"

"Together," I finished. "I know."

"Stop him from talking!" Lord Messermeen screamed at full volume. It was loud enough to nearly pop my eardrums. "Kick his mouth in! Kick it the fo in! DO IT NOW!"

Mr. Kicker reared his leg back and the last thing I saw was the toe of his boot rocketing at my face. The last thing I heard was the shattering of my teeth and the far-off sobbing of Mgurn.

Then that blessed unconsciousness came a calling finally. I'd missed that fella.

FIFTEEN

Pain took me out, pain brought me back.

"Oh, Eight Million Gods," I gasped as I opened my one working eye.

The light pierced my brain and I screamed for a good couple of minutes before the world around me came into stark focus. Okay, not so stark as blurry, but manageable focus.

"Joe," Mgurn said as he put a wet rag to my lips.

Lips that were ten times their normal size and felt like they'd been run through a garbage disposal.

"Try to sip some of this," he said as he squeezed water past my lips and into my mouth.

The pain increased and I wanted to just die, but I let the water trickle in past the broken shards that had been my teeth once. He kept at it, wetting the rag again and again since most of the water just dribbled down my face and onto the hard floor I was laid out on. Maybe it was a hard floor, I didn't know. I hurt so bad that it could have been a feather bed and I would have cried like a baby about it.

My tongue unstuck itself from the roof of my mouth once wet enough and I did a little exploring. Not a single tooth survived. Some were kicked right out of their sockets, but most were just jagged peaks of bone and enamel.

"Can you sit?" Mgurn asked.

"Can you suck my unit?" I replied.

It didn't sound anything like that. It was more of a mumbled and jumbled grunting, but Mgurn got the picture from my tone of voice.

"You can't lie there forever, Joe," the voice in my head said. "You need to tap into your gift and force your will upon your body."

"Like you were forced to kick the teeth out of me?" I asked, using my inside my head voice.

"That is over with," he said. "In the past now. Focus on the present and then try to plan the future."

"You want me to plan for the future?" I laughed internally. "Like what? Invest in stocks and prepare for retirement? Ha, foing ha!"

"Pay attention!" the voice shouted and I winced.

"Joe? What is it?" Mgurn asked.

I shook my head as much as I could without dying and Mgurn frowned.

"What is going on, Joe?" Mgurn said. "I can sense an electrical pulse around you, but I cannot find the source."

"Perceptive assistant you have," the voice said. "Leforians have always been more attuned to what we can do than the other races. It's why Mgurn was chosen for you."

"Yay for me and Mgurn," I thought. "And please don't yell at me again. You'll turn my brain to jelly."

"That yell wouldn't come close to turning your brain to jelly," the voice said. "It takes a much harder push and a lot more mental volume to do that."

"I was kidding," I thought.

"I'm not," the voice replied. "I've done it on more than a few occasions. Not pretty, Joe. Brains start leaking out of ears and then the screaming starts. Try to avoid, if you can."

"I'll remember that," I thought. "So, you're him? You're really Salvage Merc One?"

"That's me," he responded. "This isn't how I wanted us to meet, but here we are. It's nice to finally talk."

"Nice isn't the word I'd use, but my synonym skills aren't up to snuff right now, so nice will have to do," I thought. "You got a name, Salvage Merc One?"

"I did at one time," he responded. "But just call me One for now. I prefer not to think about who I was before I was given my number and these extra gifts."

"Extra gifts? Like what?" I thought.

"I'm talking to you from halfway across the palace," One said. "So there is that."

"Nice trick," I thought. "What's the range on it?"

"Joe? What is going on? Can you hear me, Joe?" Mgurn asked.

I opened my eye, which I hadn't realized I'd closed, and winked at him then tried to nod. Failed at nodding, started to cry a little then took a deep, painful breath and croaked, "All...good..."

"I hear a guard coming, Joe," Mgurn said. "I need you to sit up. Last time he came by he said he'd kill you if you weren't awake. A sleeping human is just a lazy human that refuses to die, he said."

"Better do what he says, Joe," One said. "You are important, but not so important that a Skrang guard won't rip your head off because they feel like it."

"Great," I thought.

"Okay," I said through broken teeth and split lips.

"Good, good," Mgurn said and sounded relived as he helped me sit up.

Yeah, it was a hard, metal floor I was on, not a featherbed.

"Listen carefully, Joe," One said. "I am working on getting you back to me. I almost have Messermeen convinced that the two of us working together would be a million times more powerful than if he killed you and sent your body to the SMC as a warning."

"That's a thing? Lord Menstruate wants to do that?" I thought.

One's mental laughter hurt like hell.

"Stop, stop," I begged. "You're killing me."

"Sorry," he said. "I'm rusty on the full telepathy with others thing. Forgot how sharp emotions can be."

"Pretty sharp, man," I thought.

"You!" a Skrang guard yelled as he approached the cell we were in. It was an actual cell with bars and everything. No energy cage for us. "Stand up!"

Mgurn moved from my side and stood.

"No! Him! He stands or he dies!" the guard shouted. His guttural accent was almost as painful as One's telepathic giggling.

"Do it, Joe," One said. "Get your ass up and do whatever they tell you to do. If we are lucky, you'll be brought before Messermeen. That's where I'm at right now. He'll ask you to perform some tricks to prove you have the same abilities as me. Just go with it. I'll do all the heavy lifting."

"So, I can't do what you can do?" I thought.

Mgurn bent and gently grabbed me up in his four arms.

"What? No way," One replied. "You aren't even close to my level. You have years of training to complete before you can do half of what I can do."

"Looking forward to years of you in my head," I thought. "More yays."

"I'll use my regular voice," One said. "Don't be an idiot."

"Let him go!" the guard shouted at Mgurn. "He walks on his own or he dies!"

"Is every solution that he dies?" Mgurn asked and received a stun wand in the belly for his impertinence.

He went down on one knee, nearly taking me with him, but I stayed upright and faced the guard.

"I'm up. I'm on my own," I grunted.

I actually was up on my own. Gotta love some well-made battle legs. The skin covering them felt like it was on fire, but the mechanics beneath the skin were cool as a space cucumber. Which are really cold considering the vacuum of space and all. Those are some cold cucumbers.

"Mgurn?" I asked without taking my eye off the guard.

"I'm alright, Joe," Mgurn said and struggled to his feet. He instinctively reached out for me, but held back at the last second. "I'll be fine."

The guard opened the cell and pointed his shock wand at me then at Mgurn.

"The Leforian stays!" he yelled, which seemed to be his only volume setting. "You come with! Try to escape and die! Look anywhere but ahead and die! Move too slow and die! Talk and die!"

"Got it," I said then stepped away from Mgurn and out of the cell.

I wanted to run and see my faithful assistant one last time, but I was afraid if I tried I'd die. Mgurn was right that dying seemed to be the solution to every problem with this Skrang.

"You still there, One?" I asked as I walked slowly, but not too slowly, down the long, rock corridor that led away from the cell. There was no answer. Oh, well.

The corridor was lined with other cells, but I didn't dare to look over and see if they were occupied. More than a few fecal odors told me they were, but not a single sound issued out from any of them. I had the feeling that the guard had given them the "Or die!" speech as well.

I stumbled a couple of times, more from exhaustion than from my legs giving out, and waited for my fate of death to come crashing down on my head. But the guard only shoved me along and I kept on my feet long enough for us to reach the end of the corridor.

He did some hand to scanner thing and the thick door opened by sliding into the wall. I walked through and waited as the guard did that hand to scanner thing on the other side and the door closed.

"Move!" he shouted.

I moved. I did everything he asked of me. Lucky for me, he only asked me to keep walking. And did we walk. The palace was huge. It must have taken up half the Skrang city. Probably not, but it felt like it did. The guard guided me through back corridors where other guards were hanging out, shooting the breeze, smacking around servants, torturing captives of various races, doing nasty things with their nasty parts to other captives of various races, and generally having a gay ol' Skrang time.

Twists and turns, twists and turns. I started to get the feeling maybe the palace wasn't as big as I first thought. Some of the torture we walked by started to look familiar as if we'd passed it a couple times already. The guard wanted me disoriented and completely lost. If that was the case, he was a master at his job.

When we finally arrived, I was barely able to keep my legs from buckling. Even battle legs get tired and that was some serious palace hiking we'd just accomplished. Normally, after a hike like that, I'd celebrate with a beer and an energy bar, but I wasn't about to ask Lord Messermeen for a Fruity Nut Gunker at that moment. And Skrangs don't drink beer, so that was out.

"Laribeau," Lord Messermeen hissed as I was shown into the throne room. With the place empty of the Skrang peanut gallery, his voice echoed everywhere. It was more than a little spooky. "Sit. Now."

He was seated in his throne, a goblet of something in his right hand and one of my KL09 pistols in his other. I assumed it was my pistol. Could have been One's, could have been some other unlucky bastard that stumbled into Skrang hell. Or it was Messermeen's. I don't know. The only reason I fixated on it was because it was pointed right at my belly. Casually pointed, but fairly obvious.

"My sources tell me you are very, very important to the SMC," Lord Messermeen said. "That you are heir to their power. I do not understand why. Look at you. You are a sad, sad human that is nothing but weak muscles and broken bones."

"I don't think anything is broken," I replied.

"Oh?" He smiled. "Are you sure?"

Crud…

The hit to my upper left arm came so fast and hard that for a couple of seconds I didn't feel a thing. My entire arm went numb. I blinked a few times and turned my head, not surprised to see One standing there, a thick bar of metal in his grip.

Then the pain kicked in.

"Oh, fo!" I yelled as I fell to my knees, my right arm grabbing for my left instinctively. Bad move. "FO!"

Just the slightest touch sent waves of agony through me. My left arm hung at my side, a limp, useless appendage. Just the act of breathing nearly sent me into convulsions as my ribs bumped against my shattered humerus. Nothing humorous about it, though. Nothing at all.

"There are many things I would like to do to you, Laribeau," Lord Messermeen said. "Many include fire and your man-thing."

"My…man-thing?" I gasped. "You…mean…my winkie? Be…adult about…it…Messermeen."

"I knew many a Marine that joked their way to death," Lord Messermeen said. "They refused to be serious and die with honor. Joke after joke after joke. None of which I got due to the cultural barrier between our races. Your brand of humor does not make me laugh."

He stood and nodded to One.

More pain.

My shoulder was obliterated as One brought the bar down on top of it. You could have taken a dull butter knife and sliced my left arm off without any resistance at that point. It had less form than one of Ig's arms. Ig. Tarr. Hopsheer. Sure could have used their help right about then. Which made me think of Midnight and her crew.

"Hang on, Joe," One said in my mind. "You'll see them again. You'll see all of them again. I'm getting you out of here."

"I'm supposed to get you out of here," I said. Out loud.

"What? What was that?" Lord Messermeen snapped. "You think you are going to capture me and take me prisoner? You are mad. All of you salvage mercs are mad. Mad for thinking you can be neutral and mad for thinking that the Skrang Alliance will allow you to stay neutral. By this time tomorrow, your precious SMC will be declaring war and the galaxy will never be the same."

"Why so angry, Messyman?" I asked through shattered teeth. At least the searing, excruciating pain in my arm had taken my mind off my lack of teeth.

Lord Messermeen pointed to his face and then did some wiggly finger motion.

"I cannot understand half of what you say, merc," Lord Messermeen grunted. "I brought you here to interrogate, but your mouth is a mess and you will serve me no purpose."

Uh-oh. No purpose means no use which means I'm dead.

"Don't panic," One said telepathically. "He is not going to kill you here. He's going to take you to one of the breeding ponds and feed you to the young."

"Oh, well okay then!" I shouted in my head. I think I felt One wince. "I'd much rather die in a Skrang breeding pond! Nothing says happy ending like being Skrang tadpole food!"

"Calm down!" One mentally snapped.

He said it so loud that my head rocked back and I groaned a little. Okay, I groaned a lot.

"Sorry. Sorry," he said.

"What is wrong with him now?" Lord Messermeen said.

"He is dying, my lord," One said out loud. "I shall carry him to the pond so his body may be of use to the next generation of Skrang leaders."

"Do that," Lord Messermeen said. "I will join you shortly. I have a meeting with the generals then I must satisfy my sixty concubines before I can watch the entertainment."

"He may not live that long," One said. "You had said you want to watch him being eaten alive."

"That is true," Lord Messermeen replied. "Very true. I can watch dead meat be tossed into the pond anytime of any day. But to watch a live merc get eaten by my progeny, that is not something I care to miss."

"I shall take him there now, my lord," One said.

"Do that," Lord Messermeen said. He turned to a row of guards standing by the wall. "You and you will help drag the merc to his fate. The rest of you will send word to the court that today's entertainment has been moved up. If they want to witness the death of the merc then they will be at the royal breeding pond in ten minutes."

The guards snapped to attention and moved off to perform their duties. One of those duties was picking me up and hauling my ass out of the throne room. I passed out for that journey since one of them had my left arm gripped in his taloned hand. A light breeze could have brushed that arm and I would have gone night night.

When I came to, I was outside in the oppressive heat, my body wrapped in something like thin plastic, but smelled like it may have come from the insides of a dead terpig. When my eye finally focused, I could see veins and sinew threaded through the wrap. It was from inside a terpig. I was wrapped in stretched out terpig intestines. That was new.

I could barely move my neck, but I pushed through the agony and looked at my surroundings.

A large pond, black and murky, was in front of me. I was being held on a stone ledge that jutted out over the pond. Circling the water were the same Skrangs from yesterday. The court, I guess. Skrang guards were everywhere, standing like a wall behind the court, encircling everything.

"Joe? Can you hear me?" One asked.

"Yeah," I thought.

"I have good news," he said, "and bad news."

"Bad news first," I thought.

"Bring out the Leforian so the merc can witness the power of my young!" Lord Messermeen said from across the pond. I hadn't noticed him since he wasn't sitting in his throne. He was just standing there like a normal psychotic Skrang. Easy to miss.

Guards dragged Mgurn through the crowd and to the edge of the pond. Then they shoved him in.

"That is the bad news," One said.

SIXTEEN

"Mgurn!" I screamed and instantly regretted it. Every nub of a tooth in my mouth vibrated from the force of my voice. Black spots filled my eye and I could feel my vision dimming.

But Mgurn's shout brought me back around and I forced myself to focus on him, to watch him and keep him in my sight until the very end.

"Joe!" he yelled. "I will survive, Joe! Leforians are strong! Leforians are fighters! Leforians are—Ah! They're biting my toes! The little fos are biting my toes! Get them off! GET THEM OFF!"

Then Mgurn was yanked under the surface of the pond and I lost him. So much for keeping him in sight until the very end. Unless that was the end. If it was then that was unfortunate. Mgurn's last words shouldn't be "GET THEM OFF!" That's just not right.

"One! Do something!" I yelled from my mind.

"I cannot. Not yet," One said. "Your friend will have to fight his own fight for now."

"Fight his own fight? Are you foing mad? The guy is being eaten by Skrang babies in a foing pond!" I screamed. Mentally screamed. "Do something!"

"I cannot," One said, his telepathic voice sad and pitiful. "I am under the Lord's control. My physical self is not my own. If I were to help Mgurn, it would be using my other gifts, and I cannot, for the sake of the SMC and the entire galaxy, show those to him. Not yet. Not while I am in his grip."

"Then get ungripped, asshead!" I shouted. That time it was out loud and my whole face lit up like a pain-filled balloon of pain. There was pain. So much pain.

"What does he say?" Lord Messermeen asked, looking about at his court and the guards. Then he focused on One. "Tell me what he said!"

"He said to get ungripped, asshead," One responded.

"What does that mean?" Lord Messermeen growled. "Is it code? Is it some challenge to my honor? What is being gripped that must be ungripped? I want answers!"

One shook. His entire body vibrated with conflict.

"Tell me what it means!" Lord Messermeen roared. "I own your soul, Salvage Merc One! You will tell me what it means!"

One sighed. His shaking body calmed and it looked like he just gave up. I've seen it before, that body language that says it's all just too much and there's no point in fighting anymore. I've been there and I'll be there again. The pitiful circle of life for a soldier. And merc, I guess.

One lifted his head and his one visible eye began to darken. I watched it happen. It had been dusty blue then every part of it started to turn grey. The pupil, the iris, the whites, all of it. He was changing into something more than One.

"I will tell you what it means," One sighed, the weight of the universe on his shoulders expressed in those six words. No, wait. Seven words. It's hard to count sometimes when you are beaten to a pulp and wrapped in terpig intestines. You'll know what I mean if you ever get in that situation.

But, One didn't get a chance to tell Lord Messermeen what it all means. Not that it meant anything really other than me wanting One to save my friend.

Blasts ripped through the air and tore into the crowd. Skrangs of all ages, sexes, sizes, and classes screamed like little gumps as their bodies were torn apart by plasma. The court panicked and bolted, slamming into each other as they tried to escape the barrage of plasma that rained down on the area around the pond. An area I was in. Oh, crud…

A plasma blast hit the stone ledge I was precariously perched on. My intestine wrap jiggled and I was horrified to find that it was stretched so tight that it had some bounce to it. Another blast hit the ledge and the intestines made an elastic jump. Towards the pond. Would have been nice if the gory wrap had taken me away from the gross womb water, but that wasn't in the cards.

Another blast and another and I suddenly found myself off the ledge and tumbling into the murky yuck below me.

There was a splash and then I was under. Gross pond water tried to rush up my nose, but I snorted and took a deep breath before I was fully submerged in the swimming pool from Hell.

To my surprise, the water actually eased some of my pain. It took the weight off my broken arm and instantly soothed the cuts and gashes that covered my exposed skin. Not that I had a lot of exposed skin since I was wrapped in foing terpig intestines!

I tried to kick my feet and spin my body around so I could get a look at my new aquatic surroundings, but I didn't get the chance. Baby Skrangs were on me in seconds. Those hungry buggers came at me like little lizard torpedoes, their stubby arms and legs propelling them through the water faster than I've ever seen anything that size move.

Then, praise be to the Eight Million Gods, my world slowed to a tick. Clarity took hold and I nearly shouted with joy. But I remembered that shouting was bad for a human being when under the water. It tended to let all the air out of one's lungs and then cause the drowning to happen.

I let the clarity take hold and I used it. I took my time and kicked my feet, spinning my body around so I could see the rest of the pond. Skrang babies were streaming at me, but it was as if they were swimming through molasses. And I'm talking Sterli molasses, the really slow stuff.

I got myself oriented and looked for something I could push up against and get the intestines off me. All I needed to do was cut part of it and it would rip right off, it was stretched that tight. It made sense that I'd be trussed up that way. Toss me in the pond, let the little buggers bite into the intestines, the wrapping splits and falls off me, then it's feeding time.

But my search for freedom stopped the second my clear focus locked onto the murky shape of Mgurn fighting for his life. It was a slo-mo blood bath. Not Mgurn's blood, but the Skrang babies' blood. The Leforian had all four arms whirling about him, having somehow gotten free from his own bindings.

He was grabbing up the little fos left and right. Smashing their heads together hard enough that I could almost hear the pops through the water. I could certainly hear the screeches of the dying babies. It almost made me feel sorry for the things. Almost.

Mgurn ripped a Skrang baby in half then jammed one half into the open mouth of an attacking pondmate until he'd shoved the half-corpse so far down that part of it came out the other end. The attacking Skrang baby burst open and the bodies floated off into the depths of the pond.

Which was pretty deep. I glanced down and was shocked to see scores of Skrang babies coming up from below. The ones that were already swimming around were the bloody icing on the death cake. The real filling was on its way to… Oh, hell, I don't know. There were a lot and they looked hungry.

"One!" I thought as I started to feel my lungs burn. I had been so caught up watching Mgurn shred some Skrang kids that I'd forgotten I needed air to live. Good thing clarity gave me time to get my head back in the game. "One!"

"Not now, Joe," One replied. "I am busy."

"Screw your busy!" I thought. "I'm foing drowning!"

"Help is on the way," One responded. "That is part of the good news."

"Yay!" I thought. "But I have to be alive to truly appreciate the good news!"

He didn't reply. I could feel him in my head, but I could also feel other things. Visions and shadows of what he saw from his perspective. If I thought the pond was a blood bath, it was a hundred times worse up on the surface.

A half-dozen Skrang babies rammed into me and I twisted around, letting their teeth saw through the intestines. It was a tricky move, and required perfect timing so I didn't get chomped on, but clarity allowed me to move in perfect synchronicity with their nibbling teeth.

The wrap burst off of me and floated down into the dark. The Skrang babies came in for the coup de grace, but I was ready for them. I forced myself to channel the agony of my arm, and the rest of my body, and put all of my energy into my battle legs. They were the one part that wasn't weak human flesh and they were my only hope at surviving the sick game of Marco Polo I was being forced to play.

I kicked out with my left foot right at a Skrang baby and the thing bit down onto the toe of my boot. I let it pull the boot off then grimaced and winced as a second one bit down onto my toes. Pulling back, I let the synthetic skin get shredded and pulled off, exposing the raw metal of that battle leg.

I swung my leg through the water, cutting a line with my foot as I pointed it as sharply as possible. The metal sliced through one, two, three Skrang babies, severing limbs, cutting open bellies, splitting them in half. Their little screeches didn't mean crud to me anymore. It was me or them. And there was a lot of them.

I kicked out with my other foot, pushing the boot against the rocky pond wall, sending my body into a twisting spin. Slowly, I extended my exposed metal foot and angled it so it became a deadly blade that sliced and diced like a giant blender. Skrang baby after Skrang baby screeched their last screech, their nasty blood spilling out in dark clouds, making the murky pond water even murkier.

That's about when clarity left me and reality came back for a punch to my chest. I was out of air. As happy as I was that I was surviving the feeding frenzy, nothing could replace a good lungful of fresh air.

I took one last look over at Mgurn, but he was lost from sight. Even with the last bit of clarity still in place, I couldn't see through the bloody murk of the pond. Not with one eye that was quickly filling with dancing motes that told me to get up and breathe or I was going to die.

I kicked hard and shot myself up to the surface of the pond. My head had almost breached when I was yanked back down, four little buggers having clamped their jaws onto my metal foot. I panicked and opened my mouth in a cowardly shout. The pond water rushed into my mouth and filled my throat.

Coughing did nothing, just made things worse. I felt the weight of the pond water inside my lungs and those dancing motes started to fade away as I felt my life begin to dim.

The Skrang babies continued to yank and pull, dragging me deeper and deeper into the pond. They'd figured out how to incapacitate my one weapon. They also seemed to know that humans needed to breathe. Smart little buggers.

My left arm was useless, so I couldn't reach through the water and slap at them. And my right arm was busy punching new Skrang babies that had joined the fun and were trying to go for my face and head. That was until I felt a sharp pain in my right shoulder and all motion stopped.

I looked over and saw a Skrang baby firmly attached to my shoulder, its teeth sunk deep into my flesh. It had to have not only pierced the tendons and ligaments, but also the nerves because I felt one last hot flash of agony then my right arm went completely numb. No feeling. Nothing.

So, to sum up, I had no use of my arms and one of my legs was engulfed in Skrang babies that were busy gnawing away at the metal, putting some serious dents into my battle leg. I did have a second battle leg that hadn't been harmed, but let's face it, I was done. No air, no energy, no nothing. I was a sinking hunk of human crud.

I craned my neck, which surprisingly was not a painful activity, and stared up at the weak light that filtered down through the water. I felt a Skrang baby take a bite out of my left arm and I would have shrugged to say, "Oh, well, it's a goner anyway," but something up above caught my attention. I could see an outline against the surface light. A growing outline.

Skrang baby after Skrang baby detached from my body and shot up at the growing outline. I watched in fascination as the outline became a solid form. One that I recognized.

"I am here now," One said in my mind. "I will bring them to me. Can you swim to the surface?"

"Nope," I thought. "This is the end for Joe Laribeau."

"Fight, Joe," One said. "Dig deep into your soul and find that last bit of strength that we all carry."

"Yeah, I think I spent that last bit a couple times today," I thought. "I'm in last bit debt at the moment."

"Joe! TRY!" One screeched and my head nearly exploded.

Okay, okay, I would try.

I focused on myself. I put all of my thought into getting my one good leg moving. A small flip of my foot followed by a weak kick with the entire leg. It didn't really do much, just sort of spun me to the left and made me dizzy. Dizzier, considering the last of the oxygen in my brain was about to fizzle, fizzle, be gone.

Then I was shooting up through the water and breaking the surface.

My head hit open air and I projectile puked pond water about twenty meters. I heard a scream of disgust, followed by a scream of dying pain, and knew some Skrang sucker just met his or her end with Joe puke all over them. Hell yeah.

I was dragged from the pond and roughly thrown onto the rocky edge. Hands pressed down on my chest, pumping the last of the pond water out of my lungs, then rough lips were on mine and some seriously nasty breath was exhaled into my mouth. Before I could puke again, I was coughing and shoved over onto my side.

I screamed. I screamed bloody murder as my entire weight pressed down onto my left arm. My right was still numb, but my left didn't have the privilege of severed nerves. It was still connected and did the hurting for both arms.

"Get off me," I coughed. "Fo, get off me."

"Joe! You live!" Mgurn yelled and wrapped me in his four arms.

I screamed some more.

"Oh, my, I am sorry," he apologized as he gently pushed me away. "You are injured. I forgot."

"Yeah, buddy, I'm injured," I whispered.

The battle raged on around us. I could hear Skrangs shouting, screaming, dying. I could also hear others shouting, screaming dying.

"Midnight?" I asked.

"They are fighting valiantly, but they are outnumbered," Mgurn said. "They will not win. We need to get out of here fast."

"I'm not doing anything fast, buddy," I said. "I'm a broken mess."

"Not for long," Mgurn said and produced one wicked large injector from somewhere. "This will hurt a lot at first, but it will allow you to get up and escape with me on your own power."

"Hold on, what is it? Get that thing away from me!" I said just as he jabbed the needle into my neck.

I heard the hiss of the injector and felt a searing hot liquid start to pump through my veins. My body was on fire. I was melting from the inside out. Every molecule of me wanted to die.

Then it was over and I had feeling in my body that wasn't pain. It was life.

Mgurn helped me to my feet and I was shocked to be able to flex both hands and roll my arms in their shoulders.

"This is amazing," I said.

"You say that now, but…" Mgurn replied.

"That's a little ominous," I said. "What did you inject me with?"

"No time to explain," Mgurn said and pulled me to the side, skirting a pile of Skrangs that were ripping something to shreds.

Or someone to shreds.

"Is that one of the Cerviles?" I asked as we hurried past. "Mak or Kam?"

"Mak, I believe," Mgurn said. "But we cannot do anything for him now. We have to escape and get to the moltrans point."

I yanked my arm from his grip and spun about to face the pond. "One!" I yelled. "The mission was to retrieve One!"

"The mission is done," Mgurn insisted and started to pull at me again. "Our new mission is to survive."

"And you will," One said, blinking into view at my side.

He was dripping wet and looked like he'd gone ten rounds with the Seven Devils themselves, but he was upright and smiling. It wasn't the most reassuring smile. Sort of a creeper smile I could have totally done without seeing. My gut wasn't exactly liking Salvage Merc One. Can't say why, but he just unsettled me.

Could have been the completely black eyes.

"Hey, you have both eyes open again," was all I could say.

"I do," One said. "Now follow me. I know how to get out of here and have a ship waiting."

"What about the others?" I asked, but didn't argue as I let Mgurn pull me along through the gaps in the violence.

"They will have to save themselves," One said. "They knew the risks coming here."

"Man, that's cold," I said as Mgurn blocked a heavy blade from taking my head off. He grabbed the Skrang by the neck and snapped it, tossing the body into three guards rushing at us.

"It is what it is," One said as he lifted his hands before him and the three Skrang guards burst into flame.

They ran screaming towards the pond, diving in as soon as they reached the edge. I didn't see much of what happened to them, but I was pretty sure the flames didn't go out even when they were fully submerged. That's a trick and a half.

"This way," One said as if he didn't just turn some Skrangs into waterproof pool torches.

We made it back into the palace and One led us through the maze of corridors until we reached a short door just outside one of the bathrooms.

"You will not like this," he said and pulled the door from its hinges.

The smell hit us hard and I knew where we were going.

"Sewers," I said.

"Sewers," Mgurn echoed.

"I have a ship down there," One said. "Follow me."

We ducked inside and crawled our way through the plumbing access hatch until we reached another small door. One shoved it open to reveal a good twenty foot drop. Below us was a river of crap. A literal river of crap.

"No choice," One said and dove.

"I certainly wish there was a choice," Mgurn said and followed.

I had nothing to say. I didn't want to risk my mouth being open when I hit that river. I dove.

SEVENTEEN

Skrang baby pond into Skrang palace sewer. Frying pan meet stinky, disgusting fire.

We floated along as the river of crap took us from the palace and towards an ever-growing light. Hunks of please don't tell me and chunks of I don't want to know bobbed up and down next to my head. Blobs of melting toilet paper tried to adhere to my face, but I plucked them off and flung them as far away as possible.

"Stop that," Mgurn said, wiping the sixth or seventh blob of TP from his own face. "Your aim is not amusing."

Then he took a mouthful of crap and I laughed. Which meant I took a mouthful of crap as well. I stopped laughing and started throwing up.

"Prepare yourselves!" One said in my mind.

I could see Mgurn jerk and his eyes went wide, so I knew he'd gotten the same mental message.

"Prepare ourselves for what?" I thought.

"We will be coming to the end of the sewers soon," One responded. "Once we do, you will need to tuck your arms in tight and keep your legs closed. Hold that position for the entire fall or you will snap your legs, break your arms, and possibly crush your spine."

"I've already had most of that happen to me today," I thought. "I don't plan on an encore."

"Joe? Is that you?" I heard Mgurn's thoughts say. "Well, this is interesting."

"Arms in, legs closed, stay in that position the entire fall," One said.

"We heard you the first time," I thought.

"I hope so, because here we go," One said.

The sewer tunnel brightened considerably as we came flowing around a bend. Ahead of us was a wide opening and I caught a glimpse of a bright, rocky cliff just before everything dropped out from under me.

I screamed as the waterfall of crap took me out and down. I tucked my arms in, closed my legs, and braced myself as I realized that the fall was going to be a bad one. A risky glance down told me there was at least two hundred feet from where I was to the surface of the crap below.

I'll give it to the Skrangs, they know how to dig one giant latrine pit. Why, I couldn't figure out. They could build and fly spaceships with enough firepower to destroy entire planets, but they couldn't develop a way to get rid of their poo other than just filling a giant hole in the ground?

To each their own, I guess.

The surface came up at me faster than I expected and I barely had time to take a deep breath before I was submerged for a second time that day. In poo. So much poo.

I kicked hard once I knew I wasn't dead or broken and fought my way to the surface of the sewage pit. My head broke free and I gasped for air, took in more than air, spat over and over, then breathed easy as I looked around and saw Mgurn and One doing the same thing.

I started to swim my way to the edge of the pit, but One called out and I stopped.

"What's wrong?" I asked, careful not to get more poo in my mouth.

"We aren't getting out of the pit," he said. "We are going down into it."

"Oh, come on!" I yelled. "Why the hell would we do that?"

"Because my ship is floating in the middle of this sewage, ready and waiting for us," he answered.

"You can't be serious," I said.

"He is," Mgurn said. "I caught a glimpse of it as I was under."

"How about this?" I said to One. "You swim down and get your ship then you fly up out of the poo pit and we climb aboard. How does that sound?"

"It sounds good to me," Mgurn said.

"That will not work," One said. "The moment I engage the engines, where you are swimming will become a flaming pit of burning sewage. Skrang waste is comprised of ten times the methane that human waste is."

"Interesting fact," Mgurn said. "Leforians do not expel methane, but a combination of gasses such as—"

"Mgurn? Shut up," I said then choked and gagged. "Dammit! You made me swallow poo!"

The sounds of vehicles from up above echoed down into the pit and One spun his body around to face us.

"We dive now before they see us!" he yelled and then was gone.

I looked at Mgurn, he looked at me. We both shrugged and dove.

Goggles would have been nice. Actually, an entire containment suit would have been nice. But we had neither so I had to force myself not to freak out as I swam with both eyes open through Skrang excrement.

Mgurn took the lead, his four arms better at propulsion than my two arms. I thought I could make out One in the dark below, but I wasn't sure. I just made sure I didn't lose sight of Mgurn.

My lungs began to burn again and I wasn't sure if I was going to make it, but then Mgurn pulled up short and I realized One's ship was only a few feet in front of us. The hull was so dark that I could barely make it out and would have swam right past it, or right into it, if Mgurn hadn't stopped.

A light came on below us and Mgurn dove deeper. I followed and found a hatch open under the ship. We swam to it as a ladder descended into the poo. Mgurn grabbed onto the rungs and climbed up and in then shoved his hands back into the sewage to grab me. I was yanked up into the ship and the ladder rolled itself inside then the hatch closed.

The moment the hatch sealed, we were assaulted by a multitude of jets of water, half of which seemed to be aimed at my face. I ended up with so much water up my nose that if One had tried to mind talk with me he would have gotten only gurgling for an answer.

As the water jets stopped, and a surprisingly pleasant blast of warm, dry air hit us, I could feel the ship's engines start to power up.

"Better get up here to the bridge and strap in," One said, his voice coming from the intercom system and not from our heads, which was a relief. The whole novelty of telepathy had lost its charm and was beginning to get a little grating.

"This way," Mgurn said. "I know what type of ship this is and have memorized the layout."

"Of course you have," I said as I followed him through a hatch, down a corridor, up a ladder, down some more corridors, up a couple more ladders, until we were standing outside the doors to the bridge.

"Whoa," I said as I stepped onto the bridge. "This isn't standard SMC issue. How the hell did you get a ship like this?"

"The perks of being Salvage Merc One," One replied as he sat in the pilot's chair, not in the captain's. "Not that there are many of those."

"Way to sell the job," I said and took a seat at the communications station.

The view out the view screen was still a lot of poo, but that fell away as we lifted up out of the pit and One spun the ship about. He dipped the nose enough for us to see below and Mgurn and I gasped as the sewage pit ignited and hundred-foot flames lifted into the air after us.

One piloted the ship out of harm's way and took us half a mile up into the air so we could see the far off Skrang city and the smoking wreckage that was Lord Messermeen's palace.

"Nice," I said. "Looks like Midnight and her crew did some damage."

"Yes, it does," One said. He looked over his shoulder at me. "Try to see if you can raise her on the com."

"Good idea," I said and turned to the com controls. I began searching through channels until I came to one that sounded right. There was a lot of cursing and shouting and a very deep grumbling from what I guessed was an enraged Grue.

"Midnight? Midnight, do you read me?" I yelled into the com, hoping to be heard above the chaos.

"Joe?" she replied immediately. "Where are you? Give us your location and we'll come get you!"

"I'm good," I said. "Safe and sound in One's ship. Where are you? We'll come get your asses instead."

"Maybe not," One said.

I looked back at him then saw what was beginning to fill the view screen. Skrang fighters. A whole squadron of them were lifting off from the far side of the city and racing right at us.

"Yeah, huh," I said. "Hey, Midnight? You think you can call your ship and get moltransed up on your own?"

"What? Why?" she yelled.

"Because we've got about twelve—"

"Eighteen," Mgurn interrupted.

"Eighteen Skrang fighters about to engage us," I said. "We could try to come get you, but odds are we'll either get blasted out of the sky or just bring a whole lot of Skrang firepower to your position. Either way we're no use to you."

"Then go!" she shouted. "We'll figure out how to get free!"

"Call your ship," I said. "They can lock onto your location and transport you up!"

"Too much interference," Midnight replied. "They won't get a lock."

"Fo," I muttered.

"What was that?" she asked.

"Fo!" I repeated at full volume. I spun to face One. "We need to go help them."

"No," One said.

"Uh, yeah," I responded.

"No," he said more forcefully. "You are more important than a bunch of Edger separatists. My mission is to get you somewhere safe and sound."

"What? No, that's my mission!" I snapped. "Not to get me back, but to get you back! And here you are! So let's go get Midnight and her team!"

"Neither of us are at SMC headquarters," One said. "So neither of our missions are complete. We're numbers, Joe. We have been given tickets to punch and we will punch them."

"Not at the expense of my best friend's wife, we won't," I snarled and stood up from my seat.

The bridge turned into nothing but blinding light and searing pain.

"Sit back down," One ordered and I did. I didn't have much choice. It was like the words he spoke were my every thought. To not sit back down would have been unthinkable. But I was a guy that sort of specialized in doing the unthinkable. Or that's what I told myself at the time.

"Fighters will engage in thirty seconds," Mgurn announced, having taken a seat at the weapons station. "I have missiles and plasma cannons locked on, but we cannot take all eighteen of them out at once. Some will get through and they will destroy us."

"That's why we're leaving," One said.

"No," I said and fought against the pain in my head. "We are getting Midnight."

"Stop fighting, Joe!" One yelled. "Dammit! I can't fly the ship and control you at the same time!"

"Then stop controlling me." I gave a hard push with my mind and One cried out. "Get out of my head, One, or I will make this very hard on you."

"Stop it, dumbass!" he yelled. "You don't know what you're...doing..."

The pain, the light, the command to sit, all stopped at once and I leapt to my feet, nearly falling over after the weight of One's mind was lifted from me.

No, that wasn't why I nearly fell over. The reason was actually a lot simpler than that.

One was slumped over the ship's flight controls, unconscious and drooling, blood leaking from his nose and ears.

"Oops," I said.

"What did you do, Joe?" Mgurn nearly shrieked as the ship started to yaw to port and we began to lose altitude quickly.

Mgurn was up and out of his seat fast. He pushed One from the pilot's chair and took over, grabbing up the flight controls with two hands while he worked the throttle and brakes with the others.

I rushed from the com console to the weapons station and sat down fast. I glanced over at Mgurn, but I could tell by the look on his face he was not happy with me so I focused on the weapons.

"Their guns are heating up," I said as I studied the scan readouts in front of me. "They're firing in—"

I didn't have to finish as every Skrang fighter let loose on us. Our shields held, but there was no way we could survive all eighteen of those fighters firing at once again.

"Mgurn!" I yelled.

"Quiet," Mgurn said. "I am concentrating."

Yikes. I totally got the Serious Mgurn voice.

Mgurn lifted the ship's nose and hit the thrusters. We were both pressed back into our seats before the dampers kicked in and leveled our g-forces. Unfortunately, One's unconscious body had itself a hard roll into the wall before things were under control. I was fairly sure I heard a snap or two on impact. The bosses weren't going to be happy about that.

Maybe Mgurn had another one of those miracle injectors? I wonder what that stuff was. It was simply amazing.

"Firing torpedoes," I announced as I launched our full battery down at the Skrang fighters that pursued us. "Contact in three, two, one."

The ship shook from the detonations of the torpedoes as well as several of the Skrang fighters. But not all the fighters.

Alarms rang out as the ship was rocked by several plasma impacts to our aft section. I switched over the console to defense systems and was not happy to see our rear shields at less than twenty percent.

"Keep us pointed up, Mgurn!" I yelled as I watched us rocket towards the upper atmosphere and the clear black of space. "I'm diverting power from the forward shields and giving our butt some more padding!"

"What?" Mgurn yelled. "Joe! No!"

"I have to or we'll be ripped apart from behind, man!" I shouted. "I don't know about you, but I would not like to be ripped apart from behind!"

"Joe! When we hit space, we'll be exposed to other dangers!" Mgurn yelled. "Try to fight the Skrang fighters off! Take control of the weapons and target them yourself! Do not take power from the forward shields!"

"Too late, buddy!" I said. "I already did!"

The ship rocked again, but the alarms died down as the rear shields absorbed the blasts.

I checked the scanners and counted six Skrang fighters still in pursuit.

"Now I take over the weapons and do some shooting," I said to myself.

A holo display of the view behind our ship popped up in front of me and I grabbed onto the targeting stick, bringing up a bright red set of crosshairs. I moved the crosshairs onto the closest Skrang fighter and pulled the trigger. Plasma blasts shot from our ship and impacted dead on with the fighter. It exploded and half the shrapnel from the ship went one way and the other half went another way, taking out two more fighters.

That left only three to deal with.

"Bam!" I yelled as I swung the crosshairs onto the next fighter.

The bugger was a little smarter than the last one. The pilot must have been alerted that it was being targeted and took evasive actions. The fighter dove down and then rolled to the left as I pulled the trigger. Plasma blasts shot past it, falling harmlessly into the planet's atmosphere.

Or maybe not harmlessly as I caught sight of a bright flash way, way down on the planet's surface. I guess plasma blasts don't stop being deadly when they miss their target.

The other two fighters engaged and opened fire on our ship, but the shields held and I took aim again. My crosshairs locked on and I kept the trigger squeezed, following the flipping, rolling, diving ship until I nailed it on the left wing, sending it spinning out of control into space.

"Good luck getting back before your air runs out!" I yelled. "Ha!"

"Joe! We need full power on the forward shields!" Mgurn shouted.

"Hold on, hold on!" I shouted back. "One more fighter to take care of!"

"Forget the fighter, Joe!" Mgurn yelled, his voice rising an octave.

That got my attention.

I sent a few blasts at the last fighter then switched my view to the front of our ship.

"Oh, yeah, now I see why," I said.

The B'clo'no warship cluster was moving slowly to intercept us. We were a smaller ship, way more maneuverable, but that made no difference. B'clo'no warships were designed to trap and block so the collective will of the crew could suck the energy right out of the ship. In about fifteen seconds, the cluster would not only be close enough to drain our ship of all of its power, but they'd be close enough for the B'clo'nos on board to drain me and Mgurn of our lifeforce.

The B'clo'nos didn't need weapons systems when they basically lived the ethos that the best offense is a good defense. That defense being the ability to combine themselves into one hell of a battery drain.

"Fo," I said as alarms started blaring on the bridge. I gave up trying to figure out what stations they were coming from since it looked like they were coming from every station.

I checked the rear view one last time and wasn't surprised to see no sign of any Skrang fighters. They were smart enough to high tail it out of there and avoid the massive energy suck that was about to happen.

"I'm redirecting all power to forward shields," I said. "That may hold them off for a few seconds. Is that enough time to punch it and get us past them?"

"Maybe," Mgurn said as he slammed the throttle as far forward as it would go. The metal handle even began to bend under the force he was using on it.

The B'clo'no warship cluster closed on us, coming in from the left. Our ship shot ahead, but not fast enough. Not nearly close to fast enough. More alarms rang out and I watched in horror as the forward shield meter dove from green to pink to red. We had close to ten, maybe fifteen, seconds of shield power left then those B'clo'no bastards would sip us empty like a Tchalmian soda.

"Well, we tried," I said as the shields flatlined and I started to feel really, really tired. "Is there a way to turn off the alarms?"

"I can do it from here," Mgurn said, sounding equally as tired.

The alarms went silent and we both just stared out the forward view screen as the warship cluster filled the view.

"Nice knowing you, buddy," I said.

"You as well, Joe," Mgurn replied.

The explosion was surprising. Or that was what my mind told me to think. Everything was so fuzzy it was hard to have a decent reaction to the B'clo'no warship cluster tearing apart before our eyes.

"Huh," I said as I sat there and watched. "That's pretty."

EIGHTEEN

"Joe! Mgurn! Do you read?" a lovely voice asked as the com system struggled to hold a signal. "Joe! Come in!"

"Hey there, pretty lady," I replied, slapping my hand on the com controls. I must have hit the right interface because I heard a thankful sigh.

"There you are," Hopsheer said. "I thought we were too late."

"Nope. Right on time," I said as my faculties began to return. I still felt like I wanted to just sleep forever, but at least I could think well enough to know I wasn't dead. "What are you doing here?"

"There was no way we'd let you have all the fun," Tarr said. "We convinced the bosses to let us come help you out."

"You are so lying," I replied.

"Yeah, I am," Tarr said. "The bosses will can us as soon as we get back to SMC headquarters, but it'll be worth it."

"We could not live with ourselves if we let you and Mgurn die," Ig said. "Hello, Mgurn."

"Hi," Mgurn said, his voice sleepy. "Thank you."

"Joe, listen," Hopsheer said. "My scans show your ship is at less than ten percent power. That isn't enough to get you through the wormhole portal. I'm going to dock with you and transfer my ship's power to yours. That means I need you to keep your ship steady. Can you do that?"

"I don't know," I replied. "Mgurn? Can we do that?"

"I can do that," Mgurn said and his hands fumbled at the flight controls. "Or not. I may need some help."

"On my way, buddy," I said and stood up then promptly fell right on my face. "Ow."

"Joe? Are you alright?" Hopsheer asked.

"Baby, I'm always alright when you're whispering in my ear," I replied.

"Smooth, man," Tarr laughed. "But chill on the smooth and keep that ship steady. We didn't rescue you guys just to have you to crash into Hoppy's ship. Wake the hell up, Joe!"

"I'm up, I'm up," I said as I pushed into a crawling position and made my way to the pilot's chair. "Move, Mgurn. My turn at the stick."

"Moving," Mgurn responded as he just sort of collapsed out of the chair and onto the floor.

I climbed over him and struggled into the seat. I stared blankly at the flight controls for a couple of seconds then took hold of the stick and gripped it hard.

"Stick is in my hands and I'm keeping it steady," I said. "Oh, wait, sorry, you didn't want anymore smooth talk."

"That's not smooth," Hopsheer said. "That's adolescent."

"Same thing sometimes," I said.

"No, not really," she replied. "Now, keep your position and I'll dock in three, two, one."

There was a loud clang from above and I almost let go of the stick. I probably could have locked the stick in place, but my mind couldn't focus on the procedures it would take to do that. The procedure was pressing one button, but that was too hard, man. Way too hard.

I'd dozed off a little when I heard the bridge doors open behind me. I turned in my seat and gave Hopsheer as wide a smile as I could. Her rough-skinned face went from happy to see me to terrified in the blink of an eye.

"What?" I asked. "What's wrong?"

"Joe, your face," she said. "Your body."

She hurried over to me and her hands hovered in the air around me. I could see she wanted to touch me, but she didn't know where to start.

"Nah, I'm good," I said. "Mgurn gave me this miracle injection and all my bones healed and everything. I even got my teeth back. See?"

I opened my mouth wide and ran my tongue along my top teeth. The coppery smell of blood filled my nostrils and the taste filled my mouth.

"Stop!" Hopsheer cried out. "You're slicing your tongue open!"

"I'm what now?" I asked. "That can't be. I'm totally healed. Mgurn? Tell her."

"He thinks he's totally healed," Mgurn said. "It was the only way to get him moving."

"Huh? What the hell are you talking about?" I asked. "No, no, I feel great. Look! See how my left arm is back to normal!"

I looked down and moved my arm. It responded just fine, wiggling about like an empty water hose.

"All good," I said and smiled.

"Stop smiling," Hopsheer said and turned her head. "That's not right. We have to get you back to SMC headquarters and into the tanks. If we don't, you're going to die."

"Die? Who me? No foing way!" I exclaimed. "Mgurn, buddy, tell her what was in that injector cocktail you gave me! Tell her you healed me!"

"Sorry, Joe," Mgurn said as he rolled onto his back and slowly sat up. "You were never healed."

"I wasn't?" I asked. I looked closer at my wiggly, floppy, left arm and frowned. "But look. Good as new." I brought up a holo mirror display and stared at my gashed, shattered face. I gave myself a big smile, studying every jagged tooth and empty socket then shook my head. "Not seeing the problem here, people. Nothing but handsome Joe staring back at me."

"Mgurn? What did you give him?" Hopsheer asked, gently grabbing me by the shoulders and lifting me out of the pilot's chair.

"My blood," Mgurn said. "When combined with human blood, it gives them the ego and confidence to overcome anything. Right now he does not believe he is injured. He has been running on nothing but willpower for the last few hours."

"He's going to die, isn't he?" Hopsheer asked.

"Not now," Mgurn said. "I will get him into a med bay and sedate him before my blood wears off. The med bay should keep him stable enough to get us back to SMC headquarters."

"No," One said from his crumpled spot on the bridge floor. "We can't go back to SMC headquarters now. We could before, but not after three SMC ships arrived and destroyed a B'clo'no warship cluster. We go on the run and I contact the bosses through back channels. We only return when they say it is safe to return."

"Who's this guy?" Hopsheer asked. "He looks almost as bad as you do, Joe."

"Then he must be looking pretty fine," I said and pointed both thumbs at myself. My left thumb was angled totally to the side, but close enough.

"This is Salvage Merc One," Mgurn said. "Mr. One, this is Hopsheer Balai."

"I know who Salvage Merc Eight is," One responded. "Good to meet you in person, Eight."

"You're One?" she asked. "The real One?"

"I am," One said.

"Hey, I'm convulsing," I said as I started shaking uncontrollably. My back arched and my body flopped halfway across the bridge before Hopsheer got a hold of me again. "Fun!"

"Get him into the med bay," One said. "I'll pilot the ship with Mgurn's help. Stabilize him and start a field repair."

"Field repair?" Hopsheer asked. "Why not a full repair?"

"No time," One said.

He moved to the pilot's chair and began doing piloty stuff. Not sure what since a strange feeling was creeping into my mind. It was like pain, but not really pain. More like the memory of pain. I didn't like the memory at all.

"Get him into the med bay and I'll get us out of this system," One said. "Make sure he's strapped down because this is going to be a bumpy ride."

I distinctly heard some new voices start calling out and I vaguely remember Mgurn getting up and shuffling to the com station.

"Who's that?" I asked. "Who's calling?"

"Don't worry about it," Hopsheer said as she picked me up and carried me from the bridge. "You just relax. I'm taking you to the med bay so you can get patched up."

"Field patched, not full patched," I said.

"Yes, field patched," Hopsheer agreed. "But it will have to do."

"Have to do," I echoed then winced. "Ow." A strange thought occurred to me. "Hey, Hoppy?"

"Yes, Joe?"

"Do I have a tooth loose?" I asked, opening my mouth. "It feels like I have a tooth loose."

"Yes, Joe, you have a tooth loose," Hopsheer responded. She was crying.

"Oh, no, what's wrong?" I asked. "What happened? You aren't a crier, Hoppy. So it must be bad."

"No, no, I'm fine," she replied. "Just relax and we'll get you into the med bay."

"To fix my loose tooth," I said.

"To fix your loose tooth," she said.

One of her tears fell onto my face and it stung like hell. I think I had a scratch or something on my cheek.

It was a little more than a scratch. A lot more, as you know.

One thing the med bay did when Hopsheer set me in it, was to cleanse my body of any and all foreign impurities. Namely, Mgurn's blood. This meant that the illusion that my mind had created about my body being fine, just fine, was stripped away and the reality of my physical destruction hit me like a ton of space bricks.

Which are a lot heavier than normal bricks. They'd have to in order to be effective in space. That's just brick logic.

"Hey there," Hopsheer said as she sat down outside the bay and placed a hand against the thick, plastic partition that kept all the bad stuff away from me. "You feeling any better?"

"Gonna go with a big no on that one," I replied.

Which was the truth. I looked at the readout that was inside the bay and saw I'd been there for about ten hours. Ten hours of sheer hell.

"You will feel better soon," Hopsheer said. "One had a great idea of where we can regroup and it's probably the best thing for you."

"One sure does know what's best," I said. "You see my teeth? He did that. Yep. Nothing but the dental best from that guy."

"He explained to us what happened on Skrang," Hopsheer said. "He had to play a part in order to keep Lord Messermeen from killing him. It didn't help that the Skrangs have some very potent venoms they use in conjunction with spinal tech to control the actions of others."

"Is that so?" I asked. "Why didn't the Skrangs ever use the venoms during the War?"

"They only work on Skrang planet," Hopsheer said. "It has to do with specific elements in the atmosphere. Mgurn confirmed it. Leforians are venom nerds apparently."

"Mgurn's just a nerd nerd," I said then shook my head which was a big ow. "Sorry. That was mean. How's Mgurn doing? He rested up from the B'clo'no attack?"

"He's almost there," Hopsheer said. "He's still tired enough not to insist he take the flight controls. He's conceded that in his exhausted state, One is still the better pilot."

"Wow, he must really be tired then," I replied.

"He is," Hopsheer said. "Tarr and Ig say hello. They called on the com just before I came back in here."

"They still with us?" I asked.

"Nowhere else for them to go," Hopsheer replied. "Until we sort things out with the bosses, we're rogue."

"Yikes," I said and grimaced. More ow. "Rogues. That's pretty harsh."

"It's the truth," Hopsheer said. "I doubt the Edger separatists would touch us at this point."

"Especially after we gaffed up the whole rescue One without creating a galactic incident thing," I said. "Have we heard from Midnight? Is she okay?"

"She is," Hopsheer said. "She is on her way back to Crawford now. The SMC didn't abandon them, but they have a limited window of protection. They'll have to relocate as soon as possible."

"This just turned into a cluster," I said. Then something struck me. "Did we ever find out why there was a B'clo'no warship cluster orbiting Skrang? Anyone have a clue what that was about?"

"Mgurn told me it was waiting there when you arrived in the system," Hopsheer said. "He had plenty of theories, but it was One that set us all straight."

I waited. She didn't continue. It got a little uncomfortable.

"Do we need to play twenty questions?" I asked. "Is it bigger than a gump?"

"One says that lately the B'clo'nos will cluster when he stays in the same place for too long," Hopsheer finally said. "He has about twenty-four hours before they track him down."

"Well, that's not normal," I said. "Did he say why they do that? Or, better yet, how they find him?"

"The why is easy," Hopsheer said. "They want his lifeforce. Salvage Merc One puts off an intense amount of energy. The B'clo'nos somehow are able to track that lifeforce even from halfway across the galaxy. He can't be within ten systems of a single B'clo'no without all of them knowing."

"Does the same go for B'flo'dos?" I asked, thinking back to that mission on Hepnug that went south. "Because B'clo'nos I can handle. B'flo'dos? Those things are messed up. I don't even know how they travel around the galaxy when they are barely bright enough to build their own ships or anything at all."

"I wish you were out of there," Hopsheer said. "Because we have all been having this exact discussion. One surmises it has something to do with their natural disposition towards quantum entanglement. He honestly thinks they can just transport themselves wherever they want."

"That's terrifying," I said. "But it can't be or they'd have just popped out of nowhere on every civilized planet and started feeding."

"Like you said, they aren't very bright," Hopsheer replied. "They don't have the mental capacity to plan out any type of long-term strategy. They live in the moment and just bounce around until they find something they can feed off."

"I don't know," I said. "Still doesn't feel right."

"Doesn't to me either," she said.

A wave of pain ran through me and I arched my back and grunted, which was the worst thing to do because it jostled my left arm and made my healing teeth sing.

"When we get to where we're going, we'll be able to regroup and recharge," Hopsheer said. "One is confident the environment will accelerate your healing process. He says that the best thing for people like you is to be grounded and get back to their roots. He visits his home planet all the time to get centered and make sure he hasn't strayed too far from who he is."

"What does all that mean?" I asked. "I was a Marine for years. I don't have roots."

"That's not entirely true," Hopsheer said. "We all have roots. Some are deeper than others."

"Not following you here, Hoppy," I said. "Speak plain common so I can understand."

"I am speaking plain common, you are just being dense," Hopsheer replied and frowned. "If you think about it for a minute, you'll get what I'm saying."

"Or, and here's a whacky idea, you just stop talking in code and woowoo riddles and tell me where we're going," I said. "Because the only roots I have now are at SMC headquarters, which you said we can't go to. Unless you're talking about... Oh... Come on, you can't be serious?"

"Did you figure it out?" she asked.

I could tell by the look on her face that she didn't think One's plan was a good one. If my guess was correct then she was right. I've been on a lot of planets and had some very messed up things happen to me on those planets, but there is only one planet I have sworn never to return to.

"Hopsheer, please tell me we aren't going to Bax," I said.

"Yeah... I can't tell you that, Joe," she replied. "One is very insistent that you go back home. He says it is not only good for your body, but for your soul."

"One is a twat that needs a smack down for even thinking he's even close to being right," I said. "Stupid gump turd."

That made Hopsheer laugh. She started off giggling then put her hands to her mouth as it grew into a full on guffaw. It was infectious and I started to laugh with her which hurt so much. Oh, Eight Million Gods did it hurt.

"Stop, stop," I begged. "I'm going to die in this bay if you keep laughing."

"You're laughing too," she said.

"Only because you are," I replied. "So knock it off."

Her eyes met mine and I remembered our night together. Despite the pitchers and pitchers of beer, every detail slammed into the front of my mind. I think she was remembering the same thing because a blush rose up on her cheeks and she slowed her laughing down as she looked away.

"Hopsheer?" Mgurn's voice called over the intercom. "We are arriving. Your ship is back to full charge and has enough power to land separately. That would be advisable as reentry in this atmosphere can prove tricky due to the amount of moisture present."

"There is a lot of moisture," I said. "Bax is a rainy swamp planet. Nothing but clouds for most of the year. I once went from birthday to birthday without seeing the sun."

"Oh," Hopsheer said. "That sounds dreadful. Not healing at all."

I nodded. "Tell me about it. Unless One has some magic mojo up his sleeve, he's going to get a fist to the nose the second I'm out of this bay."

"I can hear you, you know," One said in my mind.

"Get out of my head, ass muncher!" I shouted.

That made my jaw hurt worse and also made Hopsheer jump to her feet.

"Sorry, sorry," I said and tapped my temple. "One is telepathic and was eavesdropping when he shouldn't have been. Not cool, dude!"

"So he can hear what you're thinking?" she asked and that amazingly beautiful sly smile crept across her face.

"No, not at all," I said, trying to act cool and casual. "So do not go asking him any personal questions about me. He won't have any answers."

That smile grew and Hopsheer blew me a kiss as she turned and left.

"Hopsheer? Hey! Come back here!" I called. "Do not think of asking him any questions! I do not give consent! No consent has been given to the divulging of my brain contents! Private! No trespassing! Keep out! Hopsheer? Hoppy? HOPSHEER!"

NINETEEN

Bax.

Yay.

The planet where my parents were butchered and their bodies were left to rot in the damp.

Good times.

One must have really dug around inside my head, because not only did he decide to take me back to the planet I grew up on, he also decided to land the ship only a couple kilometers from where my childhood house used to stand. I say used to because Bax is a swamp planet that gets more annual rainfall than the majority of inhabited systems combined. Not planets, but entire systems.

That's a lot of rain.

So everyone that lives on Bax is used to picking up and moving to find higher ground. Some tried to build dykes and canals to control the flooding and keep back the swamps, but none of it worked. When a hurricane can settle over an area and last for three months straight without tiring out and going away, you give up on engineering a solution and just let nature take its course.

Bax.

Seriously?

We'd been on the planet for a week before I was given the green light to leave the med bay and venture outside the ship. In that time, One had done some engineering of his own and built a fairly sturdy-looking habitat that we could all stay in. I was informed by Mgurn that his original design had included using the ship as an anchor, with wings splitting off to Hopsheer's, Ig's, and Tarr's ships as well, but I scuttled that instantly when I told them about the storm of '03 and how half the planet had to evacuate for six months until the swamp gas that was generated by the mini-hurricanes subsided and the planet wasn't in danger of exploding if someone lit a smoke.

Only half of that was true. The storm lasted three months, not six.

But it kept One from making a colossal mistake by hooking our only means of escape to the habitat we were to be living in. If we needed to leave fast, we didn't want to have to unhook the crapper to do so.

I stood on the rear ramp of One's ship's cargo hold and stared out at the landscape that I'd spent most of my youth around. The massive trees clumped together to form islands of earth that they could anchor themselves to. Their canopies stretched in all directions for miles. The branches and tops connected more in the air than their roots down below.

The never-ending swamp made sure nothing connected on the surface of the planet.

We'd landed on a good-sized hummock, about four kilometers square, and One had at least planned the habitat to take advantage of the huge tree trunks, spiraling it up and then over to another trunk to give it stability and also allow for enough space for the six of us.

I started to take a step down the ramp, ready to set foot on Bax for the first time since well before I'd joined the Marines, but my reunion with the earth of my birth had to wait.

"Crawford is calling," Mgurn said as he ducked his head into the hold. "He says it's not urgent, but I thought you might like to talk to him before you go out there."

"Yeah, I do," I said. "Send the link to my wrist holo, will ya?"

"Already have," Mgurn said. He gave me a smile and then ducked away, leaving me alone in the hold with a view of my past outside and a view of my past about to pop up from my wrist.

"Hey there," I said as I activated my holo and a small image of Crawford appeared above my wrist. "I know Mgurn said it wasn't urgent, but you wouldn't be calling unless it was."

"It's not urgent," he said, still covered head to toe in bandages. "It's more selfish."

He gestured to his dressings and gave me a wink.

"Any word on when I can make that trip to SMC headquarters and get some new skin?" he asked. "That was part of the deal your boss made with us."

"You are asking the wrong salvage merc about that," I said. "Not only have I been out of commission because of my own body issues, but I'm sure Midnight told you what a mess we made of things."

"She did," Crawford said, "and it doesn't seem to matter. All of our sources are saying the Skrangs aren't looking to retaliate against the SMC for what happened. Not yet, anyway. The main thing is they aren't putting one and one together to realize that a team of Edgers had helped get you and One off the planet. As far as they know, it was all SMC."

"But they don't want to retaliate? Really?" I asked. "That's not very Skrang of them."

"No, it's not," Crawford said. "It's like they have something more important going on and can't be bothered with revenge."

"That's very not Skrang," I repeated. "This is the race that burned the orphanage planet down to its core because one of their generals lost her parents in the Battle of Cvet. They retaliate if they mistake a weak wind for a fart."

"Not the best analogy, brother, but yeah, you are 100% right on that," Crawford said. "But, no worries, I'll just hang tight until we get the invitation to SMC headquarters."

"I can have Mgurn ask around," I said. "He has Leforian contacts that can be discreet."

"You have to be kidding me," Crawford laughed. "There isn't a Leforian in the universe that can be discreet."

"They can if their number's honor is on the line," I said. "Trust me. I wouldn't risk it if I didn't know Leforians and their convoluted ways."

"Yeah, do that then," Crawford said. "Hey, hold on, Midnight wants to talk to you."

He looked nervous, or his eyes did, at least. I gave him a frown and he sighed then stepped aside.

His image switched to his beautiful blue wife's and I gave her a sheepish grin.

"Sorry about your people dying," I said. "I didn't want that to happen."

She didn't return my grin. In fact, she looked very disturbed.

"They knew the risks," Midnight shrugged. "It is sad and unfortunate, but part of being in the separatist movement. We all expect to die at some point."

"You aren't foing kidding there," I said. "So, what do you need to talk to me about?"

"Salvage Merc One," Midnight said. She looked around so I did the same.

"We're alone," I said, walking back into the depths of the ship. "What's up?"

"When we hit the Skrang palace, some of us went to their security control room first, hoping to find you on one of the holo displays," she said. "We did find you, on your way to the breeding pool, but we also found One."

"He was at the pool," I said. "That's how Mgurn and I got away."

"We saw that," she said. "Later. But first we saw him talking with Lord Messermeen. They were leaning close and looking very chummy. I know you've reported that he was under Skrang control at one point, but this didn't look like that."

"What did it look like?" I asked, tired of the conversation and ready to get the hell off the ship, even if it meant setting foot on a planet that had less than happy happy memories for me. "Spit it out, Midnight."

"I copied the feed and filtered it through my system," Midnight said. "It was able to read his lips."

"And…?" I asked.

"One is in league with the Skrangs," Midnight said. "The conversation was fractured and hurried, but it looked like he was making a deal with Lord Messermeen to double cross everyone. Especially the B'clo'nos."

"B'clo'nos?" I asked.

"Yes," Midnight said. "I think the escape was planned and you're going to be sacrificed to the B'clo'nos instead of him."

"Instead of him? What does that mean? Why would he be sacrificed to the B'clo'nos?" I snapped. "You aren't making sense."

"None of it makes sense!" she barked. "But that's what I saw. I'll send you the feed right now. Watch it yourself. Filter and analyze it yourself. You tell me what you find."

"Okay, okay, sorry," I said. "Thank you for letting me know. I didn't mean to get snippy with you."

"I think I know why your boss wanted me and my people to help you," she said. "They can't trust Salvage Merc One anymore. He's been compromised."

"I don't know," I said. "It's hard to believe. But I'll look everything over. Thank you again, Midnight, for everything you've done. I owe you."

"No, you don't," Midnight said. "We captured you to use you for our own purposes. That's Eight Million Gods worth of karma right there. We're even, as far as I'm concerned."

"No, I owe you," I said.

"Whatever," she said and shrugged again. "Crawford wants to talk to you. Stay safe, Joe. Watch your back."

"I will, thanks," I said.

Crawford came back into view and his eyes were apologetic.

"You didn't call because of your skin, did you?" I asked.

"Sorry for the subterfuge," he said. "We needed time to scan the transmission and make sure we weren't being monitored."

"No worries, brother," I said. "All part of the glamourous life of a salvage merc."

"And an Edger separatist," he laughed. "We gotta go. The SMC has left orbit and we can't stay here any longer. I'll get in touch when we're settled."

"You better," I said. "And do me a favor, will ya?"

"Sure, what?" he asked.

"No more peeling your skin off to fake your death, alright?" I said. "Just blow up a ship with someone else's body on it like everyone else."

"Can do," I said. "Chat with ya later."

The holo blinked out and I stared at my wrist for a couple seconds as I gathered my thoughts.

I was faced with a dilemma. Confront One or wait it out and see what is going on. Do I involve Hopsheer? Or Mgurn? What about Ig and Tarr?

Turned out I didn't have to make the decision on my own.

"You're probably a little confused right now," One said from behind me.

I spun around and went for my pistol, but I didn't have my pistol strapped to my thigh. I just sorta slapped at my leg a couple of times then grunted in frustration.

"Were you spying on me?" I asked. "Listening to my holo conversation with Midnight?"

He tapped at his temple. "Don't need to listen when I can hear everything up here."

"That's a rude gift you have there," I snapped. "Stay the fo out of my head."

"I'd love to, Joe, but that stopped being possible as soon as you left the med bay," he sighed. "The bay helped mute your thoughts some, but not completely. Now that you're out?" He shook his head. "I can't stop listening if I want to. And believe me, Joe, I want to."

"Why should I believe you?" I asked. "You're going to sacrifice us all to the B'clo'nos then double cross them somehow. I don't know all the details, but I do know—"

"You don't know jack crud," One laughed. "About me, what my plans are, what your future is, why we are here, nothing. Right now you are a pawn that is only a move away from becoming a queen."

"You mean king," I said. "I'm a guy. Got the junk to prove it."

"No, I was making a chess analogy about when you are able to move a pawn to your opponent's far row, that pawn becomes a queen," One said. "The only problem here is that we can only have one queen on the board, never two."

"We? What we?" I asked. "Because I'm not feeling very *we* right now."

"The SMC, dumbass," he growled. He pointed to a crate up against the wall. "Sit."

"I'll stand," I said.

"Don't be a big baby. Sit," he snapped. "You are one row off, but I'm still the queen on this board. I'll make you sit if I have to."

"Well, your highness, wouldn't want to piss off the queen," I said and took a seat.

He started to pace, glanced out of the hold to make sure no one was directly outside listening, then turned and looked at me, a deadly serious look on his face.

"Do you think this has never happened before?" he asked.

I thought it was a rhetorical question so I waited.

"It's not rhetorical," he said.

"Oh, sorry. Uh, no? Yes? I don't know?" I replied. "What are we talking about?"

"Everything," he said. "The Fleet wanting to start the War again. The Skrangs wanting the same thing. One side trying to involve outside forces to fight with them. The Skrangs and B'clo'nos having differences and wanting to double cross each other. You, me, everything to do with Salvage Merc One. That's what I'm talking about."

"Then my answer is I have no foing idea, man," I said. "Read my mind. You'll see I'm being 100% honest with you. Not a damn clue as to what the hell is going on."

"Let me tell you a story," he said and sat down next to me. "It's about the very first Salvage Merc One. The man that founded our organization and changed the shape of the War and the galaxy itself."

"Is this a long story? Should I go pee first?" I asked.

"Don't be a little bitch," he said. "Just listen."

So I did.

I listened as he told me how the SMC started. How Bon Chattslan saw a business niche that needed to be filled, so he filled it. How he built the SMC from scratch, taking it from a one merc operation to what it is now. It was nothing I didn't already mostly know. There were some details and dates I hadn't heard, but overall it was straight out of the SMC handbook.

Until he got to Bon Chattslan's death.

I listened with rapt attention. The stuff One was telling me wasn't in the handbook. I doubt it was even written down anywhere in the galaxy. Not even the bosses would dare keep a permanent record of that information.

It blew my mind which made One wince since he was tethered to my brain against his will. I toned down my shock and he thanked me then continued on with the tale.

From Bon all the way up to the present, One laid it out for me. He didn't hold back a single detail, gave it to me straight. Not a punch was pulled or a care for my sanity or delicate nature was considered. Not that I have a delicate nature, but when you get told the crud that One told me, you turn delicate fast.

"Do you see now?" he asked when he was all done.

"Better than I did," I replied. "But it's still confusing and a lot to take in."

"It clears up when you stop being a pawn," he said. "Especially with the natural gift you have. Clarity won't be a problem soon. Not ever."

I tapped my temple. "So this? You reading my mind was your natural gift?"

"It was, yes," One replied. "I wasn't fully telepathic, but I could get glimpses of thoughts and feelings from people if I concentrated hard enough. Then I became One and my gift expanded exponentially."

"Why can you tune everyone else out, but me?" I asked.

"End of the game," One said. "The barriers between us are thinning, getting ready for the transition. If I concentrate really hard, I can dull your thoughts down, but that takes up more energy than just ignoring you."

"I've been told I'm not easy to ignore." I smirked. "Sorry."

"Part of the job," he said and stood. "You think you can handle this? If you can't then you need to tell me now so we can evacuate. I'll go back to the bosses and we'll figure something else out. It'll be dangerous, probably suicidal for the SMC, but if you aren't ready then we have no choice. What you need to do is not negotiable. One stutter and it all collapses."

"So, no pressure?" I laughed.

"It's all the pressure, Joe," One said. "I know you are joking because that's what you do, but you need to tell me you understand. This is all the pressure of everything and everyone."

Surprisingly, especially to myself, I didn't hesitate when I answered.

"I understand," I said, "and I'm in. But do you have to—?"

"Yes."

"There's no way we can—?"

"No, Joe. It's all been tried, trust me," he said. "Boss Four spent a full decade coming up with ideas and none of them worked."

"Okay," I said. I stood as well. "We should probably tell the others."

"That isn't a good idea," One said. "The less they know, the better."

"Not with these guys," I said. "I trust them and they trust me. Hopsheer and Mgurn will know I'm lying by the look on my face. Tarr and Ig are no idiots. Plus, like you just said, it won't matter what we tell them. They won't remember any of it anyway."

"Maybe," One said. "But it is risky. If one of them does remember then they will be in grave danger. If they let the truth slip, they'll have most of the galaxy trying to hunt them down and there will be nothing the SMC can do to stop it."

"We're stronger with them knowing," I said. "And if there is a risk any of them could die from this, which we both know has a high probability, then I want them to know what they are dying for."

He took a couple of deep breaths then squeezed the heels of his hands against his head. "Alright! Stop yelling! Fo!"

"Sorry," I said and took a couple of my own deep breaths so I could calm my mind down.

"Thank you," he said after a couple of seconds. "Eight Million Gods, I wonder what your successor will do to you. How will that clarity thing get turned on your ass?"

"I'll probably learn the secrets of the universe at the end," I said.

"Joe?" Hopsheer asked from the ramp. "Oh, One. I didn't know you were in here. I was just coming to get Joe and show him what we built."

I looked at One and he nodded.

"Actually, we were coming to find you," I said. "And everyone else. We have something to tell you."

"That doesn't sound good," Hopsheer said.

"It probably isn't," I said. "But better than all-out war and possible total oblivion."

"That really doesn't sound good," she responded.

"Help me get everyone together," I said. "I'll explain what I can, One will too, and then you all can decide if it is good or not."

She gave me a worried look and my heart nearly broke in two.

"Steady," One thought. "Do not let your personal feelings override what needs to be done."

I didn't respond. I didn't have to. He knew what I was thinking.

TWENTY

We spent the next two weeks prepping our staging ground for what was coming. When we weren't going over the plans, Hopsheer and I were in our quarters going over each other as much as possible. The time for coy flirting and professional embarrassment was over. We had maybe a couple of days left before Bax became ground zero.

So we foed like gumps hopped up on every stimulant the galaxy has to offer.

The others got a little sick of it, Tarr just flat out stopped looking at us, but we didn't care. Every waking second of every waking day that we weren't working on the plan, we were working each other. I have to admit, it was nice. Bax wasn't so bad during those last days.

Then the alerts started to come in and we knew our time with each other was about over.

"There's no other way?" she asked as we lay in our cot, which was actually two cots shoved together, our naked limbs intertwined, sweat cooling on our skin. "How about if we—?"

"It's already been tried," I said.

"You don't know what I was going to say," she grumbled.

"Yeah, I do," I said.

Which was true. As the days went on, and me and One talked more and more about the transition, I started to hear the others' thoughts. It was quiet at first, just an annoying whispering in the back of my head. But by that day where Hopsheer and I lay there, never wanting to leave each other's arms, I could pretty much hear anyone's thoughts just by focusing.

Mgurn is a messed-up Leforian. We'll leave it at that.

"I still don't understand," Hopsheer said. "Why here? Why Bax?"

"Because it's my home," I said. "As foed up of a home it is, it's where I was raised until my parents were killed. There has to be symmetry to all of this. That's something the bosses learned early. Symmetry makes the transition easier and helps break the connection by the B'clo'nos."

"B'clo'nos," she sighed. "Those jelly bastards. They're like junkies always hunting down the next great fix."

"That's pretty much it," I said. "We do this right and they'll go away for a long time. When they come back, start stalking me like they started stalking One, then I'll know it's time to find my replacement, just like he did."

"Which is why the bosses gave me the ticket to track you down," Hopsheer said. "Why they drilled it into me that you needed to be brought in safe and sound. Or I think that's what happened. I can't remember the details."

"Yeah, that happens with the bosses," I replied. "It's because of Boss One."

We lay there, holding each other. I stroked her hair as she rested her rough, rocky cheek against my chest.

"Hops?" I asked. Hoppy seemed too buddy buddy; Hopsheer too formal. She was my Hops. "You had said being Salvage Merc Eight was a burden. Why?"

"What? No, not a burden, just a heavy responsibility," she replied.

"But numbers shouldn't matter," I said. "A merc dies and the number is assigned to the next rookie that comes in."

"Not with Mercs Two through Ten," she said. "We don't have that luxury. We are handpicked for our skill sets and our numbers are carefully assigned."

"You're the what? Merc special forces?" I laughed. She didn't laugh with me. I'd made a point of not going into her thoughts while we were together, but I couldn't resist at that moment. "Oh..."

"Hey!" she snapped and rolled her head to bite my nipple. Hard.

"Ow!" I said and jumped. Well, tried to jump. She held me in place. I may have been the heir to Salvage Merc One, but she was half Gwreq and a lot stronger than me when she wanted to be. "Sorry for peeking."

"Salvage Mercs Two through Ten are special forces in a way," she said. "We all have skill sets that make us unique amongst the numbers. When the bosses need a special ticket punched, they send one of us."

"I don't know any of the other numbers," I said. "I don't know Two through Eight or Ten."

"You will soon," she said. "You'll be One."

"But One doesn't interact with the numbers much," I said. "We all know that. Even One himself said so."

"No, but his presence is felt," Hopsheer replied. "Some of us meet him in person, some of us just catch glimpses, some never come in contact ever. But he's always there. Always in the background."

"Huh," I said. "Interesting. I guess that means maybe you won't forget—"

I stopped as fast as I could, but her entire body went tense.

"Forget what?" she asked.

"Huh? Oh, nothing," I said.

Both hands went to my nipples and she had me. She rolled fully on top of me, one of her knees pressing gently, but firmly against my exposed crotch.

"Nothing?" she asked. "Is that the story you want to tell me right now?"

"Yes?" I replied.

The pressure against my crotch stayed firm, but stopped being gentle. And she gave my nipples a tweak.

"Okay, okay, you big bully," I said and leaned up and kissed her.

She didn't relax.

So, I told her.

I heard One's mind give me a slap and I slapped back. He retreated, but I knew he was hovering just outside my head, like a lurker outside a door, listening to the conversation in the room.

Hopsheer got up from our cots and began to pace back and forth. It wasn't an unpleasant sight. A naked Hops pacing is rather entertaining. She looked over and saw how entertained I was and shook her head.

"Uh-huh," she said. "Mercs with benefits time is done. I have to focus. If what you just told me is true then I can't let this go on anymore. I need to be Salvage Merc Eight, not Hopsheer Balai. You're Salvage Merc One Eighty-Four, not the man I…"

She didn't have to finish. Even trying not to read her mind that thought was like a blazing sign on her forehead. I watched her realize I could read what she was going to say then watched her watch me realize I saw her realize it.

She pointed a finger at me and it began to harden into stone. She was really agitated to get her battle skin on.

That made me think of my battle legs. I wondered if those would be imbued with the Oneness as well when the transition occurred.

"Get up," Hopsheer barked, her stone finger jabbing at the air. "Get up! You are going to go tell the others now! Right now!"

"I think it's like four in the morning, Hops," I said.

"No. No more Hops!" she growled. "No more us! We are salvage mercs and that is all from now on!"

"You know that's not true," I said, swinging my legs off the cot. I stood and stretched and grinned as her eyes strayed. "I'm up here, Hops. Eyes up."

The finger jammed right into my sternum and it took all of my strength not to collapse back onto the cot and all of my willpower not to wince and cry out. Okay, okay, I failed on the wincing and there may have been a squeak of pain.

"We tell the others," she said. "Especially Mgurn! Eight Million Gods, Joe! He's going to lose his salvage merc! It's going to be devastating!"

"But he won't remember," I said.

"Not the point!" she said and that finger hit me again. I fell back that time.

"Get dressed while I gather everyone up," she said, throwing my clothes at me. "Five minutes."

"Yes, ma'am," I said and waited until she'd stormed out of our room before pulling on my pants.

One was not going to be happy with me about that slip up.

"Ya think?" his voice grumbled in my mind. "You have complicated things, Joe."

"Oh, shut up," I snapped and shoved him out of my thoughts. It was a lot easier to do than ever before and I could even catch a piece of One's surprise as he retreated.

When I got to our improvised mess area, I was greeted with tired, annoyed glares. Even Mgurn wasn't looking too pleased to see me and he was usually fairly polite even at four in the morning.

I made sure coffee was handed out and everyone had a couple sips before I started.

"You won't remember me soon," I said. "Once this battle is done, and if we live through it all, none of you will know who I am."

"So?" Tarr asked. "You woke us up at the crack ass of Hell to tell us that? Man, I'd forget you right now if I could."

"He's not joking," Ig said. "He means it."

"No, I'm not joking," I said. "When the battle happens, which could be tomorrow or the next day or three weeks from now, I will start to change. I won't be just Joe anymore."

"Yeah, yeah, you'll be One," Tarr said. "Just like this guy here. What does that have to do with us remembering you?"

"This," One said.

He stood before them all and his eyes turned pitch black. Just like when I saw him in the Caga station cafe. The only reason I could remember him was because I was already starting on my own path to becoming One. After a couple of seconds, One's eyes returned to normal and everyone shook their heads like they were just waking up.

"What the fo, Joe?" Tarr snapped. "It's four in the morning. Why the hell are we here?"

"Hops?" I asked then cleared my throat. "Hopsheer? Do you remember why we're here?"

"Yes..." she replied carefully. "You are going to tell them something. Something about you..."

I started all over. Tarr was just as disbelieving as before. I brought up the vid feed of our conversation since we had the entire makeshift complex wired for security. If things didn't work out, the SMC needed some evidence of the coming conflict so they could maintain their place in the galaxy. Vids of Fleet, Skrang, and B'clo'nos attacking five mercs and an assistant go a long way in the court of public opinion.

"Damn, boy," Tarr said after watching the vid of my first reveal.

"That is unsettling," Ig added.

"I will not remember you?" Mgurn asked. "All of our time together will be wiped away?"

"What? No. You'll remember that Joe Laribeau existed and you were his assistant," I replied, looking to One for confirmation. He nodded and I continued. "It's just that after all of this, if you come across me, you won't see me as Joe anymore. You'll see me as Salvage Merc One. A completely different person."

"So, what, you're a Jirk?" Tarr asked. "You'll take on this guy's skin?"

"No, I'll still have my own skin, you just won't know who I am," I said.

"But we will know Joe Laribeau?" Ig asked. "We'll know we did all of this except for the final battle?"

"No, no, you'll remember the final battle too," I said. "You just aren't going to remember why you fought it except to protect yourselves. After all of this, Joe Laribeau will be dead to you. You'll mourn him, I mean me, and move on. Or something like that."

"For One to continue to exist, Joe must die," One said. "Not in the literal sense, that's up to me, but he will only be fond memories in your heads, no longer a living person in any system of the galaxy."

"You guys may have fond memories, but I'll just remember the guy that drank all my beer all the time," Tarr said then looked around the mess. "Speaking of, did we ever find that case of beer I had in my ship? I know I stashed some in there."

"I looked, but couldn't find it," Ig said.

"Let's try again," Tarr said getting up. "I could use a drink. Or six. Don't care how early it is, it's suds time."

Tarr gave me an annoyed nod and Ig gave me her weird, wobbly Groshnel smile, then they both left.

"They're more heartbroken than they're acting," Hopsheer said.

"No, they're not," I said and pointed at my head. "They're bummed, but they're also professionals. They're taking it like they take the loss of any number."

I turned and looked at Mgurn. His bug-hound eyes were locked onto mine and I could tell he had a lot to say. I stayed out of his mind, letting him get to the words at his own speed.

He stood and offered one of his hands.

"It has been an honor to work with you, Joe Laribeau," Mgurn said. "I will try not to forget you, but since that seems impossible to avoid, I want you to know that I have enjoyed our time together and will think of you fondly."

"You too, buddy," I said and took his hand. Then I pulled him into a big hug and he squirmed under my grip.

"I am not completely comfortable with this," he said.

"Shut up," I replied. "You'll forget it soon anyway."

He tolerated a few more seconds of hugging then gave me a sad smile as we parted. He gave each of us a formal nod then turned and left the mess in a hurry.

"That's one dedicated Leforian," One said. He looked at me and Hopsheer. "Do you two need a moment?"

"We've had our moments," I said.

"Good," he said and frowned. "Because it's all about to start."

"What is?" Hopsheer asked.

One tapped his temple. "Everything," he sighed. "They're here. Well, the B'clo'nos are. The Skrangs and the Fleet will be close behind."

"What?" I exclaimed. "How do you know? I can't hear anything?"

"You're a little distracted," One said. "Concentrate."

So I did and the feeling that hit me was not a good one. Nobody, and I mean nobody, should have to get inside a B'clo'no's head. Those snot blobs are freaky things. Freaky.

"I guess this is it then," I said and gave One and Hopsheer my biggest, strongest smile.

They both winced. I dropped the smile.

"We have about thirty minutes," One said. "Time to get into place."

TWENTY-ONE

One and I stood there and watched as Hopsheer, Ig, and Tarr took off in their ships. Their jobs were to swoop in as soon as the party started and make an SMC presence known. With the threat of breaking the neutrality rules, and possibly the treaty, we'd hoped at least the Galactic Fleet would back off.

It may not make a damn bit of difference to the Skrangs, but the Fleet was a by-the-books kind of organization. At least when they weren't trying to frame the Skrangs with the killing of their own Admiral of The Fleet.

The B'clo'nos on the other hand were not going to back off. That was a certainty. I'd tried to argue, but One slammed a lifetime of images into my head which shut my ass up fast. When you get mentally bitch slapped by every interaction a person has had with the B'clo'nos, you stop arguing.

Mgurn stood at the ramp to our ship. He wouldn't have any official use since he wasn't a salvage merc. The other three could identify themselves and have their identities verified. No one would listen to a SMC assistant. They'd more than likely blast him out of the sky for flying a SMC ship.

So his job was to hide. Get in the ship and hang back until when we needed him. He wouldn't have to leave the planet, just wait under one of the thick canopies of trees until the end was almost there. His timing would be crucial, and really the key component to making everything work, but I knew he could handle it. If something needed to be done with precision, Mgurn was more capable than any of us.

I gave him a wave and he entered the ship then took off immediately. We watched him fly out across the swamps, staying low so he wouldn't be detected by the approaching ships. It was another reason One had chosen Bax as the staging ground for our last stand. Tons of plant life to confuse the B'clo'no sensors and also keep them from trying to drain us instantly.

So much lifeforce to distract them with.

As soon as Mgurn's ship was out of sight, One turned to me and held out his hand.

"It's been an honor," he said. "Sorry we couldn't have worked together more. You are actually the most like me than the other Ones."

"Thanks," I said as I shook his hand. "Sorry for all the bad jokes and smart-ass chatter in my head you've had to suffer through."

"Better than some of the sick things other folks think," One said. He clapped me on the shoulder then looked out at the planet around us. "This place isn't half bad. It'll bounce back from everything faster than most places. Way better than Hapnug."

"Hapnug? Was that where one of the other One's battles took place?" I asked.

"Four," he said. "Brutal, horrible fight. Nearly lost everything that day. Before my time, but I watched the memories over and over so I wouldn't make the same mistakes. You'll see."

"Yeah, I guess I will," I said.

We stood there a while longer, just taking in the fresh, moist air and watching as heavy, dark clouds started to roll into the area.

"Can't put this off any longer," he said.

"And we have to do this?" I asked. "You have to do this?"

"Yes," he said. "Ready?"

"I feel naked without a H16 in my hands," I said.

"No tech when we join," he said. "It interferes with the purity of the transfer."

"But my battle legs don't?" I asked.

"Nope," he said and smiled. "Those are yours, a part of you. Trust me, the artifact knows the difference."

"That's kind of creepy," I replied.

"Not going to argue with that," he said. "No more stalling, Joe. Say goodbye to your old life and get ready for your new one."

"See ya later, old life," I said. "It's been fun in a horribly violent and heart-wrenching sort of way."

One grabbed me by the temples and pressed his forehead to mind.

"If you kiss me, I'm gonna hit you," I said.

"Joe," he warned.

"Sorry, sorry," I said. "Jokes done. Old Joe gone, new Joe here now."

"No Joe at all," One said. "Get ready to be the one and only One."

He didn't let me crack a joke about how that sounded. Joke time was over. Joe time was over.

We merged.

It wasn't pleasant.

You know how sometimes you feel like your head is so full of information and memories and life stuffs that you're actually worried it will explode and splatter everything with your bloody grey matter? Merging mentally with One was nothing like that.

It was like what happens after your head has already exploded and you're staring at your own grey matter that has been splattered everywhere. It hurts like a foing bitch and is not an activity I recommend.

"Son of a gump!" I screamed.

But not out loud. Out loud was gone. Everything was internal. For both me and One. Not that there was a difference anymore.

"Hold steady," we said. "Let it all wash through you. Let the artifact seep into your whole being. It cannot replace your soul, but it will feel like it is. Let it. Do not fight it. Fighting it will only prolong the feeling of disorientation and helplessness. We can't be helpless. Not now. Now we must be everything."

And we were.

It was insane. Almost literally.

One second I was Joe Laribeau, former Galactic Fleet Marine, Salvage Merc One Eighty-Four. The next second I wasn't. I wasn't even One. Not yet. What I was was everything. The entirety of the universe. All packed inside my head. Well, shared with One's head, but that was like shoving the universe into two shoe boxes instead of one. Still not the best fit.

"Don't fight it," we said again. "Touch it all. Brush your mind across every object in the universe. Feel it then move on. You do not need to remember any of them. You shouldn't remember any of them. The objects will be there. They always have and they always will."

I did what we said to do. I touched lightly each and every object in the universe. I brushed my conscious mind across them all. Not a single thing that existed was spared my creepy fondling. It took all of .00001 seconds to do.

"Now we are ready," we said. "Let the B'clo'nos come."

With our mind pulled back from the infinite, we were able to focus on the approaching warships that had just entered Bax's orbit. There were a lot of them and as soon as they punched through the closest wormhole portal they began to form into clusters, combining their power and strength.

We knew it wouldn't be enough. All the power and strength would never be enough. But we were cautious. Ego was not the solution to our problem. Quite the opposite.

"They are sending down their scout ships," we said. "They'll enter the atmosphere across the planet and absorb the energy from the trees and life along their path here so they are at full strength. Then they will attack. They will not hesitate. They know what we are and they must have us. So it has been, so it always will be."

"Damn, we are so profound," we said.

"Yes, we are," we replied.

Can you guess which we said what? Not hard to guess.

We could feel the trees and plants and swamp animals being drained of lifeforce. They didn't cry out or panic, nothing like that. It was just as if pixels on a screen started to fade and then die, one by one. It was alarming at first, but we got used to the feeling. Until it began to accelerate as it got closer.

"Something isn't right," we said. "The drain is too powerful. Too overwhelming for the numbers of B'clo'nos that they sent down. Why? It shouldn't... Oh, fo us."

The images of what were coming slammed into our mind. Not just B'clo'no scout ships, but also something way worse.

B'flo'dos. An entire legion of them. Thousands of B'flo'dos dropping to the ground and the swamps, sucking everything dry, leaving nothing but wasted death behind them.

"They've never done this before," we said. "Not in all the history of One. Those rat bastard B'clo'nos. Those cheating sons of gumps. They can go fo themselves after this. So not cool."

"Focus!" we shouted. "Turn us against the B'flo'dos! Let the B'clo'nos come, we can handle them later, but we must stop the B'flo'dos from getting to us!"

B'flo'dos were feral, nasty, just base animals compared to their cousin species, the B'clo'nos. They ate and ate and that was it. If it wasn't for the B'clo'nos looking after them, they would have probably died out millennia ago. But the B'clo'nos did start looking out for them. And started using them.

So much made sense at that moment. How the B'clo'nos could win so many battles in the War the way they did without anyone, even the Skrangs, figuring out their strategies. They came, they saw, they conquered on so many occasions that the Galactic Fleet began to fear the B'clo'nos more than the Skrangs.

All because the damn snot monsters were using B'flo'dos. It was an easy enough deception because the B'flo'dos left no witnesses and even recording devices were wiped clean.

And nobody even suspected.

On they came, sweeping across Bax like an eraser, wiping away everything they touched.

"How are they moving so fast?" we asked.

"They've been given vehicles," we answered.

And they had. We could see them in our mind. Primitive vehicles for a primitive species. Huge rolling things with giant wheels and bodies made of crude metal and a ridiculous amount of plastic. B'flo'dos aren't known for their finesse or ability to distinguish between details; they were a devour it all and sort it out later race. Not that they sorted anything out later. They weren't smart enough for reflection.

"They have been combined," we said, the images in our mind coming clearer as the B'flo'dos came closer. "They are part of the machines they drive. They aren't sucking them dry because they would see that as sucking themselves dry."

"Abominations," we said.

"We got that right," we replied.

They were maybe only a few dozen hammocks away. Their vehicles cared nothing for the swamps. They rolled on through, large enough for the water to only come halfway up those giant wheels. What they didn't drain, they crushed. Entire canopies fell, broken and destroyed by the evil that were the B'flo'dos and their massive machines.

"This is going to hurt, isn't it?" we asked.

"A lot," we replied.

"Fo," we said.

TWENTY-TWO

Part of the whole Oneness thing is that you can never truly shut something out. You learn to partition, to compartmentalize, to section-off events. That was what we did as we focused on the B'flo'dos.

But far above, flying through space, were friends of ours. Hopsheer, Ig, and Tarr.

No matter how much we shut everything off, we still had them in our mind. It was like a song playing in the background, one you know so well that you don't even have to notice it to know what comes next, which lyric, which beat, which chord change or bridge. There it was, a subconscious member of your psyche.

So, while we waited for the B'flo'dos to show themselves before us, we also watched as Hopsheer, Ig, and Tarr took on the newest arrivals to our little conflict.

The Skrangs had arrived, followed closely by the Galactic Fleet.

For the record, the Skrangs were the more civilized. They only arrived with a small armada of cruisers and destroyers.

The Galactic Fleet? It looked like they brought every ship they had, including some that were officially mothballed just after the War.

Now, being a hair distracted by the B'flo'dos and their monster truck attack, we couldn't concentrate on every single itty bitty detail of the firefight above, such as what our friends were saying to each other, but we got the gist of the action. We caught all the plasma blasts and pertinent explosions.

It went a little something like this:

Hopsheer had been about to engage the B'clo'no warship clusters, hoping to break a few apart and weaken their attack capabilities, but the Skrangs punched through the wormhole portal at just the moment she had weapons hot and targeted on the B'clo'nos. It wouldn't do any good to fire some plasma blasts at the B'clo'nos and give away her position and intent, so she changed directions and shot out at the Skrang ships that were filing into the system.

She dove down, sending her ship way below the oncoming Skrangs. Her intent was obvious, she would get way low then come up at the Skrangs from underneath, blasting at their tender bellies. Not that Skrang ships had tender bellies, they were just as armored as the rest of the ship, but nothing was more upsetting than getting hit with a hard belly attack.

She pulled up on the stick and aimed her ship right at the Skrangs. They saw her coming, no way not to. They had scanners and sensors just like everyone did. But she was a small blip on their screens compared to the huge blips the B'clo'no warship clusters made. And she registered as a SMC ship, so technically she should have been neutral.

That was until she hailed them and started to order them to leave the system immediately or they would be breaking all treaties and neutrality agreements in place with the SMC.

There is one thing Skrangs absolutely hate and that is ultimatums. They love giving them, but detest it when they are thrown at them.

She was answered with a barrage of torpedo fire and quite the array of plasma blasts. It was actually impressive how much they threw at her.

But this was Hopsheer and that woman knew how to fly.

In and out of the torpedoes' trajectory she flew, tossing out countermeasures left, right, up, and down. It was incredible to watch even if it was only an after image in the back of our mind. The plasma blasts she only attempted to avoid, letting many impact with her shields. It would drain her defensive resources, but taking a direct hit from a torpedo would kill her, so it was a calculated loss of shield energy.

Then she started to fire. Like we said, the bellies of Skrang ships are just as armored and protected as the rest of the ships. But with Skrang ships, unlike Fleet ships, they launch all of their individual fighters from below. Fleet ships launch from side pods that extend out during battle. Skrangs open their guts and let the fighters fall out.

That there is the soft spot and Hopsheer was well aware of that.

The second the Skrang fighters started to fly out, she began emptying her guns on them. She took out a dozen before the fighters realized they needed to switch their attack to the little SMC ship instead of the B'clo'no warship clusters. By the time the Skrang fighters had turned about to take her on, she'd already fired all torpedoes at three of the Skrang cruisers.

The explosions were spectacular. Three Skrang cruisers went up in a display of fire and shrapnel that even the Eight Million Gods couldn't ignore.

The Skrang fighters had to hit the throttle to avoid getting taken out by their own ships' debris, giving Hopsheer time to escape their attack and return close to Bax.

That was where Tarr and Ig were busy sending B'clo'no warship clusters to Hell. They attacked relentlessly, forcing the clusters to break apart back into individual warships.

Ig would blast at the clusters until they weakened then zoom off before retaliatory fire could lock on. Tarr would come up right behind her and take up the attack, but at a different point at the cluster, creating an entirely new weak point the B'clo'nos couldn't ignore. It wasn't an original strategy. In fact, it had been a tried and tested strategy during the War.

For some damn reason, the B'clo'nos never figured out a defense against it. Probably because it only broke clusters and didn't destroy the actual warships. The logic behind that became very apparent as three clusters splintered into separate ships then drifted close enough with each other to form new and different clusters.

Tarr always did a lot of swearing as he fought. Ig was more restrained, but even she couldn't help but let loose with a string of expletives as the B'clo'nos regrouped and reformed. The two of them just couldn't keep up.

Luckily, Hopsheer arrived in time to give them a hand.

She swooped in and pretty much emptied her weapons on the B'clo'nos that had begun to cluster once again, letting Ig and Tarr focus on breaking up the other warship clusters. She managed to take out six warships before the Skrangs reached Bax orbit.

By that time, the Galactic Fleet was in the system and in play. That took a lot of the burden off Hopsheer, Ig, and Tarr since there was no question where the Fleet's alliance lied. Or didn't lie. It wasn't with the Skrangs or the B'clo'nos.

But that did present a bit of a problem for Hopsheer. She had to give the Fleet the same ultimatum she gave the Skrangs and order them to leave Bax alone and exit the system or they would be in violation of the War treaties and neutrality agreements. The Fleet ignored her, of course, which meant she, Ig, and Tarr now had three major enemies to fight.

Yet, despite the overwhelming odds, we could tell that all three of those crazy mercs were having the time of their lives. You just couldn't buy that kind of excitement.

Not that the excitement wasn't without risks. Deadly risks. We all knew our plan was thin and the odds of all of us making it out alive were slim.

Tarr was the first to prove that to be true.

He dodged a breaking B'clo'no warship cluster, diving between two warships as they separated, and came up on the other side right in front of a full squadron of Skrang fighters. Dozens of ships rocketed towards him and he had nowhere to go. He couldn't reverse course or he'd fly right into the breaking cluster he'd just created. He couldn't dive any more or he'd risk hitting the outer atmosphere of Bax which would incapacitate his ship and make him a sitting duck. He couldn't even go up or he'd just face the same scenario, but with Fleet fighters instead of Skrangs.

So he chose the evil he knew and sent his ship at the Skrang fighters, his throttle pushed to full and his weapons blazing. He didn't deviate from his path, didn't waver or flinch. He rode that ship of his right into the center of the squadron, his guns red hot and all torpedoes out.

Three quarters of the fighters were taken out before Tarr's ship went up in a blaze of honor and glory. If he'd been trying to live, been trying to defend himself, he wouldn't have gotten even close to the number of kills he did. But the kamikaze strategy is a hard one to defend against and his relentless attack was only stopped because his weapons quit on him and his shields couldn't take anymore fire.

We felt and heard the anguish from Ig and Hopsheer. It was impossible not to. We shared in that anguish, knowing that Tarr wanted to live. He had no intention of going into the battle with a death wish hanging over his head. He'd been 100% confident he'd make it. It made his loss even more painful.

The ship's explosion and Tarr's death snapped our attention away from the B'flo'dos that had arrived, putting us in deadly jeopardy of being taken down before our fight even began. But something at the last second gave us the confidence to leave the space fight and focus entirely on our planetary problems.

Midnight's ship, as well as several dozen Edger ships of various sizes, strengths, and capabilities, punched through the wormhole portal and sped right at the fight. We knew what side they were on and all of a sudden odds had been, well not evened, but at least semi-balanced.

So, we let the coldness of space disappear from the back of our mind and put all of our energy on the B'flo'do monster truck army that had just flattened the last canopy of trees before reaching ours.

Time to get at it.

TWENTY-THREE

They were disgusting. Those monster trucks with their huge wheels and their burning fuel that made the air stink. Even with their primitive design, they still seemed like more than a B'flo'do should be able to operate. They had gears and wheels and buttons and such. B'flo'dos were simple minded creatures, barely able to work a lever mechanism.

But seeing was believing and we saw thousands of B'flo'do vehicles coming right at us.

"What do we do?" we asked.

"We extend our control to those loathsome things and we shut them down," we replied.

"We have to touch those with our mind?" we asked.

"We do," we responded. "We have to touch them with our mind and end them. Turn them into piles of useless parts. Make them inoperable even if the B'flo'dos do know how to repair machinery."

"And we do that how?" we asked.

"We start punching holes," we said. "Punching holes into anything and everything our mind comes in contact with. We do not hesitate, we do not think, we just destroy. We have the ability to sort it all out later. That is what makes us different from the abhorrent beings."

"After us," we said.

"No, after us," we replied.

Then we started punching.

It wasn't much different from physical punching. We just used our mind to dish out the pain. Sure, we were punching monster trucks, not people or alien beings, but in the end, punching is punching is punching.

The first wave of vehicles to reach us crumpled. They just folded in on themselves again and again until they were tight squares of metal and squished B'flo'dos. We couldn't mentally harm the B'flo'dos themselves since they were living, sentient beings and we weren't one of the Eight Million Gods. Harming them directly wasn't in our wheelhouse of powers.

But damn if we didn't fo up those monster trucks something nasty!

The second wave of vehicles didn't even pause. They rolled right over the first wave that we'd turned into smashed squares and kept coming. The far tree line on our little hummock of earth fell hard under the advance of the B'flo'dos. The sound of wood ripping and breaking was almost too much to bear as we actually heard the trees crying out before us. Being that tapped in was not something we were prepared for even though we were prepared for it.

It hurt our head, but we pushed on.

We aimed our focus on the second wave of vehicles, but instead of total demolition, we went for a more refined approach. Our first attack taught us a lot about the way the vehicles worked. They were of an ancient technology, one that should have been lost to the wasteland where it came from. Earth. Stupid, gross Earth.

We put our thoughts into the dirty fuel that allowed the monsters to move. In the disgusting liquid our mind went. We agitated it, churned it, got it so riled up that it started to burn well before it was supposed it. It started to burn in the tanks where it was held, not in the cylinders it was being pumped towards.

A thousand vehicles exploded all at once. It wasn't spectacular like the explosions of the Skrang ships up in space. It was terrifying and nightmarish. The heat the explosions generated reached us and we could feel our physical self flinch in pain. Not severe pain, but pain enough to pull our thoughts back to where we stood instead of out at the attacking vehicles.

That gave the third wave time enough to roll through the flaming wreckage, climb over the mounds of crushed truck squares, and get so close that we were afraid we'd messed up and our sly offense would become our foolish death.

But we had that ace in the hole. We had that ally waiting in the wings. We had a Leforian assistant that took his job very seriously.

In came Mgurn, plasma blasts raining down on the third wave of monster trucks that roared towards us. He lit up half of them before he had to climb back up into the air to avoid their energy-sucking abilities. But half was all we needed. We could handle the rest.

We learned from our second attack and instead of agitating and igniting the fuel in the tanks, we ruptured the tanks themselves. We did even better than that, we followed the fuel to the engines and broke down all of the hoses and connectors that delivered the liquid to the cylinders.

The air around us smelled of fuel and fire and dead B'flo'dos, not to mention the earth and trees and plants of the swamp that burned on and on. The fourth wave came and we disassembled those vehicles. Then the fifth and the sixth. We turned the swamps before us into monster truck graveyards, spilling out thousands of gallons of that disgusting fuel into the precious waters of our home planet.

My home planet.

That brief thought nearly split One from me as I panicked at what we had done.

I was burning down Bax. I had sent tens of thousands of gallons of poison flowing into the swamps which would then be spread across the planet. Yeah, Bax didn't have the greatest of memories for me, but it had been a place I had called home. And despite their grisly ends, it was where my parents were laid to rest. I was killing it; I was killing Bax.

"Focus!" we yelled. "We are almost done!"

I focused and became we again.

With the B'flo'dos incapacitated in their fuel-less vehicles, we turned back to our original strategy and crushed those monster trucks with our Eight Million Gods dammed mind! Whump, crump, thump, crunch, munch, mash, slam! Every last one of those vehicles became giant paperweights, their drivers nothing but lifeless jelly.

The B'flo'do remains leaked out into the swamps as well, but we didn't panic over that. Their biomass would be added to that of the swamps and possibly offset the fuel leakage. That was what we hoped.

The B'flo'dos had come close to getting us, close to stopping our plan and ending the legacy of One. But they hadn't and we still stood, our heads pressed together just as they had been before the ships had started to land.

That left the B'clo'nos.

Far above, out of our hands and current reach, a battle raged on between the Skrangs, the B'clo'no warships, the Galactic Fleet, and the Edgers. Hopsheer and Ig had disengaged and were flying down through the atmosphere to reach us after witnessing the B'clo'nos launching a squadron of heavy fighters right at our coordinates.

We wanted to tell them to stay above, to remain in space and fight that fight, but there was no way to get a message to either of them without losing focus on the ground. So we let them come and turned all of our energy onto the advancing B'clo'no forces.

On they came, their intent to destroy us blazing the trail before them. Their ships dove, aiming themselves for where we'd built our little camp. The time we'd spent there, planning and plotting, resting and recuperating, getting to know each other even more than before, getting to learn so much from One and all he had to offer, was something we could never forget.

No matter what the B'clo'nos did, they could not take that time away from us.

So we waited. Joined at the head, in mind and spirit, knowing that the attack would reach us well before Hopsheer or Ig could. Mgurn could come help, but he was instructed not to. His job was to clean up after it was all done and make sure that the only story told was the story that we wanted told.

It blew us away that the Ones before us had managed to keep the illusion of death going without the assistance of so many friends and comrades. How they did it was mind-boggling.

That was what went through our mind as those last seconds ticked off and the B'clo'nos flew directly to us. Their heavy fighters opened fire and we sent out one last wave of mind energy, obliterating the ships from the sky just as the plasma blasts hit the ground around us.

Well, not only around us.

We felt the plasma rip into our bodies and we knew it was time.

I hadn't believed what One had told me would happen could happen. It wasn't the joining of our minds that had me squeamish. I hadn't ever objected to that part since we had been in each other's thoughts for days, even weeks. That part I got. That part made sense.

It was the dying that didn't. Because there was no way a person, or persons, could survive direct hits from plasma blasts. Maybe an H16 blast, if they were lucky, but not dozens of blasts coming from B'clo'no heavy fighters.

Yet, survive we did. Or I did. The we stopped when I felt One's lifeforce leave his scorched body and rocket from the planet. I actually felt it happen. He left Bax and his dead body fell to the ground, a burning, bloody mess.

My body wasn't anything like his. Yeah, I took direct hit after direct hit, but the damage done healed instantly as One transferred what was inside his body into mine. I felt the artifact absorb into every cell of my being and the entire world turned pitch black.

But I could see. I could see everything. It was like a smaller version of what happened when One and I first joined. I knew where every single object in the entire universe was hidden. Nothing could be veiled from my sight. If it existed, I could find it. I could track it down. I could salvage it.

In that very moment, Joe Laribeau stopped existing and there was only Salvage Merc One.

There was one problem, though. I no longer had the destructive power at my fingertips that had been there when One and I were joined. I couldn't stop the B'clo'no ships from reaching me and destroying my new body. Yes, I had healed from the first attack, but that was because the artifact had possessed me, entered my cells and fixed them as it fused with my soul.

That was a one-time gig.

But I did have a last resort. A trick I could fall back on and it was the trick that would completely change everything. Literally.

My clarity hit me so hard that I thought time hadn't slowed, but stopped completely. I looked up into the sky, the blackness draining away from my sight, and saw B'clo'no heavy fighters only a half mile above me, all aimed at my location, all about to fire their weapons one last time.

The clarity helped me to concentrate and use the last singular power the transition gave me. The power to make all forget. Everything. If it had the ability to remember then it was fair game to me. Not a square inch of the entire universe, let alone the galaxy, was free from my influence.

I did as One had instructed and I took a deep breath and let go, then said the words, "Now we start again, as we have before, and as we will do forever."

The world snapped back into real time and the B'clo'no heavy fighters didn't fire. My telepathic strength wasn't anywhere near what it was before, but I could sense the confusion amongst the B'clo'no pilots. They didn't know why they were fighting a single human being standing in the middle of a smoking swamp. They knew they had come to wage war, but the reason had slipped from their mucousy minds.

Still, they didn't pull up. Sure, they hadn't started to fire on me, but their instincts told them to go with it, to keep the attack up because they wouldn't be there unless they needed to fight.

"B'clo'no fighters!" Mgurn announced over all channels and even with the loudspeakers on the ship. "You are invading sovereign territory and have no right to wage war on this planet! You have broken the War treaties and neutrality agreements set forth in the armistice and contracts with the Galactic Fleet and the Salvage Merc Corps! Be advised that to proceed will be considered unforgivable and you will forfeit all and any rights you have as an independent race!"

The heavy fighters still flew.

"That means you'll be a bitch slave race, morons!" Mgurn yelled. "So turn your ships around and go home before the SMC and every organization in this galaxy are granted rights to own your asses!"

That got their attention. Couple that threat with their confusion as to why they were fighting and they whipped those heavy fighters in the opposite direction before Mgurn could take a breath to start shouting again.

In seconds, the B'clo'nos were gone from Bax and I was left standing by Salvage Merc One's ship, which was now my ship, just watching them go.

Reports started coming in from the Edgers above that the Skrangs, as well as the Galactic Fleet, were turning their ships around and heading for the wormhole portal. As soon as they all were gone from the system, I cleared my throat and opened my com to address the folks left behind.

"On behalf of the SMC, I want to thank the Edgers for their assistance in this conflict," I said. "Midnight, you and your people are in our debt. We do not take that lightly and neither shall you. While this debt does not nullify any of the SMC's neutrality, it does mean that if the scales are out of balance, we are obligated to come balance them in your favor."

"Uh…thanks?" Midnight replied. "It was our pleasure?" I could hear her whispering to her crew about not quite knowing what they had done or why, but no one seemed too freaked out about it since they'd just discovered they had the SMC in their debt. "Yeah, we're going to take off now. But, before I go, who am I speaking to?"

"You are speaking to Salvage Merc One," I said.

"Oh, fo," she said. "Then it's been an honor to assist you, Salvage Merc One."

"The honor is mine," I said. "Safe travels. Oh, and Midnight?"

"Yes, Salvage Merc One?" she replied.

"Tell Crawford hello for me, will you?" I said. "And that we still owe him some new skin when you get a chance to safely travel to SMC headquarters. They know you're coming, so stop by anytime."

"Okay," was all she said and then the transmission was dead.

I watched as Mgurn landed his ship by mine and climbed out. He studied me for a second and was about to speak when Hopsheer and Ig landed as well.

Those two came out of their ships looking like they'd they just been gang foed by a planet of gumps. Their eyes were wild and I could almost see the adrenaline pumping through their systems. Not that Groshnels have adrenaline. It's more like a maple syrup substance, but still it gets them all jacked up.

"Salvage Merc One!" Hopsheer nearly shouted as she gave me a salute. "Thank you for the honor of allowing us to… Uh… Do whatever we did!"

Nice finish. I smiled.

"You are?" I asked.

Hopsheer blushed and put her hand down.

"I am Salvage Merc Eight. This is Salvage Merc One Fifteen," Hopsheer replied. "I believe we are here to... I think we're here to—"

"You are here to accompany Salvage Merc One back to SMC headquarters as there has been increased aggression from both the Skrang Alliance and the Galactic Fleet towards the Salvage Merc Corp," Mgurn interrupted. "Return to your ships and ascend back into the planet's orbit. We will join you shortly."

"Mgurn? What are you doing here?" Hopsheer asked. "Shouldn't you be with...?"

"Yeah, you're what's his name's assistant," Ig said, putting four of her hands to her face as she thought it over. "You know. That guy. Salvage Merc One Eighty-Four."

"Sadly, One Eighty-Four was killed during this conflict," I said. "Mgurn will now be my assistant until he is reassigned to a new rookie merc."

"I will?" Mgurn asked.

"You will," I said.

"Okay. Works for me," Ig said and shrugged her eight shoulders. "Hoppy? Come on. We better do as Salvage Merc One instructs because of reasons that I can't really seem to bring to mind."

"Right," Hopsheer said and her eyes locked onto mine. For the briefest of seconds, I saw recognition flash to the front, but she shook it off, saluted again, and turned to follow Ig back to their ships.

Mgurn and I waited until they were gone before we turned to face each other.

"Well, Mgurn, it looks like you will be officially assisting me until we can—"

"I remember, Joe," Mgurn said.

Yeah, that stopped me.

"Uh...what?" I asked. "That's not supposed to be possible."

"I remember everything," Mgurn said. "For a second, I had lost it all then I sat down and saw you face to face and it all came back. You are Joe Laribeau, now Salvage Merc One, and you are a pain in my ass."

"Wow, you do remember," I said. "Huh. Go figure. This is new."

"Is it?" Mgurn asked.

I thought for a while, accessing shared memories from all the Ones that came before me.

"Yeah, it is," I said. "No one has ever retained their memories of a One's former self."

"I guess that makes me an exceptional assistant," Mgurn said.

"Eight Million Gods damn right it does," I said as smacked him on the back. "This is great! I'm not all alone!"

"Were you going to be alone?" Mgurn asked. "You have the SMC bosses. They know who you are, who you were, and everything about Salvage Merc One, don't they?"

"Oh, right, those guys," I said. "We should probably get back to headquarters so I can report in and start my new job officially."

"Excellent idea," Mgurn said and started to walk to my ship.

"Hey, where are you going?" I asked.

"To the ship," Mgurn replied.

"That's my ship, buddy," I said and pointed to the ship that he'd just flown. "I am more than sure the assistant to Salvage Merc One gets his own ship. Hey, look! There's one sitting right there!"

Mgurn's jaws opened and closed a few times then he started to tear up and there was nothing I could do to stop the hug that came rushing at me. Getting his own ship seemed to counteract the discomfort Leforians have with the hugging.

"Oh thank you, Joe!" he cried. "My own ship! An assistant with his own ship! This is a glorious day, indeed!"

"Indeed, buddy, indeed," I said and patted him on the back.

The hug went on for a very long time.

TWENTY-FOUR

The seven bosses sat before me, looking bored as I recalled the entire fight. There was a good reason they looked bored. They'd watched it all. In fact, Boss Seven had been there.

"That was a great report, One," Boss Four said. "Full of descriptive words and lots of pew pew noises and such."

"I enjoyed the part where you used your hands and pretended they were B'clo'no heavy fighters," Boss Six said.

"No, the best was when he spit all over us while making explosion noises," Boss Two said.

"What's going on?" Boss One asked. "I dozed off there for a minute. Oh, One, are you still here? Have you given us your report yet?"

"Yes!" the remaining bosses shouted.

Except for Boss Seven. He just gave me a smile and a wink.

"What's it feel like to be the new Salvage Merc One?" Boss Seven asked. "Because I have to say, it feels weird being Boss Seven instead of being you. Or the former you which was the former me. You get the picture."

"I get it," I said and laughed. "And it feels fine. Not a whole lot different than being Joe Laribeau."

"Yeah, about that," Boss Four said. "You have to make sure this assistant of yours, Mgurn, only calls you One or Salvage Merc One. He cannot call you Joe while in SMC headquarters, got it? That'll blow everything. Joe Laribeau died on Bax. We clear?"

"Clear," I said. "I keep reminding him."

"Well, remind him harder," Boss Five said.

"I will. I promise," I said.

"Then that's that," Boss One said and clapped his hands together. "What's for dinner? I am foing hungry!"

"Can I ask a question before I go?" I asked.

"Just one, One?" Boss Three asked. "Because we get really bored around here, so if you have a list, we can talk about them while we eat. What is for dinner, by the way?"

"Spaghetti," Boss Two said.

"Oh," Boss Three said.

"Klatu spaghetti," Boss Two added.

"Oh, snaps!" Boss Three said. "Evil pasta! Yum!"

"What's your question, One?" Boss Seven said.

"You guys are all dead, right?" I asked.

"Yep," Boss Seven said.

"You died during your own transitions, right?" I asked.

"Yes, One," Boss Seven said. "You were there for my death."

"Then how the fo are you here now?" I asked. "You are all living and breathing, and about to eat dinner even though Klatu spaghetti is technically poisonous, so how could you die and still be here?"

"Because we are only here," Boss Three said.

"No, Boss Four visited me on planet C," I countered. "He was alive there."

"Yeah, I was," Boss Four said. "Good point."

"So...?" I trailed off and waited. They all blinked at me.

"What was the question?" Boss One asked.

"Never mind," I said. "It's one of those mysteries of the universe, isn't it?"

"Was that a rhetorical question?" Boss Five asked. "I'm awful at answering those."

"You aren't supposed to answer those," Boss Six said. "They're rhetorical."

"Perfect," Boss Five said.

"I always get the answers right to rhetorical questions," Boss Four said.

"Listen, One," Boss Seven said. "Now that you are who you are, you are going to be disappointed that there aren't more answers available to you. We've all lived with the artifact inside us yet none of us really know what it is."

"I do," Boss Two said. "It's a lost remote control."

"No, it's a nuft," Boss Three said.

"A special magical nuft?" Boss Six asked. "Because that would make sense."

"No, just a normal nuft," Boss Three replied.

"Oh," Boss Six said. "That doesn't make sense."

"See?" Boss Seven chuckled. "Just relax and get used to being who you are. Don't ask so many questions. Answers will arrive when you need them to. That's how it's worked for all of us."

"Including when my next ticket comes up?" I asked. "Or do you guys know and assign those to me?"

"A little of this, a little of that," Boss Four said.

"Spaghetti's ready!" Boss Two announced and they all had steaming hot plates of some very scary-looking pasta appear in front of them.

"I'll leave you to your dinner," I said and turned to leave.

They'd already forgotten I was there as they dug into their food.

I started off heading to my quarters, which by the way are some spectacular digs. Salvage Merc One lives the life. I still had to share with Mgurn, but we each got our own rooms. And there's a pool table.

But I changed my mind, and instead of heading to my quarters, I decided to go to the mess and have a pitcher or two of beer. Maybe strike up a conversation with some numbers and see what the latest news was.

As I walked my way to the mess, I was passed by tons of numbers. They acknowledged me then frowned like they should have known me, but didn't. By the time they'd passed by, I knew they had forgotten they even saw me. I had a lot of new abilities with my position, but there was one serious drawback.

Other than Mgurn and the bosses, no one could recall my specific existence. I was Salvage Merc One. The man of legend and story. I wasn't a real guy that walked the corridors of the SMC headquarters. That just wasn't possible.

Yet it was possible because I did it and I walked my tired self to the mess hall, poured a pitcher, grabbed a pint glass, and found my seat in the corner where I watched mercs look my way, shake their heads, then make a subconscious point not to look in my direction again. And I didn't even have my black eyes on. I really messed with people's minds when I got those obsidian eyes rocking.

I was down three pitchers and finally losing the novelty of mixing with the regular numbers when something strange happened.

A merc turned her head, but didn't turn back away. She stared at me for several long seconds. Long enough to get my hopes up and make my heart flutter. I gave her a wave and she jumped, like she'd come out of a dream then she shook her head and turned back to her conversation with Ig and a couple of mercs I didn't know.

I have no idea if she had a memory of me or not, but Hopsheer lasted longer than any of the other numbers. I, of course, blew it by waving at her. I always mess that stuff up.

A thought occurred to me and I decided what the fo, why not try it out.

I went and fetched two pitchers then walked over to the table Hopsheer was sitting at.

"Hey," I said.

"Hey," she replied, looking me up and down.

The other mercs looked at me then immediately looked away. I could see the memory of me standing there fade from their conscious minds as soon as they averted their eyes. But Hopsheer continued to stare.

"You new?" she asked.

"Not really," I said. "I work a special division."

"What's your number?" she asked.

"Hoppy? Who are you talking to?" Ig asked then glanced my direction and looked away fast.

Hopsheer frowned, but didn't look away from me.

"You didn't say what your number was," she said.

"One," I replied, deciding to be honest. "I'm Salvage Merc One."

"Sure you are," she laughed. Then nodded at the pitchers. "One of those for me?"

"One of these are for you," I said. "Care to come sit and talk?"

"Why not, Salvage Merc One," she said. "Not every day I get to drink with a legend."

She physically made air quotes when she said "legend." I smiled at that.

"Nope, not every day," I replied. "Just some."

That made her frown again, but she still got up and took a pitcher out of my hand.

"Where are you sitting, Salvage Merc One?" she asked.

"I was sitting back there," I said and nodded towards my former table, which had been taken over by a bunch of rookie mercs. "But not anymore, I guess."

"Well, we can sit anywhere," Hopsheer said.

"I have a better idea," I said. "Do you like pool?"

"I do," she said. "Haven't played in a long time, though."

"Me neither, but I have a pool table in my quarters," I said.

"No you don't," she laughed. "No merc has room for a pool table."

"I do," I said. "Want to see it?"

For a moment I saw her resolve waver, but then she straightened her back, took a look at me, realized she could crush me without even hesitating, and nodded towards the mess hall doors.

"Lead the way, Salvage Merc One," she said.

So I did.

THE END

Jake Bible, Bram Stoker Award nominated-novelist, short story writer, independent screenwriter, podcaster, and inventor of the Drabble Novel, has entertained thousands with his horror and sci/fi tales. He reaches audiences of all ages with his uncanny ability to write a wide range of characters and genres.

Jake is the author of the bestselling Z-Burbia series set in Asheville, NC, the Apex Trilogy (DEAD MECH, The Americans, Metal and Ash) and the Mega series for Severed Press, as well as the YA zombie novel, Little Dead Man, the Bram Stoker Award nominated Teen horror novel, Intentional Haunting, the ScareScapes series, and the Reign of Four series for Permuted Press.

Find Jake at jakebible.com. Join him on Twitter @jakebible and find him on Facebook.

 SEVERED**PRESS**

 facebook.com/severedpress
twitter.com/severedpress

CHECK OUT OTHER GREAT SCIENCE FICTION BOOKS

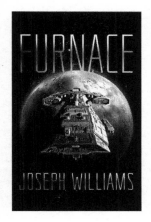

FURNACE
by Joseph Williams

On a routine escort mission to a human colony, Lieutenant Michael Chalmers is pulled out of hyper-sleep a month early. The RSA Rockne Hummel is well off course and—as the ship's navigator—it's up to him to figure out why. It's supposed to be a simple fix, but when he attempts to identify their position in the known universe, nothing registers on his scans. The vessel has catapulted beyond the reach of starlight by at least a hundred trillion light-years. Then a planetary-mass object materializes behind them. It's burning brightly even without a star to heat it. Hundreds of damaged ships are locked in its orbit. The crew discovers there are no life-signs aboard any of them. As system failures sweep through the Hummel, neither Chalmers nor the pilot can prevent the vessel from crashing into the surface near a mysterious ancient city. And that's where the real nightmare begins.

LUNA
by Rick Chesler

On the threshold of opening the moon to tourist excursions, a private space firm owned by a visionary billionaire takes a team of non-astronauts to the lunar surface. To address concerns that the moon's barren rock may not hold long-term allure for an uber-wealthy clientele, the company's charismatic owner reveals to the group the ultimate discovery: life on the moon.

But what is initially a triumphant and world-changing moment soon gives way to unrelenting terror as the team experiences firsthand that despite their technological prowess, the moon still holds many secrets.

SEVEREDPRESS

 facebook.com/severedpress
 twitter.com/severedpress

CHECK OUT OTHER GREAT SCIENCE FICTION BOOKS

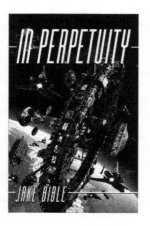

IN PERPETUITY
by Jake Bible

For two thousand years, Earth and her many colonies across the galaxy have fought against the Estelian menace. Having faced overwhelming losses, the CSC has instituted the largest military draft ever, conscripting millions into the battle against the aliens. Major Bartram North has been tasked with the unenviable task of coordinating the military education of hundreds of thousands of recruits and turning them into troops ready to fight and die for the cause.

As Major North struggles to maintain a training pace that the CSC insists upon, he realizes something isn't right on the Perpetuity. But before he can investigate, the station dissolves into madness brought on by the physical booster known as pharma. Unfortunately for Major North, that is not the only nightmare he faces- an armada of Estelian warships is on the edge of the solar system and headed right for Earth!

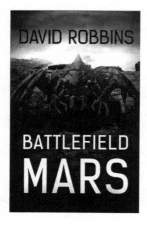

BATTLEFIELD MARS
by David Robbins

Several centuries into the future, Earth has established three colonies on Mars. No indigenous life has been discovered, and humankind looks forward to making the Red Planet their own.

Then 'something' emerges out of a long-extinct volcano and doesn't like what the humans are doing.

Captain Archard Rahn, United Nations Interplanetary Corps, tries to stem the rising tide of slaughter. But the Martians are more than they seem, and it isn't long before Mars erupts in all-out war.

SEVERED**PRESS**

 facebook.com/severedpress
 twitter.com/severedpress

CHECK OUT OTHER GREAT SCIENCE FICTION BOOKS

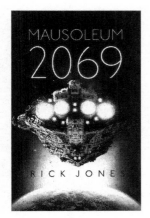

MAUSOLEUM 2069
by **Rick Jones**

Political dignitaries including the President of the Federation gather for a ceremony onboard Mausoleum 2069. But when a cloud of interstellar dust passes through the galaxy and eclipses Earth, the tenants within the walls of Mausoleum 2069 are reborn and the undead begin to rise. As the struggle between life and death onboard the mausoleum develops, Eriq Wyman, a one-time member of a Special ops team called the Force Elite, is given the task to lead the President to the safety of Earth. But is Earth like Mausoleum 2069? A landscape of the living dead? Has the war of the Apocalypse finally begun? With so many questions there is only one certainty: in space there is nowhere to run and nowhere to hide.

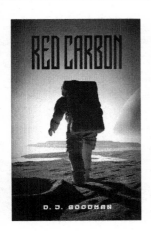

RED CARBON
by **D.J. Goodman**

Diamonds have been discovered on Mars.

After years of neglect to space programs around the world, a ruthless corporation has made it to the Red Planet first, establishing their own mining operation with its own rules and laws, its own class system, and little oversight from Earth. Conditions are harsh, but its people have learned how to make the Martian colony home.

But something has gone catastrophically wrong on Earth. As the colony leaders try to cover it up, hacker Leah Hartnup is getting suspicious. Her boundless curiosity will lead her to a horrifying truth: they are cut off, possibly forever. There are no more supplies coming. There will be no more support. There is no more mission to accomplish. All that's left is one goal: survival.

SEVEREDPRESS

 facebook.com/severedpress
 twitter.com/severedpress

CHECK OUT OTHER GREAT
SCIENCE FICTION BOOKS

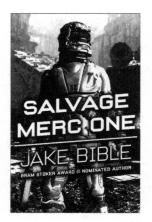

SALVAGE MERC ONE
by Jake Bible

Joseph Laribeau was born to be a Marine in the Galactic Fleet. He was born to fight the alien enemies known as the Skrang Alliance and travel the galaxy doing his duty as a Marine Sergeant. But when the War ended and Joe found himself medically discharged, the best job ever was over and he never thought he'd find his way again.

Then a beautiful alien walked into his life and offered him a chance at something even greater than the Fleet, a chance to serve with the Salvage Merc Corp.

Now known as Salvage Merc One Eighty-Four, Joe Laribeau is given the ultimate assignment by the SMC bosses. To his surprise it is neither a military nor a corporate salvage. Rather, Joe has to risk his life for one of his own. He has to find and bring back the legend that started the Corp.

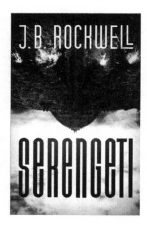

SERENGETI
by J.B. Rockwell

It was supposed to be an easy job: find the Dark Star Revolution Starships, destroy them, and go home. But a booby-trapped vessel decimates the Meridian Alliance fleet, leaving Serengeti—a Valkyrie class warship with a sentient AI brain—on her own; wrecked and abandoned in an empty expanse of space. On the edge of total failure, Serengeti thinks only of her crew. She herds the survivors into a lifeboat, intending to sling them into space. But the escape pod sticks in her belly, locking the cryogenically frozen crew inside.

Then a scavenger ship arrives to pick Serengeti's bones clean. Her engines dead, her guns long silenced, Serengeti and her last two robots must find a way to fight the scavengers off and save the crew trapped inside her.

31770019R00143

Made in the USA
San Bernardino, CA
18 March 2016